Seashells in the Desert

Susan Tornga

WhoooDoo Mysteries and
Sundowners
Divisions of
Treble Heart Books

A Crossover Novel from
WhoooDoo Mysteries and SUNDOWNERS
Divisions of
Treble Heart Books
Sierra Vista, AZ 85635-5512
http://www.trebleheartbooks.com

Published and Printed in the U.S.A.

With the exception of true historical figures, Fred Harvey and John Lorenzo Hubbell, the characters and events in this book are fictional, and any resemblance to persons, whether living or dead, is strictly coincidental.

ISBN: 978-1-936127-61-0
ISBN: 1-936127-61-X
LCCN: 2011931907

Thank you for choosing another
crossover novel from
WhoooDoo Mysteries (Historical)
and Sundowners (Western) Selection

Dedication

For the brave women who sacrificed so much to open the West for others. And for Mark, with my love. Thank you.

Author's Note

I began research for *Seashells in the Desert* in 2007, and completed the manuscript in 2008. Subsequent to its acceptance for publication, Arizona border issues and the resulting immigration laws have made nationwide headlines.

The reference to treatment of Mexicans in the Arizona Territory in the late nineteenth century is provided solely to give my readers an insight into the conditions of that era.

In no way have I intended to use *Seashells* as commentary on the current controversies in my beloved home state.

Foreword

In 1876, Fred Harvey, an English emigrant, opened a small depot restaurant at the Santa Fe Railroad station in Topeka, Kansas. This was the beginning of what was to become the Fred Harvey Company. Lunch counters, dining rooms, hotels and even newsstands bearing the Harvey name sprung up along the Atchison, Topeka and Santa Fe Railway line from Chicago west to San Francisco and south to Galveston. By the late 1880s, there was a Fred Harvey dining facility located every 100 miles.

Before Mr. Harvey opened his facilities, train passengers were forced to eat when and what they could, which would often be cold beans and rancid meat at a roadhouse located by a water stop.

Until 1883, patrons to the Harvey Houses were served by waiters. In Raton, New Mexico that year, Mr. Harvey fired all of his waiters for poor service and began hiring attractive and well-educated young women. There were contracts to sign, rules to follow and rigorous training to complete, but that didn't stop thousands of women from applying each year.

Early on, the Harvey Girls had to overcome the perception that they were prostitutes masquerading as waitresses. Strict rules of behavior and dress and oversight by a chaperone helped banish that stigma. The women who applied for the positions did so for a variety of reasons. Some needed to provide an income to help their struggling families, others were seeking adventure in the American West.

Fred Harvey's mission was to provide excellent meals to the Santa Fe passengers, in elegant surroundings, served by charming young women. The Harvey Company had its own dairies and refrigerator cars, enabling the chefs, many of whom were European-trained, to count on fresh fruit and vegetables, prime meats and even ice cream. The menus rivaled those of the best restaurants in Chicago or New York City. When dining cars were introduced on trains, the Fred Harvey Company contracted with the Santa Fe Railroad to provide "on the way" meal service, prepared and served to the same high Harvey House standards.

Some of the original Harvey Houses stand today, like El Tovar and Bright Angel Lodge at the Grand Canyon and La Fonda in Santa Fe.

The Santa Fe Railroad established a terminal and roundhouse in Winslow, Arizona in 1881. In 1887, the Fred Harvey Company built a dining room next to the depot. It wasn't until 1929 that La Posada, an elegant Harvey House hotel, was open for guests. Closed in 1957, the beautiful building fell into disrepair. Today, renovated, it is open for business as an elegant reminder of the romantic era of train travel through the American West. Guests can tour the grand hotel, escorted by a guide clad in authentic Harvey Girl attire.

The Harvey Empire thrived until the middle of the 20th Century. During World War II, the Harvey Company provided meals to GIs traveling on troop trains across the country. The end of WWII was also the beginning of the end for the Harvey Girls, the women who tamed The West.

Chapter One

The wail of the approaching locomotive's whistle should have sounded different that morning, but it did not. Another octave higher, perhaps, like a woman's scream, because today it heralded more than just the arrival of tired, hungry travelers. In addition to mail, supplies and passengers, the noon train from San Francisco brought something to Winslow, Arizona that no one wanted: trouble.

Tessa Crane, standing ready to provide the first class service for which the Harvey House was known, tensed. The hammering of angry voices reached her ears only seconds before a rotund man, dressed in the navy blue uniform of a Santa Fe Railway conductor, lurched into the dining room, his face puffed and reddened with anger. His skin glistened with fear-scented sweat. He stumbled forward, shoved by the scrawny arm of a man half his size.

Tessa stared at the two men, surprised to see a conductor

submitting to such humiliation. These men, always neat in dark suits, shiny fob watches hanging from weskit pockets, were the self-professed masters of the passenger trains that chugged into Winslow several times each day. When she saw the reason for the large man's acquiescence, she gasped. The smaller man encouraged his prisoner forward with the business end of an angry pistol.

"Where is the sheriff?" he demanded of no one in particular. "The station master told me that I would find him here."

His tinny voice matched his height, yet Tessa recognized the keen eyes and upright bearing of a man aware of his own authority, traits characteristic of her father and his fellow Army officers. Clearly, this man knew he was in charge, even without the gun to prove it.

Sheriff Jed Bowman, a large man himself, yet with none of the porcine characteristics of the conductor, pushed his chair back from the counter. With a longing glance at his half-eaten lunch, he walked toward the two men, each step announced by the thud of a boot on the wooden floor.

"I'm the sheriff. Name's Bowman."

His towering stature, aided by the deep tenor voice, accorded him immediate command of the situation. Tessa heard the unmistakable sound of porcelain shattering as a serving bowl slipped through the shaking fingers of a nervous waitress.

"You must be the Santa Fe's spotter," Bowman said. "I received a telegram this morning to expect you. It appears that you've caught your culprit."

He pointed to the now-obsequious conductor.

"Follow me to the jail so we can lock him up and get this situation sorted out."

Tessa knew about spotters, detectives hired by the Santa Fe Railway to expose conductors who pocketed passengers' ticket money instead of adding it to the till. There had been three previous arrests here in Winslow. This particular spotter looked ill suited for the job, which could very well have been the reason for today's success.

The three men marched through the dining room, creating a curious spectacle for the entering passengers, who pointed and whispered amongst themselves. One couple, however, seemed oblivious to the strange parade. They looked only at each other as they crossed the dining room on a collision path with the spotter and his captive.

When the conductor saw them, he stopped abruptly, causing the spotter to bump him with the gun. The conductor glowered at the petite woman, ignoring her male companion.

"You!"

He pointed one stubby finger at her. Spittle rained from his mouth.

"I knew you were trouble the minute you boarded my train. I've seen tramps like you before. They never got the better of me and you won't either. I know some things about you and I'll make you sorry that you ever told the tales that got me in this fix."

He flung the last words over his shoulder as Sheriff Bowman dragged him out the door.

As unexpected as the outburst was, what surprised Tessa more was the woman's indifference to it. The enraged conductor might as well have commented on the weather. She ignored the venom that lingered in the air, and instead, smiled at her companion. She offered her hand as he escorted her to a seat.

Even from her vantage point across the dining room, the violent temper of the conductor frightened Tessa. She couldn't understand how the woman on the receiving end of such vehemence could remain unaffected by it. If her calmness was pretense, then she was an excellent actress.

As the door closed behind the jail-bound trio, the Harvey House once again echoed with the familiar sounds of excited travelers ready for solid ground under their feet and delicious food in their bellies. This afternoon however, Tessa felt none of the usual comfort she took in the diners' satisfaction. The menace that had entered the room with the enraged conductor remained even after he walked out.

"Miss Crane? Miss Crane, the soup is ready to be served."

Tessa jerked her head around. Frank Clifton, the Harvey House manager, traversed the dining room like a puma stalking its prey. His unnerving ability to move quietly, almost invisibly, was a popular after-hours topic of conversation among the staff.

Tessa set down the urn she had pretended to polish while watching the conductor's arrest.

"Yes, Mr. Clifton," she said, and flashed what she hoped was a conciliatory smile.

She had her reasons for avoiding his attention. She cautioned herself to be more alert to his presence. It was difficult, but necessary, to always be on guard, to walk carefully. One misstep and she could fall, literally, creating unwanted questions. How would she explain that she wasn't clumsy? What other excuse was there? Certainly not the truth.

As she entered the kitchen in search of the hot soup,

she caught the eye of her roommate and good friend, Lupe Castillo. Lupe was elbow-deep in soapy water, facing a mound of soiled dishes and blackened pots.

Tessa lifted the tureen of English pea soup au gratin from the countertop. Risking further rebuke from Mr. Clifton, she detoured by the sink before returning to her work station.

"Did you hear the commotion out there?" she asked Lupe, pointing toward the connecting door.

"Cook said they arrested the conductor."

Lupe continued to attack the stacks of plates and bowls as she spoke. Tessa thought of all the dishes she would add to the pile before the meal was over, and immediately regretted the fact that she'd interrupted her friend's work with idle chatter. However, she knew that, to Lupe, there was nothing idle about any conversation that brought stories from the dining room into the kitchen.

The waitresses frequently spoke with the travelers. The Mexican women who made up the majority of the kitchen staff were afforded no such diversion. They weren't allowed in the dining room when the Santa Fe passengers were present. Lupe had studied diligently under Tessa's tutelage to perfect her English. Nevertheless, she was not provided the opportunity for advancement. This unfair treatment rankled Tessa, but she was powerless to change it. She did, however, attempt to keep Lupe apprised of any exciting occurrences, which, of course, Lupe would pass along to her kitchen co-workers.

"That's not all," Tessa said. "He threatened one of the passengers. I'll tell you about it later. I have to serve the meal." She hefted the soup tureen several inches for emphasis.

As she walked through the kitchen, she inhaled the aromas of roasted pork, warm applesauce and just-baked pies. Today, as always, the Harvey House patrons would savor a delicious dinner.

The door between the kitchen and dining room swung shut behind Tessa, muffling the clanging of pots and pans. She was surprised, therefore, to hear an equally loud commotion, this one emanating from the far corner of the dining room.

"*He* threatens me. *You* threaten me. I only want what is rightfully mine."

The voice belonged to the woman who had been accosted by the enraged conductor. No longer insouciant, she was now hysterical. Tessa stared across the room, engrossed in the spectacle.

Her male companion spoke, his tone so low that Tessa could not make out the words.

"Don't tell me about trouble,"the woman replied, her loud voice a counterpoint to his soft one. "It won't be me who's in trouble."

Glowering at the man, she threw down her napkin and grabbed a tapestry satchel from beneath the table. She pushed through the front door as if it were made of paper instead of heavy oak and leaded glass. The resounding thud as it banged shut was further testimony to the tiny woman's fury.

As Tessa watched the drama unfold across the room, she ladled the soup into delicate china bowls, miraculously spilling only a few drops on the sideboard that functioned as her workstation.

She noticed that most of the diners were captivated by the discordant spectacle as well. Heads turned in unison as they followed the young woman's exit. As she marched past the front window, Tessa could see tears carving rivulets down her well-powdered face. Undoubtedly, the scene would be told and retold, and enhanced, as the train crossed the next barren stretch of desert on its way to New Mexico.

The woman's companion, who had risen politely as she stormed out of the dining room, sat back down. He watched her walk away with a rueful look that belied the twinkle in his eyes. Unexpectedly, he laughed, a hearty guffaw that caused his tablemates, bent intently over their plates, to look up. He nodded at them and resumed eating. They, in turn, began conversing amongst themselves, as if the departure of the troubling woman had relaxed their tongues. The man listened, or perhaps pretended to listen, as conversation flowed around him. As far as Tessa could tell, however, he hadn't uttered a word.

A sharp intake of breath caused Tessa to turn toward the kitchen. Lupe, silhouetted in the doorway, stared toward the front window. Her olive skin was drained of color, giving it a sickly yellow cast. Her left hand trembled as she grasped at the collar of her uniform dress, and her teeth gnawed at the fingernails of her other hand.

"Lupe, what's wrong?" Tessa asked as she hurried into the kitchen with the empty tureen.

Lupe stepped back, allowing the kitchen door to close. Her black eyes focused on Tessa. She blinked twice as if trying to erase an image burned there.

"Wrong? Nothing is wrong. It is hot in the kitchen and I am a little tired. That's all."

She took the bowl from Tessa's hand and hurried to the sink.

Tessa didn't follow her friend. There wasn't time now to question Lupe further. Soon the stationmaster would announce the "all aboard" as this train headed east toward Chicago. Two hours later, the California-bound train would arrive with its flock of tired and hungry travelers, and the well-orchestrated tableau of meal service would begin once again.

Tessa gathered up the prepared plates and hurried out to serve the waiting diners. A hectic afternoon lay ahead for the entire staff of the Harvey House, but Tessa was never so busy that she didn't remember Lupe, wide-eyed and tight-lipped, standing still as a statue in the kitchen doorway as she stared at the retreating back of the enigmatic beauty.

Tessa's childhood had been spent on Army posts throughout the West. She had witnessed Indian assaults, fires, robberies and wild animal attacks. She knew what fear looked like. It was not fatigue or heat that had molded Lupe's face that afternoon. It was fear.

Chapter Two

That evening, the upstairs sitting room buzzed with gossip as the girls discussed the unusual events of the day. Tessa heard snippets of conversation, but her mind was on Lupe. She wanted to ask her friend what she knew about the beautiful stranger, but Lupe had not returned to their room.

"They were traveling together and I heard they aren't married," one shocked girl said.

"Maybe he's her brother."

Tessa guessed the reply came from one of the new girls, fresh off an Iowa farm.

"I'm glad the sheriff arrested that conductor." Charlotte Hubbard said. "He's been in the dining room many times, as you can imagine, and he never fails to flirt with one of us. He makes me uncomfortable and we're all better off with him gone."

Charlotte had been at Winslow's Harvey House since its opening in 1887. Unlike most of the Harvey Girls, she had not left to marry a rancher or a railroad man at the end of her first twelve-month contract. She stayed on year after year and seemed to enjoy the role of big sister to each new recruit.

Charlotte's words brought to mind Lupe's frightened face as she had watched the mercurial woman leave the dining room that afternoon.

"Charlotte," Tessa said, "you've lived in Winslow for several years. Did you recognize that woman or the man with her?"

"Oh, Tessa," Charlotte answered, "I've seen thousands of people come and go for the past eight years. I thought she looked familiar but then I was sure I'd seen Olive before, too." She pointed to the new girl from Kansas. "Olive has never been west of Colorado and I've never been to Kansas."

"Girls, girls, it's ten o'clock. Lights out."

Ardella Gibson's authoritative voice echoed up the stairwell. She was the eagled-eyed housekeeper/cum surrogate mother for Winslow's Harvey Girls, and she kept track of time with a military precision that would have made Colonel Thomas Crane, United States Army, proud.

Tessa was glad that, unlike her father, Mrs. Gibson was lazy and very seldom expended the effort required to climb the stairs at night to issue her curfew edict in person. Had she done so tonight, she would have noticed Lupe's absence and looked to Tessa for an explanation. Tessa had none, only a nagging fear that her roommate was hiding something.

The next night and the one after passed in the same manner, with only a different subject for gossip. The previous Friday's excitement seemed to have fled from everyone's mind except Tessa's. As far as she could tell, Lupe didn't return to their room during that time, although she was always hard at work in the kitchen when Tessa went downstairs each morning. And, as eager as Tessa was to speak to her, Lupe was even more intent on avoiding any conversation with her roommate.

By Sunday night, Tessa was frantic. If Lupe's absences were discovered, she would no longer have a job. Lupe had never been one to break the rules. Her mother and sisters relied on the meager amount she sent to them in New Mexico and Tessa knew that her friend took that responsibility seriously. Whatever was causing Lupe's odd behavior had to be very important.

Tessa woke with a start Monday morning. She opened her mouth to scream when she realized the noise she heard was coming from the dressing table where Lupe was opening drawers. Relief at seeing her roommate translated into a desire to shake some sense into her.

"Where have you been every night?" Tessa demanded, not caring that she sounded like a long-suffering wife whose husband spent too much time at the saloon. "And why didn't you wake me? Look at the time."

She threw off her nightgown and pulled on her undergarments and stockings in rapid succession, in hopes that Lupe wouldn't finish dressing and leave the room, and their conversation, before she was fully clothed.

Lupe grabbed a clean apron from the hook beside her bed and tugged it over her head so hard that Tessa thought the heavy cotton might tear.

"I've been visiting my friends and family," she responded, curtly.

Tessa tied her shoes, then her apron. Her cap would hide her unruly hair. She silently thanked Mr. Harvey for his edict forbidding his Girls to wear make-up while working. Even on the best of days, the rule was a time-saver. This morning, it allowed her to keep pace with the frenetic Lupe.

Tessa spoke again, this time with more pleading and less accusation in her voice. "Lupe, please tell me what's wrong. You know what will happen if Mrs. Gibson finds out that you've missed curfew."

"Nothing is wrong, , " Lupe said in a shaking voice that suggested the opposite. She turned away from Tessa. "And I know ways to fool Mrs. Gibson. We all do."

"Well, I hope she isn't waiting by the kitchen door with a clock in her hand this morning," Tessa said, as she and Lupe hurried out the door.

Since Lupe had refused to discuss her strange behavior, and because they were late reporting for work, Tessa didn't press her roommate for details. Not right then, at any rate.

They walked quickly down the stairs, Tessa grasping the banister in an effort to match Lupe's rapid pace. Her leg ached more than usual this morning, which she attributed, unaccountably, to her distress over Lupe.

"Umm, do you smell that?" Lupe asked, as if she hadn't a care in the world. Wonderful aromas wafted up the stairwell.

"It's cinnamon," Tessa said, in the lightest tone she could manage as she tried to imitate Lupe's nonchalance. "That means sweet rolls this morning. I hope we're not too late to have one."

She thought that perhaps, if the morning trains ran on schedule, she and Lupe could share a couple of the gooey rolls, coffee and, most importantly, information, after breakfast service was complete.

"I'm glad I'm not a baker," Lupe replied. "Every morning Oswald is kneading mountains of dough long before--" She stopped abruptly, and turned toward Tessa, dark eyebrows knitted in confusion. "Something's wrong," she whispered.

"It's too quiet." Tessa's low voice matched Lupe's.

There was no laughter, no clatter of utensils. The sounds coming from the dining room weren't those of a dozen women setting the tables, brewing coffee, preparing for a busy day. What she did hear was the muted buzz of deep, masculine and very serious voices.

Lupe reached for Tessa. "I hope…"

Tessa felt her friend's icy fingers grip her wrist. Thoughts of three nights of missed curfew filled her head.

"This doesn't have anything to do with you, does it?"

They had reached the foot of the stairs. With one final squeeze, Lupe dropped her hand.

"I don't know," she said.

It wasn't the answer Tessa expected, or wanted. Without another word or a glance at Tessa, Lupe turned toward the kitchen. When Tessa entered the dining room, she saw her fellow Harvey Girls sitting at tables still barren of place settings. The newest additions to the staff, the ones Tessa had only recently met, sat rigid, hands in their laps, worrying at the folds of their spotless white aprons. The more experienced girls waited calmly for whatever was to come from the unusual morning. A few even chatted about their favorite topic: men.

"Ah, Miss Crane. Take a seat please," Frank Clifton said. "Sheriff Bowman has something to say when everyone arrives."

Tessa complied. She studied her seatmate.

"Kansas?" Tessa whispered.

The girl, who didn't appear to be much older than sixteen, frowned at the question, then smiled as she realized what Tessa was asking.

"Yes. I'm Olive Gillespie from Topeka, Kansas, home of the first Harvey House. I remember meeting you just after I arrived, but I'm sorry I don't remember your name."

Tessa reintroduced herself. "Don't apologize. I had forgotten your name, too."

Tessa watched the seven members of the kitchen staff shuffle into the dining room. Lupe came in next to last, followed only by Dorothea Parks, the head cook. Lupe's eyes never left the floor.

"Who is that woman talking to the sheriff?" Olive asked, forcing Tessa's attention away from the solemn kitchen troop. She matched Tessa's voice with her own whisper. "I don't recognize her as one of us."

"That's Dr. Dahlgren. She's new in town, too."

Tessa started to tell Olive what little she knew about the fair-haired Norwegian woman when Sheriff Bowman spoke.

"I think you all know that I'm the sheriff here," Bowman began.

He looked around the room, pausing to make eye contact with each person. When he came to her, Tessa could feel the heat rising in her face. She was sure that his sharp eyes bored into her mind, picking up the doubts that lodged there. What did Lupe know? He moved on.

"Early this morning a young woman was found dead in the alley behind this building."

He waved his massive arms toward the kitchen, in the general area of the back door, waiting out the gasps and murmurs that undulated through the room.

"It's obvious that she was murdered, strangled."

This news was met, not with louder cries, but with absolute quiet, as the assembled staff struggled to grasp the severity of the sheriff's words.

Bowman let the silence drag on for what seemed to Tessa to be a full hour, but was, more likely, little more than a minute. The tension increased with each tick of the clock. An occasional cough echoed through the room like gunfire and had the same nerve-racking effect. If his intention was to set the staff on edge, it had worked, at least on Tessa. Finally, mercifully, he resumed speaking.

"The reason I'm here this morning is that I need your help. The woman who was murdered arrived on the noon train Friday. She ate dinner with the other passengers. I was sitting at the lunch counter at the time."

He pointed, unnecessarily Tessa thought, toward the horseshoe shaped bar that was a popular dining spot for Winslow's male population.

"One of the railroad's spotters came in looking for me. He brought in a conductor who had been caught stealing fare money."

Bowman explained the confrontation between the conductor and the young woman. Tessa stifled a groan. The sheriff verified what she had suspected but hoped wasn't true. He was talking about the woman whose appearance had so upset Lupe. And now she was dead. Tessa forced herself to concentrate on the sheriff's words.

"I took the prisoner to the jail and I never saw this woman again. Mr. Clifton told me that she sat at one of the tables over there." Again, he pointed, this time toward the front of the room.

"From Mrs. Crook at the hotel, I know that the murdered woman called herself Deirdre Sweeney. She was in the company of a prosperous-looking man named Stanton Perry. Mr. Perry seems to have disappeared, so I'm asking all of you to tell me anything you know about either Miss Sweeney or Mr. Perry."

Bowman gazed out at the sea of attentive faces. The group seemed to be holding its collective breath and no one spoke. Tessa risked a glance at Lupe and saw her friend's dark head bent toward Delia, another Mexican who worked in the kitchen. The girl probably understood only a fraction of what the sheriff said. It would be frightening, Tessa thought, to sense such tension in the room and not be able to understand the sheriff's rapid speech. She supposed that Lupe was whispering a few reassuring words in Spanish.

"What I do know," Bowman continued, "is that the conductor from Friday's St. Louis-bound train made threatening remarks toward Miss Sweeney. No one needs to repeat that story to me. It isn't relevant to this murder, however. I personally put that conductor, Winston McCauley, on a westbound train on Saturday. He left Winslow in handcuffs, accompanied by a Santa Fe detective. I'm certain that he had nothing to do with Miss Sweeney's death."

Olive leaned close to Tessa's ear.

"Is he sure?" she whispered. "I saw that conductor when he was arrested. He looked mad enough to kill that woman."

Tessa held up her hand to shush the girl, and smiled at the same time, to soften the effect. The poor child was probably wondering what she had gotten herself into, moving from civilized Kansas to the wild Arizona Territory.

"Some of you must know something about Miss

Sweeney," Bowman said, more a command than a statement. "I need you to tell me anything that you saw or heard that concerns her. You may think it's not important, but let me decide that. If you don't want to speak here, you can come to the jail. I'll be grateful if you tell me what you know, or even just suspect."

Bowman strolled back and forth in front of his audience, as if he were a lawyer addressing a jury. The thump of his boots and the crisp pivot he made at every corner added to the tension in the dining room.

Tessa kept her eyes on the sheriff, avoiding any further glance in Lupe's direction. She was afraid that something in her expression, or Lupe's, would alert Bowman to the fact that the two of them knew more than they were saying.

Tessa decided that she would tell the sheriff something, anything, about the murdered woman. After all, she had been serving a meal when Miss Sweeney and Mr. Perry first arrived. It would be a decoy to distract him with other information so he wouldn't ask the questions that she didn't want to answer. She took a deep breath and broke the silence in the dining room.

"Sheriff Bowman," she began. "Several of us saw this Deirdre Sweeney as we were serving dinner. She was sitting next to the man you described. At least, I think it was the same man. They had a disagreement about something and she left the dining room in a fit of temper. The man with her didn't seem the least bit upset. He didn't go after her, just finished his meal. He seemed interested in what his tablemates were saying, but I can't say that he actually joined in the conversations. Then, a day or two after that, I saw the two of them walking together, right out front."

Tessa was surprised by her own chatter. She hadn't planned to say so much. The words kept tumbling out. She only hoped that no one else had seen Lupe's surprise and fright when she spotted the young woman leaving the dining room.

Tessa kept talking. "Beryl Turner should know more about the couple. She was serving the table where they sat. Beryl isn't here this morning, so it must be her day off. She usually goes home to see her family when she's not scheduled to work. The Turners live outside of town, maybe a mile south of the railroad tracks."

"Thank you, Miss Crane. Yes, I know where the Turner homestead is. I'll ride out there after I'm finished here." He nodded to Tessa, then looked out at the sea of strained faces. "Can anyone else add anything to Miss Crane's information?"

Again, silence prevailed. Tessa noticed Mr. Clifton pull his watch from his pocket and frown. He fidgeted, and finally spoke.

"Sheriff, why don't we let these good folks return to their duties? I'm sure they'll tell you if they remember anything about either Miss, um, Sweeney, was it? Or the man with her."

He indicated the four tables where his employees sat, some restless, most still as stones.

"Right now, they need to prepare these tables. The morning train will be here," once again he consulted his watch, "in less than one hour."

Bowman nodded his assent.

"But," he said, addressing the entire staff, "please think about what you might have seen or heard in the past three days that could help find this murderer."

"Thank you, sheriff," Clifton said. He turned from the sheriff to face his employees. "I have one more thing to say, and it's important. Remember that we don't want our diners to hear about this tragic murder, so please refrain from any discussions about it when they're present."

Tessa wondered if he honestly expected that the passengers wouldn't hear about the murder within minutes of the train's arrival. Four decades earlier, in the heyday of the California gold rush, such a murder might have been, if not unnoticed, at least not unexpected. However, in 1895, Winslow was a quiet town. There were churches and schools, and, of course, the elegant Harvey House Dining Room.

Murder was a rare occurrence now. Occasionally there would be a drunken brawl and someone would end up on the wrong end of a Colt 45, or a rustler would get his due from an irate rancher, but the murder of an attractive young woman was different. Of course, people would talk.

"Okay, let's get to work," Clifton said. "There will be three trains today and you know what that means: no rest for any of us."

"Miss Crane?" the sheriff called, as Tessa rose from her chair. "Could I speak to you for a minute?" Although it was phrased as a question, it was obvious to Tessa that he expected no answer, only compliance.

"Drat," Tessa said, under her breath, earning her a curious look from Olive. She had hoped to scurry to her table before either the sheriff or Mr. Clifton could question her further.

Bowman waved, summoning her to his side. He was talking to Clifton and Dr. Dahlgren, and seemed to want her participation in their discussion. Her heart sank.

"Miss Crane, have you met Dr. Elsa Dahlgren?" Bowman asked.

The doctor supplied the answer. "Miss Crane served me a delicious lunch recently. It wasn't busy in here that day so we talked for a few minutes."

She turned to Tessa. "I believe you told me that your father is stationed south of here at Ft. Apache. I think you were expecting a visit from him. Do I remember correctly?"

"Yes, you do," Tessa answered. She couldn't think of anything more to say. She wanted to turn around and leave but didn't dare.

Frank Clifton spoke, surprising Tessa. She expected the questions to come from Sheriff Bowman.

"Miss Crane, what can you tell me about this disagreement you witnessed here on Friday? When did you say you saw Miss Sweeney with Mr. Perry? Where were they and where were you?"

Tessa frowned. She was having difficulty sorting through the manager's rapid questions. She concentrated. In the days since the conductor's arrest, she had served many meals and polished mountains of silver. Mostly, however, the time had been filled with worry over Lupe, and her roommate's terse words that morning had done nothing to alleviate that concern. She let her mind wander back through time.

"It was yesterday, Sunday." Could it have been only one day ago? Tessa shook her head in disbelief.

"Not yesterday?" Bowman asked, misreading the motion.

"It was yesterday, for sure," Tessa said. "We commented on the people we saw returning from church."

"We? Who was with you?"

"Choppy, one of the cooks, came outside while I was there. We sat on the back step to get some fresh air. It was hot in the kitchen. Hot outside, too, but at least there we could get a breeze. That couple, the ones you asked about, strolled by."

"Were they arguing"? Bowman asked.

"No, that's the strange thing," Tessa replied. "Both of them were smiling, and he held on to her arm gently, like he was protecting her."

"Protecting her? From what?" Dr. Dahlgren asked.

"Oh, from tripping on a loose board or stepping in mud. Something like that. He treated her like he really cared for her."

"Anything else?" Bowman asked.

"She knew she was beautiful. She turned the head of any man who passed her and she would smile back at them. Choppy admired her, too."

"What did he say?" The sheriff was instantly alert.

"Only that he had a weakness for red-haired women. Her hair isn't, wasn't," Tessa corrected herself, "what I would call red, but that's the word Choppy used. I'd say it was auburn. She was carrying her straw hat in her hand, so her head was uncovered. The sunlight reflected brown and gold, like a crown. Yes, she was lovely."

"What was she wearing?" Bowman asked.

"Her clothes were stylish. They reminded me of pictures in the fashion magazines my cousin sends me from New York. Most women around here don't dress that fancy. We'd only get dirty. I'm sure her dress and hat were silk, maroon silk, with one of those bustles that are so fashionable now in the big cities. She wore thin boots that looked like they'd fall apart the first time she got them wet, with pointed toes and high heels and tiny buttons that went up the side. I remember wondering if they were difficult to put on."

Tessa looked down at her own low-heeled serviceable shoes. "No wonder that man held on to her. One misstep and she would have fallen off the boardwalk."

Bowman nodded. Tessa wanted to ask him if the clothing she described was what the woman had been wearing when her body was discovered, but she was leery of expressing too much interest.

"So, they weren't arguing. Were they talking?" Bowman asked.

The sheriff apparently had learned enough about fashion, and his expressionless countenance provided no clue as to the importance of Tessa's information.

"I think so, sheriff, but, if they were, I didn't hear any of the conversation."

Tessa hadn't heard anything because she had been thinking about the woman's earlier temper tantrum and Lupe's reaction to it. She couldn't explain that to the sheriff, however, without exposing Lupe to more of his questions. She didn't want to do that, at least not until she had a chance to ask those questions herself.

"You could ask Choppy. He might have heard them talk. I only remember that Miss Sweeney seemed to be flirting with her companion."

"I'll do that, Miss Crane. Now, what about Beryl Turner? You mentioned that she served Miss Sweeney and Mr. Perry that day."

"Yes, she did and she must have overheard at least some of their conversation, or argument, if you will," Tessa said.

"Beryl might also be able to tell you something about some of the other passengers who were seated near Miss Sweeney. Maybe they were the ones who made her angry."

Tessa was pleased with herself for that thought. In her heart, she knew that Lupe's fear of Deirdre Sweeney couldn't have had anything to do with her death. She needed to give the sheriff other options.

"Mr. Clifton, may I go back to work now? I can't tell you any more about the murdered woman."

Clifton looked at Bowman for approval. The sheriff nodded at the manager, who in turn, nodded at Tessa. She glanced at the doctor, in case she, too, wanted to join in the approvals.

With three trains and their passengers, the day passed in a whirlwind of preparation, service, cleaning, and preparation once again. Tessa was numb with exhaustion by the time she served the last meal and readied the dining room for the next day. Supper consisted of two thick slices of cold ham and a fruit salad.

She sat alone in a far corner of the kitchen, seeking peace in solitude. The most recent letter from her father crackled as she retrieved it from her apron pocket. Pushing her empty plate aside, she unfolded the letter and smoothed out the creases. She read it for at least the tenth time. By now, she could have recited it word for word. However, she bent her head over the table, pretending to concentrate on the paper in order to forestall any attempts at conversation. She didn't want to discuss the murder, at least not until she could talk to Lupe.

She returned to an empty bedroom, an all-too-familiar occurrence of late. Tessa removed her shoes and stockings.

It felt good to wiggle her toes in the open air, good enough that it made her smile. She sat on top of the coverlet, fully clothed save for her bare feet. She pulled her skirt above her knees and began rubbing her stick-thin left leg. The rhythmic massage helped calm her mind, but couldn't erase the doubts caused by Lupe's uncharacteristic absences.

Tessa's mind kept repeating the same question. "What does Lupe know?" The problem was, she wasn't sure she wanted an answer.

Chapter Three

Jed Bowman rode south from Winslow, coughing at the cloud of dust kicked up by his palomino, Lucky. The dust abated as Lucky slowed to pick his way over terrain that had turned rocky as they neared the Turner home. Bowman wondered why the Turners had chosen to homestead here among the boulders when there was so much flat land to be had.

At last, he saw signs of life. Two small boys ran toward a house that seemed to be held together with baling wire and mud. They were returning from the chicken coop, each carrying two eggs. He softened his usually deep voice so as not to scare them.

"Is your sister, Beryl, here?"

The smaller child pointed an egg-filled fist toward the dilapidated house. The older one said, "she's inside helping Mama sew up some fancy clothes."

"Please tell her the sheriff is out here and would like to talk to her for a few minutes."

"You're the sheriff?" one boy asked, staring at Bowman. "Do you have a badge?"

Bowman opened his jacket to reveal the star pinned to the breast pocket of his denim shirt.

"Wow," they said in unison.

Excited about the notoriety of a lawman at their house, both children dashed up the porch steps and through the front door. Bowman, noting the barren garden and the scrawny cow that scrounged for grass in a near-by corral, hoped that the boys wouldn't drop those eggs. Four eggs would hardly feed a family of at least five, and he didn't want to be the cause of an even more meager meal.

More quickly than he would have expected, a diminutive girl, he could hardly call her a woman, came out on the porch through a screen door that had too many unplanned holes in it to be of any use whatsoever in keeping insects from entering the house.

In contrast to the sparse surroundings, Beryl Turner wore a bright blue dress that complimented her developing figure without appearing provocative. Bowman thought that, if he were her father, he would approve of the high cut bodice and flowing skirt.

Two rickety chairs sat forlornly by the door, rocking in the gentle breeze. Beryl sat in one and motioned for Bowman to join her. He was glad to do so because he didn't want his height to intimidate her, especially after he saw how small she was. Far better if they were both on the same level. He sat down, hoping the chair would hold his weight. It did.

"They're stronger than they look," she said, as if reading his mind. "My daddy makes them from cedar saplings."

She pointed toward the southeastern hills where autumn-kissed trees glowed yellow in the late afternoon sun.

"He'll make you some if you want, but I know you didn't come here to talk about that." She paused, studying Bowman. "What do you want with me, sheriff?"

"Miss Turner, may I call you Beryl?"

She nodded politely, keeping her eyes fixed on his. Despite her tiny size and obvious youth, she held his gaze with the poise of a much older woman. Fred Harvey picked his Girls wisely, seeing in the young women of the American West a potential that others might overlook.

"A woman was found in the alley behind the Harvey House last night. She had been murdered."

Bowman waited for a response, got none, so continued his narrative.

"She was a passenger on Friday's east bound train."

He watched Beryl's hazel eyes for any flicker of knowledge. She acted neither surprised nor dismayed, as if she heard this sort of news on a regular basis.

"I spoke to the staff at the Harvey House today. Tessa Crane told me this woman was seated at your table. I was also told that she was the only woman there at the time. I'm hoping that you remember her."

Beryl continued to regard him with her startling eyes. Flecked with gold, they resembled green ponds glittering in early morning light.

Finally, she said, "Tessa's right. She always knows what's happening in the dining room. What did she tell you about this woman?"

"All she said was that I should talk to you."

"I remember her, dressed up real fancy, like she was

still in San Francisco. She loved San Francisco. She couldn't stop talking about how wonderful it was, and how dirty and plain it is in Arizona. She wore a brown suit, satin, I think. It was the color of the chocolate pudding that cook sometimes makes for dessert. It was tight, too. Fit her like a glove. Whoever made the dress used yards of lace. There was lace on the collar, the sleeves and the hem. She not only had a sense of fashion, but money too."

"You know a lot about fashion," Bowman said. He instantly regretted his words, thinking that it sounded like he was surprised that someone who lived this hardscrabble life would have any idea about haute couture.

"My mother is a seamstress. You've probably seen some of the dresses she's made on women in town."

Beryl didn't appear to be offended at Bowman's statement. She spoke with pride.

"If your wife needs a pretty dress, well-made, at a good price, she should talk to my mother." She laughed. "Listen to me. I'm peddling my father's chairs and my mother's sewing. I'm sorry, sheriff. You want me to tell you about that woman, not try to sell my family's wares."

"Don't apologize, Beryl. I'm not married, but I might consider a couple of these chairs." He knocked on the arms of his chair. "You're right, though. I need to know about Deirdre Sweeney. You said she didn't like Arizona."

"Deirdre Sweeney? That was her name?"

"Yes." Bowman had purposefully delayed mention of the woman's name, hoping that Beryl might let slip the fact that she knew her. Her surprise seemed genuine, however.

"Well, sheriff, Deirdre Sweeney was a city girl, for sure. Winslow was too wild, not cultured enough for her. She talked sort of funny, too. Not like east coast funny. I don't think she was an American, at least not one who'd lived here very long. I liked listening to her talk, though. It was, um, sweet, I guess."

Bowman had no idea what *sweet* meant when it came to speech, but somehow, when Beryl said it, it made sense. He would ask Mrs. Crook at the hotel if Miss Sweeney spoke with an accent.

Beryl stared at her boots. Bowman figured she was thinking about fashionable women from across the ocean. He gave her a verbal nudge.

"Was she traveling with someone? Was she upset about something that was said during dinner?"

"First off, yes, she was upset when she got to my table. You know about the conductor. You arrested him. Did that woman turn him in? Is that why he yelled at her?"

Bowman ignored the question. "You say she was upset when she got to your table, Beryl? I was told that she laughed off the conductor's threats."

"At first she smiled, but it was one of those smiles that aren't real. You know, like when you have to be nice to someone you don't like. Just her lips turned up. She wasn't smiling with her whole face."

Bowman realized that Beryl Turner was a very observant young woman.

"Anything else?"

"Yes. She was more upset that you'd think to look at her. She picked up her spoon to eat her soup and it was shaking so bad she had to put it down. Then, her companion whispered something in her ear. Pretty soon she picked up that spoon again and ate every drop of soup. Whatever that handsome man said soothed her right down."

A dreamy look came over Beryl's face. Bowman guessed that she would like to meet a handsome man of her own. He cleared his throat to get her attention.

"I was told she left the table in a temper."

"Well, while they ate the soup and salad they talked, with each other and with the other passengers at my table. They had come together from San Francisco, and that's all they talked about. He agreed with her every time she said how fantastic that city was. Then, one of them would remember something that happened there and they would both laugh."

"What made her mad?" Bowman asked.

"Truthfully, sheriff, I don't know. I went to the kitchen to get the coffee, and when I came back, she was berating him. I couldn't understand what they were arguing about, but she said something about wanting to find someone she knew in Winslow."

When Beryl didn't continue, Bowman asked, "What did the man say to her then?"

Talking to this woman tried his patience. He sure liked looking into her eyes, though.

"Well," Beryl said, "he laughed and told her to put the past behind her. He said, 'We're going to be married. We shouldn't dwell on what might have been.' By then, I was serving the folks across the table, so I didn't hear what he said next. Whatever it was, she was up and out that door in a flash. She was crying, so what he said really upset her."

Beryl rocked gently for a few moments. Again, Bowman wanted to rush her, but forced himself to wait quietly. He focused on the view across the desolate Turner homestead toward the craggy mountains to the south. Maybe the scenery was what drew Mr. Turner to this land, without regard to its potential as a working ranch. Beryl finally spoke, bringing him back to the troublesome issue of murder.

"After she ran out, the man went on eating his dinner, calm as can be. Like he didn't care about her or her problems. But, you know what, sheriff? He didn't get on that train. I'm sure of that, because he was still sitting at my table when I heard the whistle blow."

Beryl, expecting some indication of surprise from Bowman, frowned.

"You already knew that, sheriff?" she asked.

"Yes, Beryl. Other people saw them together on Sunday." He didn't elaborate.

The young woman nodded, but said nothing. Bowman figured he had learned all that he was going to from Beryl Turner, but he decided to try a few more questions.

"Who else heard the conversation at your table?"

"Certainly all the other passengers who were sitting there," she replied. "Of course, they all left on the train. Maybe some of the folks at the nearby table, but they were passengers, too. The woman was angry, and she wasn't trying to keep her voice down. I suppose almost everyone in the dining room heard at least part of what she said. What about the men at the lunch counter?"

When the residents of Winslow came to the Harvey House for a meal, they would sit at the lunch counter. The local railroad men were frequent diners, happy to take advantage of special meal rates they received at all of Fred Harvey's establishments. Cowboys, ranchers and business owners from town would often join them.

Some male train passengers also preferred to perch on one of the counter's dark wood stools, where the atmosphere was less formal and they could drink something stronger than lemonade.

"That's a good thought, Beryl," Bowman said. "I'll ask around among the railroad men. What did her companion do? Did he follow her?"

Bowman had been told by Tessa that the man stayed behind, but he wanted to see if Beryl would tell the same story.

"No," Beryl answered. "After she left, mad as a cornered wildcat, he finished his meal. Then he had a drink, brandy maybe, at the bar. That was after the train left. I never saw him again." She paused.

What she said next surprised Bowman.

"I saw her again, though."

"You did? When?" He wondered why she hadn't offered that piece of information earlier in their conversation.

"My work day ended after the three o'clock train yesterday. That means I started for home about four in the afternoon."

"How do you go back and forth? Do you keep a horse in town?"

Beryl gave the sheriff a rueful smile. "Sheriff, we don't have horses to spare, let alone the money to board them. I mostly walk. It takes a half hour or so, unless I'm real tired, like last night, then maybe closer to one hour."

"Tell me about seeing Deirdre Sweeney yesterday."

"Do you know Hiram Frye?"

"Yes," Bowman answered, wondering what that old sot had to do with the beautiful stranger whose body now rested with the undertaker. "He's the night watchman at the Santa Fe roundhouse."

"He also spends a lot of time at the lunch counter, or, as in this case, the Harvey House bar."

Bowman realized that Beryl's guise of farm-girl innocence belied her real-life experience.

"He was sitting at the bar yesterday afternoon. I was busy with the last train, but after those passengers left, it got quiet in the dining room. He was still there, complaining about his wife to the bartender. I had finished cleaning my work area and was ready to leave. He held the door open for me so we walked outside together."

Beryl picked at a loose reed in her chair seat.

"What does Hiram Frye have to do with Deirdre Sweeney, Beryl?" Bowman's heart sank with the sun. He wanted to get back to Winslow before dark.

"I didn't want to walk with him, sheriff, so I said that I forgot something and came back inside. I waited a few minutes before I left. But, when I went back outside again, he wasn't gone like I'd hoped. He was talking to the woman."

"The woman? You mean Miss Sweeney?"

"Yes. They were standing in front of the post office. It was close enough that I could see them, but I didn't hear what they were saying."

"What did you see?"

"They were facing each other, talking serious. It reminded me of when two cowboys square off to fight. They're not really mad at each other, just fighting to fight. Oh, I don't know, sheriff. When I say it, it sounds stupid."

"You're doing a good job, Beryl." Bowman wanted to reassure her. This was information he needed.

"What surprised me," Beryl looked at her shoes, embarrassed, "was that he wasn't looking at her in that odd way of his. You know, that leer he has that makes me uncomfortable. Tessa feels that way, too. She always tries to avoid him, but she wasn't so lucky yesterday."

Bowman was instantly alert. "What do you mean 'she wasn't so lucky yesterday'? Was she with you when this happened?"

"No, sheriff. She was serving at the lunch counter yesterday when Mr. Frye was there. I don't think she saw him talking to the woman. She winked at me once when Mr. Frye was going on about his wife. Tessa's so nice, sheriff. She would just smile at that repulsive man. She doesn't seem afraid of him or anything, just doesn't like to have him around."

Bowman made a mental note to speak to Miss Crane again. Was she keeping something from him?

"What happened after you saw them talking?" Bowman asked.

"Nothing, really. He didn't try to grab her, like he does with most pretty women. They talked for a few minutes. He acted surprised at whatever she said, then, all of a sudden, she just turned away from him and walked down the street. Only, it was more than a walk. She seemed angry and in a hurry. Mr. Frye followed her. I've never seen him walk so fast."

"Thank you, Beryl." Bowman rose to leave.

"Maybe she deserved to die."

Beryl said the words so matter-of-factly that Bowman wasn't sure he heard correctly.

"What do you mean?" he asked, retaking his seat in the rustic chair.

"That woman came to Winslow, showing off her fancy

clothes and her handsome man, who, by the way, was not her husband, acting like she's better than us. She made people angry, maybe too angry."

Beryl's words surprised Bowman. This quiet farm girl who seemed content to help support her struggling family had just shown a fire in her belly, a desire for a better life, perhaps a city life in San Francisco where she could wear the elegant clothes her mother sewed for others. Was Beryl one of those people whom Deirdre Sweeney had angered?

"I'm different that most of the girls, sheriff. I live here." She gestured at the pathetic homestead. "I sleep at the Harvey House when I'm scheduled to work, but I don't socialize much with the other girls. You need to talk to them about the people in town. I'm needed here."

Bowman had no trouble believing that last statement. He wondered how much she resented the obligations that kept her away from the dances and parties that the Harvey Girls occasionally hosted. He sighed. Beryl had provided him with a lot of information about the murdered woman, but she had also raised more questions that he would now have to answer.

He thanked her again, mounted Lucky and headed north. As he rode, he swung around in the saddle, gazing at the distant White Mountains, a beautiful area where clear lakes dotted vast green meadows. He was an avid fisherman, too long away from the water, but the mountains didn't offer a man much in the way of a livelihood. Towns sprang up along the railway line, and towns, not lakes, needed lawmen. The mountains would have to wait. In Winslow, he had a murderer to bring to justice. At the moment, he was flummoxed as to just how he was going to do that.

Chapter Four

Tessa's concern for Lupe grew with each tick of the clock. Where did her friend go night after night? Winslow was not Chicago, or even Albuquerque. Here, there were few places for a respectable woman to frequent in the evenings. She pushed thoughts of the not-so-respectable places out of her mind.

Lupe said she had been visiting friends and family. Tessa knew that Lupe's brother, Joaquin, was a wrangler at the Silver Spur, a nearby ranch. Her mother and three sisters lived in Albuquerque. There might be an odd cousin or two in Winslow, but no close relations.

As for friends, Tessa was befuddled about that, as well. Lupe worked hard, sent every spare penny to her mother in New Mexico, and very seldom went visiting. She might have a few friends at the Catholic Church where she attended services, but she had never, to Tessa's knowledge, gone to anyone's house for tea or dinner. Despite her concern, the thought of Lupe dressed in ruffles and lace, calling on the socialites of Winslow, amused her.

Restless, she flung herself off the bed, deciding that activity would ease her anxiety. She removed her uniform and donned a soft robe. Her hair, which she had released from its net as soon as she'd gotten to the room, was now tied back by a bright red ribbon, a festive splash of color in what Tessa considered dull brown hair.

She often wished she had the dark, almost black tresses of the Mexican girls, or Charlotte Hubbard's seductive blond curls. Instead, she was cursed with an unimaginative brown shade that lay somewhere between the beautiful extremes.

She began to restore order to her half of the bedroom. She smiled as she picked up a lace-trimmed undergarment from beside her bed, folded it and tucked it into a drawer. Lupe had flung that very camisole at her one morning a week or two earlier.

"Amiga, don't leave your clothes in my half of the room," she had said. "You can keep your part as messy as you like, although I can't figure out how you ever find anything."

Her impish grin told Tessa that she was being teased, although what Lupe said was true enough.

Lupe kept her bed wrinkle-free, hung her clothes neatly in the armoire, uniforms on one side, day dresses on the other, and stashed her books out of sight under the bed.

"I don't understand it, Tessa. Your uniforms are always spotless and tidy, yet you put other clothes, letters or books in a different place each time."

Lupe indicated Tessa's side of the bedroom with a quick jerk of her head.

"And sometimes," she continued her lecture, "when you get into bed at night, I hear the crunch of paper that has yet to find a home. How you ever locate anything is a mystery to me."

The memory of Lupe's lecture shamed Tessa into straightening the room. It would be a pleasant surprise when Lupe returned, whenever that might be. After folding clothes and placing letters in a drawer, she dusted the table and chest.

As she worked, she remembered how her father used to look into her bedroom and sigh at the disarray. Once, when she was perhaps eleven years old, she caught him standing by her door with tears in his eyes.

"Papa, have I made you cry? I'll clean my room, I promise."

"No, sweet Tessa," he'd said, coming to sit beside her on the bed. "I want to tell you something. I know you don't remember your mother very well, but she was always so proud of how neat you kept your toys, even though you were so small. And, you always made your bed. She would often give you a sweet and say, 'What a good little housekeeper you are, Tessa. You'll make a fine wife one day.'"

Her father wiped a tear from his cheek.

"I'm sorry that I can't remember, Papa. Are you sure it was me she was talking about?" Tessa remembered her father laughing at her silly question.

"Oh, yes, Tessa, it was you. Then she died, and ever since, your room has been untidy. At first, you would push me into your room and ask me when Momma was going to come and tell you to straighten it. Not dirty, mind you, but so disorganized. By the time you were seven, you quit asking, but you never kept you room neat again. I think that, in some strange way, it is how you keep your mother's memory alive. I couldn't bear to chide you about it, because I wish she would come back, too."

Tessa smiled through her tears at the memory. The room was now immaculate and she would try harder to keep it that way. She owed it to Lupe, who had, Tessa realized as the clock chimed ten times, missed another curfew.

She sat down to read a two-month-old New York Times that she had unearthed in her cleaning spree. Her cousin, Sarah, sent parcels of newspapers and magazines at least once a month, always with the entreaty, "Please come to New York, Thérése," as if the fashion and society pages, as well as the use of her formal given name, could lure Tessa away from her home in the West.

She caught herself reading the same paragraph at least three times and still couldn't recall what it was about. Instead, her mind dwelled on Lupe's strange behavior since Deirdre Sweeney's arrival. Then there was this morning's shocking news of her murder. Was there a connection?

"You're awake." Lupe stated the obvious when she opened the door to find Tessa staring idly at the open newspaper.

"Where have you been?" Tessa asked. An accusation more than a question.

"I was at Elena's. Do you know Luis' aunt, Tia Elena?"

"I can't remember all of your relatives, Lupe," Tessa said. "I know that Luis is a distant cousin, but I don't think I've met his aunt."

"Don't worry. I forget their names sometimes, too." She looked at Tessa. "Joaquin was there."

Lupe said her brother's name so softly that Tessa had

to strain to hear. And, there was a hesitation before she mentioned him, as if she didn't want to speak his name aloud, that made Tessa's skin crawl.

Joaquin was Lupe's much revered older brother. He had been a father figure to Lupe and her three sisters after the frightened family escaped political persecution in Mexico following the imprisonment of Lupe's father. The family held no hope that *Señor* Castillo was still alive, so the entire Castillo family looked to Joaquin as their patriarch.

"Joaquin? What was your brother doing in town at night?"

"He asked *Señora* McAllister if he could visit me. He heard about the murder and wanted to talk to me about it. Oh, Tessa," Lupe cried, "he knew her."

Her chest heaved as if she couldn't catch her breath.

"Joaquin knew Deirdre Sweeney?"

At first, Lupe's story confused Tessa, then the pieces fell into place.

"You recognized her that day, didn't you? I knew you were frightened, but you told me you were just tired."

"Yes," Lupe said, answering both of Tessa's questions with one word.

"I recognized her from a long time ago. She called herself 'Deirdre' then, too, but I don't think I ever knew her family name."

Lupe picked up a brightly painted statue of Our Lady of Guadalupe, a much-revered Catholic saint, as well as her namesake. The intricate wooden carving was all that graced her Spartan bedside table. As she spoke, she looked at the statue rather than at Tessa.

"Deirdre lived here in Winslow, maybe five or six years

ago. She worked at the Silver Spur for perhaps four months. *Señora* McAllister would probably remember her. Many people in town might not have known her because she stayed out at the ranch, but…"

Tessa tried to wait out the pause, but grew impatient. "What, Lupe? What are you trying to tell me?"

"Joaquin knew her. I think maybe he knew her very well, if you know what I'm saying."

The blush on Lupe's dark cheeks told Tessa all she needed to know about how well Joaquin and the murdered woman were acquainted.

"One day she just disappeared." Lupe waved her hands in the air, like a magician with a disappearing rabbit. "No one knew where. However, before that happened she told Joaquin she was going to have his child and she would tell the sheriff that he had taken advantage of her. Of course, what she wanted from my brother was money. She should have known that he didn't have any. I was just a maid for the mayor's family then. I couldn't help my poor brother. I was frightened for Joaquin, but he had already decided to return to Mexico. That was far better than facing prison. He knew he wouldn't be able to convince a jury here in Winslow that he was innocent. A Mexican's word against a beautiful white woman? Ha!"

"What happened?" Tessa was tense with apprehension.

Lupe studied her dishwater-toughened hands, clasped as if in prayer. Perhaps that was exactly what she was doing.

"I don't know what happened. All of a sudden, she was gone. Of course, I went to church and thanked *Dios* for that. Joaquin was doubly happy. He didn't have to face her accusations, and he wouldn't have to return to Mexico.

Then, last week, she comes back to Winslow, maybe to try again to get Joaquin to give her money."

"Did she go out to the Silver Spur?" Tessa asked.

"Joaquin says that he hasn't seen her since she left five years ago."

The emphasis Lupe put on the word *says* gave Tessa pause. Could Lupe possibly not believe her brother?

"How did Joaquin find out about the murder so quickly?"

"He came into town this morning for supplies. Mr. Mulliner told him about it. After he left the General Store, he went to the saloon and heard the same story from Mr. Morris. So, he came back to town tonight to talk to me."

"What did you tell him?" Tessa's voice quivered.

Tessa liked Lupe's brother. He had a reputation as an excellent ranch hand. He was a good-looking man, older than the other cowboys, and he seemed to prefer solitude over sharing whiskey at one of Winslow's two saloons. Tessa didn't want to see him in trouble, and murder was big trouble indeed.

Instead of answering Tessa's question, Lupe said, "Tonight wasn't the first time I've seen Joaquin since Deirdre came back."

She seemed uncomfortable with the conversation, wishing perhaps that she had never broached the topic. Tessa sensed Lupe's hesitation. The troubled Mexicana looked like she wanted to reach through the air and snatch her words back.

"The sheriff and Mr. Clifton want us to tell them if we know anything about Deirdre Sweeney, Tessa, but I can't tell him this. I know," she pounded her fist into her hand for emphasis, "that Joaquin didn't have anything to do with the woman's murder. Oh, I never should have said anything." She started to cry.

Tessa could see the direction of her friend's thoughts and she was quick to put her mind at ease.

"Lupe, listen to me. I am your friend, your *amiga.* You and I both know that Joaquin is a good boy, or rather, he's a responsible man. I believe you and I promise that I won't say anything to Mr. Clifton or the sheriff. Now, please tell me what happened after you saw Deirdre on Friday."

Lupe took the handkerchief Tessa offered and swiped at her nose and eyes.

"I was worried that she could still accuse Joaquin of rape." She hesitated as if that distasteful word should not come from her lips. "I was afraid for Joaquin when I saw Deirdre last week. Now that she has been murdered, I am even more afraid. My dear *hermano* is a good man, if a little temperamental. I had to talk to him, so I rode out to the Silver Spur."

"Alone? At night?" Tessa was incredulous.

"No. Oh, Tessa, I lied to Miss Parks." Again, tears dribbled down her cheeks, but she kept talking. "Saturday afternoon I told her that I wasn't feeling well. I got a horse from the livery and rode out to the Silver Spur. I went to confession as soon as I got back."

"And you talked to Joaquin?" Tessa tried to keep her aggravation with Lupe's circuitous story out of her voice.

"I warned him to stay out of Deirdre's way, to remain at the ranch. The roundup is Friday night and I asked him to find a way not to come into town. Of course, now that she is dead it doesn't matter, except that maybe he should avoid seeing the sheriff, who might ask too many questions."

"Does Anna McAllister know about Deirdre and Joaquin?"

"Of course she knows that Deirdre and Joaquin worked for her at the Silver Spur at the same time, but I don't know if she knew about the rest." Lupe blushed again.

"Are you certain the murdered woman is the same person who worked at the Silver Spur?" Tessa asked. "That was a long time ago. You might not recognize her now, and, even if she is the same one, this woman obviously does not have a child."

"I'm sure, *amiga*. She doesn't look much different than she did five years ago. Yes, she wears fancier clothes, but the person inside those expensive dresses was the same woman. I know she came back to ask Joaquin for money."

Lupe covered her mouth with trembling hands. Her mumbled words tugged at Tessa's heart.

"No one will believe Joaquin, or me, that he had nothing to do with her death. I'm sure she was going to demand money from him. I wonder if she had a picture of a child with her. That could be very bad for Joaquin. Oh, Tessa, what are we going to do?"

Lupe was right when she said "we." Instinctively, Tessa knew that Joaquin had not killed Deirdre Sweeney. The difficult thing would be proving it to the sheriff. Tomorrow was her day off. She would start by riding out to the Silver Spur and talking to her friend, Anna McAllister. While she was there, she also intended to speak with Lupe's brother. Tessa wanted to know what Joaquin Castillo intended to do about Deirdre Sweeney. What he had intended to do short of murder, that is.

"Oh, I almost forgot." Lupe's words interrupted Tessa's

dark thoughts. "I brought you a tamale. That's why I'm so late. I couldn't talk to Joaquin until the children went to bed, and they stayed up to help make the tamales."

She reached into her pocket and handed a parcel to Tessa. As she did, her eyes grew round with surprise.

"Ay, Dios, the room is glorious." She frowned. "No, that's not the word. I meant to say *gorgeous.* I can't believe I didn't notice your hard work earlier. Here, eat your tamale."

"This smells wonderful," Tessa said as she removed the soft cornhusk that covered the fragrant bundle, and took a large bite.

"Thank you, Lupe," she mumbled through a mouthful of tamale. She pushed all thoughts of murder from her mind for a few minutes as she enjoyed the delicious cornmeal and chili creation.

"Tia Elena's son, Enrique, wanted to fold over the cornhusks for the tamales. He is a handsome boy and very smart. He's only five but he knows his alphabet already."

Lupe babbled on, obviously hesitant to return to the serious conversation about Joaquin and Deirdre Sweeney.

"Did you know that Elena adopted him from the Sisters at Madre de Dios Church? What luck for the two of them to have found each other. He finally fell asleep on the floor. Elena put him to bed so we could talk."

"Did you tell her about Deirdre?"

"I didn't need to tell her. She saw Deirdre, that 'devil woman' as she calls her, in the post office and knew instantly who she was and why she had come back to Winslow. Years ago, Elena would invite Deirdre and Joaquin to her home when they'd come to town from the Silver Spur. She never liked Deirdre, but she would welcome her for Joaquin's sake."

Lupe's hands worried at each other, an invisible rosary between them.

"Tessa, I saw the look on Elena's face when Joaquin walked into her house. I can tell she is afraid for him like I am, and for what the sheriff might do if he finds out what happened five years ago. The worst part, *amiga*, is the doubt I see there. I don't think Tia Elena is as sure of Joaquin's innocence as I am. If she doesn't believe him, what chance does he have against the sheriff and this town full of white people?"

Chapter Five

Rays of morning sunshine kissed Tessa awake. She purred with pleasure, knowing that the bright sky meant late morning, and today was her day off. Her pleasure was short-lived, however, as she remembered last night's conversation with Lupe. It was time to find out what Anna McAllister knew about Joaquin and Deirdre.

Tessa dressed quickly, donning a suede split skirt in a luscious shade of yellow, a white shirt and a dark brown bolero jacket. She squatted to check under her bed for her gloves, remembered her cleaning spree, and located them instead in a neatly organized drawer. She wondered how long it would be until she would once again find them in some unlikely place. She shook her head at her own idiosyncrasies, pulled on her heavy leather riding boots and headed downstairs, hoping she wasn't too late for breakfast.

"Good morning, Dorothea," Tessa said, as she entered the kitchen.

"You're today's lucky one, I see." Dorothea Parks greeted Tessa with a smile. "Coffee, dear?"

"I'll get some tea, thank you. It's quiet in here today. No trains?"

Quiet was a relative term in referring to the Harvey House kitchen. Oven doors slammed, pots banged and Choppy shouted orders at one of the kitchen helpers. But the extreme hustle that accompanied meal service for perhaps one hundred diners was absent.

"The eastbound train was due at ten o'clock, but the stationmaster received a telegram that it will be two hours late. Not much happening in here now, but that only means that we'll have two trains within one hour of each other later. Aren't you glad you're going out for the day?"

"Yes, and a beautiful day it is," Tessa said, as she helped herself to a warm bun.

Tessa looked at the older woman. Years of work in a hot kitchen had weathered her face and plumped her hips. She had kind eyes and, as Tessa knew firsthand, a warm heart.

"That's not much to eat, Tessa," Dorothea said, pointing a spatula at the tiny roll on Tessa's plate. "I could fry up an egg or two for you if you'd like?"

"No, thank you, Dorothea."

Tessa thought about the cook's sympathetic eyes and Lupe's troubled ones. She could postpone the ride to the Silver Spur for a few more minutes. Still, she hesitated. She might learn a lot from Dorothea, but to ask forthright questions could give away more of what she knew than was wise. Putting her concern aside, she plunged ahead.

"You've lived in Winslow a long time, haven't you?" she asked.

Dorothea turned the question into an invitation. She pulled out a chair and sat down opposite Tessa before answering. Tessa took a bite of the warm roll, smiled her appreciation at the cook.

"I certainly have," she said, pride creeping into her voice. "I made the trip west with my sister in '78. She was a young bride. A mail order bride, actually. Our parents were both dead, so I came along to see that she was safe. My, what a trip that was. We didn't come by train, but with a group of wagoners. My sister, Sally, met her husband for the first time when we arrived in Albuquerque. She stayed there, of course. I intended to stay with her, but..."

The cook stopped her remembrances when she saw the disinterested look on Tessa's face.

"Sorry, dear. Of course, you're not concerned with the ramblings of an old lady, are you? I think you want to know if I have any idea about this murder, right?"

"Did you know that woman, Dorothea?"

"Well, I think, but I'm not sure, that maybe this Deirdre girl lived in Winslow several years ago. You know, we get so many of these women with their big city clothes and high-class airs, that I can't be sure. They all look alike, too, as if they stepped out of the pages of one of those *Ladies' Home Journals.* They think they're too good for the likes of our little town."

She sucked in an audible breath and her large bosom heaved with the effort.

"If she did live here, it wasn't for long, or maybe she took a position out at one of the ranches. That was fine with us devout women. We never saw her in church, although the Good Lord Himself knows she should've been there."

Tessa almost laughed. *Devout* was not quite the right description for good-hearted Dorothea. She hardly ever attended church. In fact, she seemed to make it a point to be working most Sundays. And Tessa had heard her use some pretty descriptive language while talking to Choppy and Oswald.

Tessa donned her hat and gloves, thanked the cook and headed toward the livery. She greeted a few of her fellow Harvey Girls as she walked through the dining room. To a person, they were well groomed, poised and hard at work. Their uniforms were clean and crisp. When working, Tessa, too, took great pride in presenting herself as a model representative of Mr. Harvey's empire.

Today, however, she was looking forward to a ride through the high desert, where the autumn air was crisp and dry, permeated by the pungent aroma of sagebrush, still lush from the summer rains.

The smell of horses and hay wafted up the street from the livery. Images of soldiers in smart blue uniforms, sitting ramrod straight atop their mounts sprang into Tessa's mind. Until she became a Harvey Girl, Army posts and cavalry brigades were all that she knew.

She wasn't surprised to find Jed Bowman absent from his livery. Most of the time, he was a part-time sheriff and full-time stable owner. She supposed that, with this murder, the roles were very much reversed. Most likely, he was out asking questions, looking for anyone who might have information about Deirdre Sweeney or the man who had been with her and was now missing.

She was glad that she wouldn't have to answer any of those questions. Yet. She found Edward Barnes, Bowman's able assistant, in the back stalls, feeding bits of hay to a young appaloosa.

"He's a pretty one," she said, startling Edward. He jumped and dropped the entire handful of hay into the lucky horse's stall.

"Sorry, I didn't mean to scare you. Would you saddle Ben for me? I need to ride out to the Silver Spur."

She pulled a colorful saddle blanket off the fence rail. "Here, let me help."

She reached behind the young man to grab the bit and reins, but gladly left the heavy saddle for Edward to wrestle with. He gave Tessa a gap-toothed grin, easily forgiving her for the fright, and strode to the back paddock to retrieve the gentle mule that Tessa preferred over any of the livery's horses. Ben was surefooted on the rocks, obedient as a child, and seemed to enjoy their time together as much as she did. He stood quietly as she mounted and she could have sworn he was smiling.

"Miss Crane, I'd like to speak with you." Sheriff Bowman's booming voice stopped mule and rider in their tracks.

Tessa looked back to see the sheriff walking quickly down the boardwalk from the jailhouse.

"If only I hadn't spent time talking to Miss Parks," she whispered to Ben, who blinked his eyes in agreement.

Tessa dismounted and waited for Bowman to arrive at her side. She felt her hands going numb and realized that she was gripping the reins as if she were riding a bucking stallion. She willed herself to relax.

"Yes, sheriff?"

"I spoke to Beryl Turner yesterday. She told me that you served Hiram Frye at the lunch counter Saturday."

Tessa dropped the reins in her surprise. She hadn't known exactly what Bowman wanted to ask her, but a question about the town drunk was not at all what she expected.

"Yes, I did. Has something happened to him?"

"No, should it?" Bowman asked.

His question confused Tessa even more.

"I'm not sure what you mean, sheriff. Mr. Frye ate lunch at the counter, created a little scene and finally left."

"A little scene?"

Bowman removed his wide-brimmed hat, scratched his head, and plunked it back on his head. It landed slightly crooked across his forehead, giving him a comical appearance. Tessa didn't laugh.

"You must know that Hiram Frye eats his noon meal at the lunch counter almost every day." Tessa said.

"I know that he's there frequently, but I understand that he often drinks more than he eats," Bowman said.

"Thank you, sheriff."

"For what?" Bowman asked.

"For saving me the embarrassment of explaining the true situation with Mr. Frye," Tessa said. "You asked what happened Saturday."

"Yes, Beryl told me he was there."

"I'm used to his ranting, sheriff, so I didn't think much of it. He was going on about his wife, how she wants new clothes for herself and for their daughter. Now, apparently, she also wants a piano for the girl to play."

"Did it sound like he would threaten his wife?" Bowman asked.

"Hiram talks like that most of the time, especially after he's had a few drinks. We girls have learned to ignore him, but I think Mr. Clifton was annoyed. He gave the bartender the chopping motion with his hand to get him to stop serving Hiram any more liquor. When he was out of Frye's hearing, he whispered that he wanted someone else to deal with him for awhile. 'That old troublemaker' is what Mr. Clifton called him."

"Did he leave?" Bowman asked.

"He did," Tessa said, "but not before I heard him say that he used to be the sheriff in Winslow. Is that true, sheriff?"

"I'm afraid that's right, Miss Crane. We've got a lot more sense around here now."

He seemed to realize that he was boasting about himself as sheriff and blushed. Tessa found his obvious embarrassment endearing. Jed Bowman was an enigma, a large man with a powerful position in the town, yet he seemed to have a gentle side that manifested itself in his respectful treatment of her and the other single women of Winslow.

"How long ago was he Winslow's sheriff?" Tessa asked, in a voice she hoped conveyed a reciprocal respect.

"It was some five or six years back. It was when his wife was expecting their child. He cleaned himself up and the townsfolk rewarded him by electing him sheriff. He treated his wife like a queen and was pleasant to everyone. Unfortunately, it didn't last. Once she had the child, he quickly lost interest in family life, although I have to say, his wife still seems to have some influence on him. I think he's afraid of her." Bowman said.

He patted Ben as he talked. "Did you see Hiram after he left the Harvey House?"

"No, he hasn't been back since Saturday," Tessa answered. "Why?"

"Beryl Turner told me that she saw him talking to the woman who was murdered. I'm wondering how they knew each other."

Tessa froze. The harmless conversation she was having with Sheriff Bowman just turned dangerous. She couldn't tell him that Deirdre had lived in Winslow several years ago without disclosing Joaquin's involvement. Not wanting to lie to the lawman, she merely shrugged.

"I don't know anything more about Hiram Frye than I've told you, sheriff."

It was not a lie. The subject of that old coot was safe territory, and Tessa relaxed.

"Can I leave now?" she asked, in what she hoped was a lighthearted voice. "I'm on my way to the Silver Spur."

He dismissed her with a wave of his hand. Soon she was headed east toward the McAllister ranch. She never tired of gazing at the Arizona landscape, painted in a palette of warm golds and soft oranges. Today, white clouds speckled the blue sky, which in turn melded into the red rock mountains in nature's own version of the American flag. Ben provided a tranquil ride and a friendly ear as she poured out her confusion about Lupe and Joaquin.

"What is Lupe hiding from me?" she asked Ben.

"Did Joaquin have something to do with Deirdre Sweeney's murder? And what does Hiram Frye have to do with it?"

Ben remained silent, preferring to concentrate on the rocky path.

They covered the two miles from town to the Silver Spur without incident, which suited Tessa just fine. There had been a few rides punctuated by coiled rattlesnakes and howling coyotes. Ben had never bolted in the face of danger, but Tessa didn't want to test the depth of his serenity.

By the time she and Ben arrived at the ranch gate, Tessa had figured out the answer to her last question. If Deirdre had tried to get money from Joaquin for her non-existent child, then she probably had tried the same thing with Hiram Frye. How many other men in Winslow had fallen victim to her charms and consequent threats?

Chapter Six

Tessa was several hundred yards from the McAllister house when Candy and Rebel, the ranch dogs, ran out to greet her, barking happily.

"I've got some nice bones from the Harvey House kitchen for you two mutts," she told the excited dogs as they escorted her and Ben to the house. Before Tessa could dismount, Anna McAllister opened the screen door, shrieked with joy, and ran down the porch steps to greet her.

"I'm so glad you're here," Anna said as she folded Tessa in a smothering hug.

Anna towered over Tessa and stood eye-to-eye with most of the ranch hands. Young widowhood and an outdoor life had robbed her of traditional beauty. Pitching hay and wrestling cattle added muscle bulk to her stocky frame, yet she moved with the grace of a dancer as she walked with Tessa toward the barn. Dignified, gracious, impressive, was how Tessa thought of her friend.

Tessa studied the interior of the barn. "Where's Joaquin?"

During the ride to the ranch, her mind dwelled on Joaquin Castillo and Deirdre Sweeney. The discovery of his absence from the Silver Spur filled her with apprehension. Anna's answer eased her mind.

"He's breaking my new thoroughbred in the far pasture," Anna said with pride.

Tessa had heard talk amongst the local ranchers of Joaquin's amazing skill with horses. "He speaks to them in Spanish, and they actually seem to understand," said one of the Harvey House's regular patrons. "He can break the most spirited stallion with quiet words and simple gestures. It's uncanny. Mrs. McAllister is lucky to have him as one of her ranch hands."

"This horse is strong-willed," Anna said, bringing Tessa back to the present, "but I have no doubt that Joaquin will have him ready to ship with the cattle. C'mon, I'll help you unsaddle Ben and get him some food and water. Then I have some fresh coffee on the stove for us."

Anna continued to chatter as the two women cared for the mule.

"We're only shipping fifty head to St. Louis this week, plus the stallion. It's not many but it will keep us in flour and salt over the winter. I'm grateful to have this sale, too, I'll tell you. That Aztec Cattle Company is so large that they can sell their cattle cheaper than the rest of us. The small ranchers around here, and I'm one of them, know exactly what Aztec wants to do: drive us out of business so they can buy up our land for a song. Do you know they bought over one million acres of land from the railroad for only fifty cents an acre?"

"My goodness, Anna," Tessa said, "I don't know much

about land prices, but I do know that that price sounds more like stealing land than buying it."

Anna shook her head violently as if to dispel her angry thoughts. "Don't get me started on the Aztec's Hashknife Cowboys."

She kicked at the dirt, displaying the fireball temper that was both feared and respected among her cowhands.

"Shorty is always telling me to forget about those big guys and just concentrate on doing what we do best: raise quality cattle and deliver them on time and well-fed. But how can I simply ignore their presence? Running cattle is struggle enough without the big ranchers undercutting us every which way."

Tessa laughed, earning a puzzled look from Anna.

"I know you are worried about the competition from the Aztec Company, but every time you mention Shorty, I have to laugh. What is he, at least six feet tall?"

"And skinny as a rail." Anna smiled too. "I don't know what I'd do without that grizzled old man, Tessa. Not only did he keep the Silver Spur profitable after John died, but he has taken Johnny under his wing."

"And that boy is well on the way to being another Shorty himself," Tessa said.

Her smile vanished as she asked, "will Joaquin be at the roundup Friday night?"

If Anna thought the change of subject strange, she gave no such indication.

"Yes, he will. We'd have a difficult roundup without him. Next to Shorty, Joaquin is the best hand any rancher could ask for."

As the only woman in that group, Anna was justifiably proud to include herself among the local ranchers.

"I hope you'll join the fun, Tessa. The cattle will go out on Saturday's train, but we'll have them penned up next to the depot by Friday afternoon. The boys love having all you pretty young girls there to help pass the time while they're watching over the herd."

"I'll be there, of course," Tessa said. She always enjoyed these roundup parties, and she knew most of the other girls did too."

"I'll be cooking for the crowd. Won't be fancy like the Harvey House, just plain ranch food and lots of it."

The two women sat down at Anna's kitchen table, steaming mugs of coffee in hand.

"Did you hear about the murder in town?" Tessa asked, without preamble.

"Joaquin rode into Winslow for supplies yesterday. He told me that a woman arrived from San Francisco, stayed on in Winslow and was later found murdered. That's all anyone was talking about."

Anna looked into her empty mug, stood up to retrieve the coffee pot, looked again at the mug, and sat down with a force that startled Tessa.

"Tessa, what is this all about? And don't look at me like you don't understand. Twice since you've been here, which hasn't been very long, you've asked about Joaquin. There's something else you may not know. Your roommate, Lupe, rode out here Saturday. She talked to Joaquin in the barn for a long time. Then she rode away, I presume back to town, without saying hello to me."

Tessa had been debating whether or not to mention Joaquin's connection to Deirdre Sweeney. Anna's questions made the decision for her.

"Do you remember a woman named Deirdre Sweeney?" she asked.

Anna's face blanched. She didn't run a successful cattle ranch by being stupid.

"Is that who was murdered? Joaquin didn't tell me her name. Yes, I remember her. She worked here for a short time."

She looked at Tessa, mouth forming a perfect 'o'.

"Joaquin was here back then, too. Is that why you're asking? And Lupe's visit, as well, has something to do with all these questions?"

Tessa told Anna about Deirdre's threats and Lupe's fears.

"At first, Lupe was afraid that Deirdre wanted more money from Joaquin. Then, after she was killed…"

She let her voice trail away, leaving unsaid the greatest fear of all. Could Joaquin be a murderer?

The women talked on as Anna prepared the noon meal. Their idle chatter was punctuated by additional speculation on Deirdre's murder.

"These are the last from the summer garden," Anna said, as she placed a bowl of lima beans on the kitchen table to accompany the fried chicken and applesauce. "Johnny is helping me plant a winter garden. Be prepared for cabbage in any form."

Tessa helped Anna tidy the kitchen. Anna repaid the favor by saddling Ben. What was a difficult task for Tessa was mere child's play for the hardy Anna.

"Give Johnny a hug for me."

"He'll be sorry he missed you," Anna said. "That freckle-faced kid is growing up so fast. This house is meant for more than just me. After John died, I didn't think I could bear it, but Johnny, tiny as he was, filled up the space. Now, whenever he's gone, it again feels like one heartbeat is missing. I know I have to let him grow up and find his own life, but it is so difficult."

Tessa hugged her friend and laughed. "Goodness, Anna, he's only ten. Hold those tears for awhile."

Chapter Seven

Tessa rode up Second Street, Ben's gentle gait stirring up only a few wisps of dust. As the Santa Fe roundhouse came into view, she thought of Hiram Frye, who was the night watchman there. Before she could ponder the puzzling questions that Sheriff Bowman had asked about him, a familiar figure appeared around the corner. She reined in Ben and dismounted.

"Hi, Johnny," she called to the small figure.

The boy, who seemed to be studying his horse's mane, looked up at the sound of his name. A broad grin broke out across his freckled face when he saw Tessa. When he reached her, he dismounted as well and allowed himself to be enveloped in a generous hug. He returned the hug quickly and gently, fearful, Tessa guessed, that one of his friends might see the display of affection and tease him about it later.

"Hello, Miss Crane."

He was very courteous when he saw her in town. When she visited the Silver Spur, she insisted that he call her Tessa. She didn't consider herself to be the severe person envisaged by the Miss Crane moniker, but she respected Anna McAllister's determination to instill good manners in her son. Tessa noted the stack of books tied to the saddle horn. "Looks like Miss Kingsley assigned a lot of studying for you tonight."

"Yes, Ma'am. And Momma wants me to plant some winter vegetables when I get home. Seems like there's always some woman with an idea about how I should be spending my time."

Tessa laughed. "You might as well figure that out right now, young man. You've got a lifetime of answering to women in front of you."

"Tessa?" The eyes that met hers glistened slightly with impending tears and the smile disappeared. His voice deepened, a boy assuming the serious demeanor of a man. He momentarily forgot the social formalities instilled by his mother.

Tessa noticed the change in tone and let her own face reflect his solemn manner. "Yes, Johnny?"

"That woman who got killed? Did you know her?"

"No, Johnny, I didn't. The first time I saw her was when she arrived on the train last Friday." Thinking that there must be a reason for his questions, she asked, "Did you ever meet her?"

"I don't know. I heard Miss Kingsley tell another teacher that she worked at the Silver Spur, so maybe I did know her. I didn't see her when she was in Winslow last week so I can't be sure. It's just..." The pause lengthened, so Tessa filled the silence.

"Johnny, if this was the same woman who worked at the Silver Spur, it was more than five years ago. You would have been too small to remember her. Is that what is bothering you?"

Tessa sensed his unease and wondered if he, too, knew about this woman and Joaquin.

"Well…" he seemed incapable of saying what was on his mind. Finally, he blurted out, "Is my momma safe?"

"Oh, Johnny," Tessa held out her arms to the young boy. This time, he fell into her warm hug without hesitation. Did this frightened child think that because one woman with connections to the Silver Spur had been murdered, his mother was in danger? Or, had he heard talk of Joaquin as the killer? Whatever demons his young mind conjured up needed to be laid to rest. Tessa took on the task.

"Your momma will be fine. Don't you worry about her. Whatever this was, it doesn't have anything to do with you or your mother." She prayed that her words were true.

"You get along home now. You have a long ride in front of you and don't forget that garden and those books. Scoot now, young man. Tell your momma you want some of those chocolate cookies she gave me for lunch."

His eyes widened as he slung his leg over the saddle and pointed his horse toward his mother's ranch. He was a good-looking boy who would grow into a handsome man. It was easy to understand his fear. He had lost his father and he would be very, very afraid of losing his mother, too.

Tessa was close to the livery now, so she didn't remount the mule. She paid Edward Barnes, gave Ben the carrot that she'd been saving all day, and walked home. Soon the depot came into view, with the Harvey House peeking out behind it. Her heart leapt. Four cavalry horses were tied to the hitching post. Her father was in town. Thoughts of murder and mayhem fled from her mind.

Her weak leg was stiff from the time in the saddle, but she pushed herself forward as fast as she could. As she reached the top step of the kitchen door, she slipped, knocking her shin on the edge. Pain shot through her leg, but she gave it no thought, because, sure enough, there was her father, sitting at the scarred oak table, drinking coffee and talking to Dorothea Parks.

"Papa, how wonderful to see you. What are you doing in Winslow and how long will you be here?" Questions tumbled out of Tessa's mouth as she hobbled toward her father. She planted an enthusiastic kiss on his whisker-roughened cheek then wrapped her arms around him.

Colonel Crane reached up to unclasp his daughter's arms from his neck. He kept her hands gently encased in his.

"Are you all right, Tessa? I thought I saw you limping."

"Of course, Papa. I'm fine. I banged my leg rushing up the steps because I saw your horse and I couldn't wait to see you."

She saw distress as he eyes met hers. When he looked at her like that, she thought that he wasn't seeing his daughter, but rather his wife. "You have your mother's blue eyes, so bright, so beautiful," he often told her.

When Tessa was six years old, Lucille Crane contracted a spinal infection that paralyzed her, quickly spreading from limbs to lungs. Two days after she died, young Tessa fell ill. She survived with only one deformed leg to attest to the devastation of the disease that had taken her mother.

"Who's with you, Papa?" Tessa asked, partly out of

curiosity and partly to distract him from worry about her. "I saw four horses tied up outside."

"Two soldiers from A Company, and a new lieutenant who needs to familiarize himself with the area. We're looking for a pair of men who killed a miner up near Antelope Wells. We think one of them is a deserter from Fort Apache. They might have come through here on a train recently, then stole a couple of horses somewhere. I hope they're traveling together because the contrast in the two of them would make them very noticeable. Corporal Foran is quite tall and very blond. He has pale skin, despite his life in the Arizona sun. The other man, Edward Miller, is short, stocky and very dark. Anyone who sees them would be struck by their differences. Have you seen them, by any chance?"

Tessa thought back to all the passengers she had seen in the past week. It was impossible to give her father a definite answer.

"I'm afraid I don't know, Papa. So many people eat here, town folk as well as train passengers. We are always so busy. I can ask the other girls and let you know if anyone remembers such an odd pair."

"Thank you, dear. I would appreciate any help you can give me. Now, tell me, how you are. You say you hit your leg. Is that the only reason you were limping? You know how I worry about you."

Tessa frowned and shook her head slightly, an almost imperceptible caution directed toward her father. In a low voice she said, "please don't talk about that here, Papa. I'm fine, really I am. You know I can't let Mr. Clifton find out about my leg."

Colonel Crane acquiesced. "Okay, Tessa. Whatever you

want, but please don't let yourself be hurt, either physically or emotionally. You always have a home with me. And you know I would love to have you come back to Ft. Apache."

He acknowledged her sharp intake of breath and added, "Now, don't say yes or no. Just remember it, okay?"

"Okay, Papa."

"So, Miss Harvey Girl, what is on the menu for dinner?"

Father and daughter linked arms and marched, in proper military rhythm, into the dining room.

"Miss Crane, I'm glad you're here," Mr. Clifton said, hurrying to her side.

"Colonel Crane," he gave Tessa's father a cursory nod, obviously distracted.

"Could you please help out with dinner service? Two of the girls have taken ill. I'm sorry to take you away from your father," once again he nodded at the colonel, "but it will only be for this meal. It's the last train of the day. I promise we'll feed him well, then the two of you can share dessert and coffee in the kitchen later."

"Of course, Mr. Clifton."

Tessa guided her father to the lunch counter, where she left him, beer in hand, with a promise to join him after dinner service was complete. She hurried to her room to don her uniform and comb the tangles from her wind-tossed hair.

Tessa was disappointed to miss dinner with her father, but she couldn't leave Mr. Clifton short-handed. Besides, this train had come from San Francisco and the passengers invariably had tales to tell of that exciting city.

"Welcome to the Harvey House, sir." Tessa greeted a beanpole of a man who she mentally dubbed "Abe" after the dead president. She had created the game shortly after she came to Winslow's Harvey House as a way to add a touch of mystery to the mundane task of meal service. She would invent a name for each person, based on her first impression. Often she would conjure up a brief story to explain a traveler's presence in Winslow.

Only one of the nine diners at her table inspired her imagination this evening. A small man appeared from behind the two women he followed into the dining room. When she greeted him, his eyes quickly darted to the floor, as if she had told him a scorpion was climbing up his shoe.

This man, thought Tessa, has embezzled money from the Wells Fargo Bank in San Francisco, where he was a teller. He left his wife, who constantly criticized him for not providing a better life for her and their children. He was generous enough to leave a note of explanation and some of the money behind to help her out, but he never expects to return to California. He'll leave the train in Santa Fe and head for the mining country of Colorado. He met a dancer in one of the San Francisco saloons who later moved to Cripple Creek. He plans to join her there and become a black jack dealer.

Tessa shook herself back to reality with an inward laugh. The poor man was probably a bank auditor, heading home to St. Louis with a satchel full of gifts for his adoring wife and children.

"My goodness," bellowed one of the two women at Tessa's table.

She was middle-aged, tending toward stocky. *Big Bertha*, Tessa thought, and almost said the name aloud.

The high-pitched voice continued, "I thought I'd just die of boredom, looking at nothing but brown dirt and gray rocks for days." She emphasized each word with a cut of her knife through the air, a conductor leading the orchestra.

"Well, at least we didn't run into any of those wild Indians," the other woman countered. She was a younger version of her friend, thickset as well, but with more spark in her eyes and shine in her hair.

"Mercy. That would have been terrifying," Bertha agreed. "California is certainly more civilized than this place. I wish we could have stayed there, Henry," she addressed her male companion, to whom Tessa had assigned the role of long-suffering husband. "St. Louis will seem dull after San Francisco."

The woman stared at Tessa, apparently seeing her for the first time. With a broad gesture toward the dusty street, visible through the large windows, she asked, "How ever do you live in this wild, dirty place?"

Tessa opened her mouth to answer, then thought better of it. In the nine months she had been a Harvey Girl, she had learned that most customers didn't expect an answer to their questions, and more likely, didn't want one. She also knew that it was useless to try to describe the raw beauty of the Southwest to people who refused to see it. Any attempt to convey an accurate description of the peaceful Navajo Indians who lived on the nearby reservation was futile. Certainly, this sort of person couldn't possibly believe that any sane woman would actually prefer the high desert of the Arizona Territory to life in such a cosmopolitan city as San Francisco.

"How was your dinner?" Tessa asked her father as she plunked two mugs of Arbuckle coffee down on the kitchen table.

"I don't think I've ever had a meal at a Harvey House that I didn't enjoy. And the boys," he said, referring to the other three cavalry men, "couldn't say enough about how much better this is than Army grub. Actually, I think you could have fed them anything. What they really liked was seeing all you pretty girls. You women are a sight for a poor soldier's eyes."

He took a gulp of the coffee, a special blend that the Arbuckle Coffee Company provided to all of Fred Harvey's establishments and bestowed an affectionate smile on his daughter.

"Umm. That tastes as good as it smells. Thank you, my dear."

The smile disappeared. "There was a lot of talk at our table about this murder. What do you know about this, Tessa? The bartender said that you're the one who told the sheriff who she was."

"No, no, no. That's not what happened, Papa."

Although her tone was emphatic, she kept her voice low so as not to draw attention to their conversation. She repeated what she'd told the sheriff but omitted any reference to Lupe or Joaquin.

"Sheriff Bowman talked to the waitress who served the table where Deirdre sat. She told him more than I could, and the woman who runs the boarding house was the one who gave the woman's name to the sheriff. I certainly don't know any more than that."

She folded her hands on top of the table and stared unblinkingly at her father. She had said all she intended to about that subject.

Colonel Crane drummed a finger against his lips.

Something Tessa said seemed to have triggered a thought. He wrinkled his eyebrows, then, remembering whatever it was that had puzzled him, he nodded to himself.

"We stopped at Hubbell Trading Post yesterday, looking for the deserter and his companion. There was a man there from San Francisco, who said he had come from Winslow. His fine-cut suit, tie and polished shoes were out of place up there. He even wore a diamond stickpin. I know you haven't been able to visit Hubbell's yet, but when you do, you'll realize what an unusual contrast he presented in those rustic surroundings."

The colonel tipped his cup to swirl the coffee, decided it was worthy and took a long swallow before he spoke. "According to him, he was buying some Navajo rugs to take to St. Louis to sell to the rich folks there. I wonder if this could be the missing companion of the murdered lady. What did he look like?"

Tessa, blushing slightly as she remembered how handsome she had thought the man was when she first saw him, described him to her father in significant detail. If Colonel Crane thought his daughter's power of observation unusually keen, he didn't mention it.

"Did he tell you his name, Papa?" Tessa asked. "The woman who runs the boarding house told the sheriff that the man who was with the murdered woman gave his name as Stanton Perry."

"No, he didn't give a name, but my boys and I can ride back up that way when we leave here, unless we get some other information on our outlaws and have to head another direction. It's unlikely that this man will still be there though, especially if he's running from murder. But, it's possible that

Lorenzo Hubbell knows him and maybe where he went. If he is carrying hundreds of dollars worth of those beautiful Navajo weavings, he's bound to attract some attention."

The colonel, who spoke of the long ride to the Trading Post with weary resignation, suddenly brightened.

"I met the new doctor this afternoon. She is quite a change from old Doc Benton."

"Are you sick?" Tessa, ever fearful of losing her only parent, was instantly on the alert.

"No, of course not" Crane said. "We were riding by the cemetery, which, by the way, is the bleakest final resting place I've ever seen. A group of mourners came out and we stopped to pay our respects."

"Deirdre Sweeney's funeral was today," Tessa said.

"Yes, that was it. There were only a few people there, including the sheriff and the preacher, and the undertaker, of course. I suppose the churchwomen felt the need to provide a Christian burial, even though she was a stranger here. You didn't attend."

Although her father was stating the obvious, Tessa could hear the question in his voice. She couldn't tell him that she hadn't gone to Deirdre's funeral out of fear, fear that the sheriff might wonder what interest she had in the murdered woman. She said nothing.

The colonel shrugged off Tessa's silence.

"Doctor Dahlgren came over to me and asked if I was your father. She seems happy enough to be out west. Quite a change from Sweden though. I suppose Doc Benton was getting too old for middle of the night emergencies and riding all over the desert tending to the ranchers."

"I was sorry when he quit," Tessa said. "He was

concerned about my leg, but never said a word to Mr. Clifton. The last time I saw him he told me that his eyesight was failing and he would have to give up medicine. He seemed real sad about it. The gossip around town, however, is that he hadn't treated several of his patients properly, and they died."

"Wherever there are people, there are rumors, Tessa. You just remember how well Doc Benton treated you and pay no attention to the town gossips."

"Yes, Papa."

As Tessa hugged her father goodnight, she thought about his words. Were there gossips in town now who remembered Deirdre Sweeney and her connection with Joaquin Castillo? If so, she hoped that Sheriff Bowman wasn't listening to them.

Chapter Eight

The eerie quiet of the upstairs sitting room puzzled Tessa. The church clock had chimed nine o'clock as she bade her father goodnight only minutes earlier. This was the time of night when the girls sat together and relived the day, chatter that was always punctuated by shrills of laughter.

Tonight, however, Beryl Turner sat alone, hunched under the kerosene lamp with a needle and thread in hand and a uniform apron on her lap.

"Where are the rest of the girls, Beryl?" Tessa asked without preamble.

Beryl laid her mending aside and leaned toward Tessa, suddenly animated. Tessa could tell that she was about to impart a juicy tidbit of gossip.

"Well, Tessa," Beryl began, "Violet, the newest girl here, got a stern lecture from Mr. Clifton this afternoon. She couldn't remember the cup code, so the diners at her table all got the wrong drink. Most of them were nice and just set about trading coffee for tea, but one man complained to Mr. Clifton."

"We've all made that mistake at least once," Tessa said. "Especially when we're in a hurry. Several times, I've put the cup in the coffee position, when the customer wants tea, or worse yet, lemonade. Was Violet upset?"

"Upset?" Beryl harrumphed. "She walked out. She's got family nearby, so I suppose she went to them."

"That's too bad," Tessa said, and meant it. She wished she would have known what was going on, so she could have consoled Violet. It always helps to know that others have had the same kind of problems. If her mind hadn't been so caught up in murder, perhaps she could've have done something to save the young woman's position.

"What about the others?" Tessa motioned around the near-empty sitting room.

"Several of them are sick, as you know, since you helped us out tonight. Thank you, by the way. It's always difficult to wait on extra tables and still meet the railroad's requirement for swift service."

"Is Lupe sick, too?"

"She complained of a headache, so she went to bed at least an hour ago. I don't think she's got the grippe that the other girls have. Lucky her. Mrs. Gibson sent for that new doctor this evening for Emily and Olive."

"I feel sorry for Olive," Tessa said. "She's only been here a few days and we've had a murder and now this sickness."

"The sheriff came out to talk to me about the murder," Beryl said. "That poor woman, she seemed so sad that day."

"Sad?" Tessa was surprised. From what she had seen of the San Francisco beauty, she appeared to be coy and flirtatious, not sad.

"Well, she didn't look it at first," Beryl said, "but I could see that the conductor's threats upset her."

This, too, was a surprise to Tessa, who had marveled at the woman's composure in the face of such evil.

"Then," Beryl continued, "she argued with her companion. He wasn't her husband, by the way."

Beryl's tone conveyed her attitude about unmarried women traveling in the company of handsome men.

"They were on their way to St. Louis to get married, but she wanted to stay in Winslow 'to take care of something', she said. He told her to leave the past alone. That's when she became so angry, but she was still sad, too, if you know what I mean." Beryl looked at Tessa for confirmation. "Like she wanted to yell at him and cry at the same time."

"Did she say anything else to him?" Tessa asked.

"Yes, she threw down her napkin and said 'the past is all I have now'. That's when she ran out the door. She looked like she didn't have a friend in the world." Beryl seemed ready to burst into tears herself. "And now, she's dead, so she must've had at least one enemy."

"Sheriff Bowman told me that you also saw her talking to Hiram Frye."

Beryl shuddered. "That old drunk. Yes, I told him about the next day when Frye ate at the lunch counter. Didn't you see him talking to that woman later?"

"No," Tessa said. "I didn't go out in the street after he left. Were they arguing, too?"

"That's the strange thing, Tessa. You know how Hiram,"

Beryl shuddered again as she said his name, "looks at all of us like we should be dancing in the saloon? Well, here's this beautiful woman and he stood there, hat in hand, like the gentleman he is not. He listened to whatever she had to say, and then followed her down the street like he's a lost puppy she's taking home. Unfortunately, he was back to his old self today."

"Today?" Tessa asked.

"Yes. My bad luck. I was assigned to serve the lunch counter today. As soon as he came in, he ordered a double shot of whiskey. I knew when the bartender winked at me that Mr. Frye had been to one, or maybe both, of the saloons already. That man drinks more than he eats. My papa has tales to tell about the time he was sheriff here." Beryl was delighted to have an audience for her discourse on the evils of Hiram Frye.

"I don't know why his wife is so smitten with him," Tessa said. "I suppose she figures she's lucky to have a man who puts up with her wild nature."

"I've heard tell that she's been seen more than once smoking cigars with the men. She probably plays poker, too. And they have a child, poor thing. What is she now, four, five? Can you believe that her father brings her into the bar with him?"

"I've seen her," Tessa said. "What's her name? Annabelle? Allison? No, Agnes."

"Yes, Agnes," Beryl said. "She's a pretty little thing, but she's in for a difficult childhood with a mother and father like that."

Tessa thought of her own childhood. She had been six when her mother died. Lupe had told her that Tia Elena's adopted son, Enrique, was five. Yet, she and Enrique had been raised in homes filled with love and attention, albeit by only one parent. Yes, Beryl was right, poor Agnes.

"Good night, Beryl. After I check on Lupe, I'm going to bed, too. Don't strain your eyes sewing in that light."

Chapter Nine

Tessa's heart pounded as she descended the stairs. Lupe had been asleep when she got to their room the previous night. She had color in her cheeks and her breathing was even, so Tessa had left her to rest. However, this morning she awoke to find Lupe's bed empty. Had Lupe felt ill in the night and gone in search of help? When she entered the kitchen and saw the familiar profile across the room, she exhaled with relief, surprised to realize that she had been holding her breath.

"How are you feeling, Lupe?" Tessa asked as she hurried to her side.

"It was only a headache." Lupe all but spit out the answer.

Her friend's unusual curtness took her by surprise. She was pondering what to say next, when the arrival gong sounded.

"Okay, girls," Dorothea Parks said, "this will be breakfast service, so make sure to keep things moving." She raised her voice to be heard over the clanging of pans and the rattle of silverware. "There's nothing worse than cold eggs."

Tessa was in and out of the kitchen several times, taking to heart the cook's words to hustle the scrambled eggs to the hungry passengers. Coffee, too, was much in demand. She was pouring the last cups of tea and coffee at her table when a thought that had been niggling at her mind struck full force.

She hadn't seen Lupe in the kitchen since the gong had sounded. She grabbed an armload of soiled plates and hurried through the swinging door. Her fear was confirmed when she saw the mountain of dirty plates and cups stacked beside the sink. The tension in the room told her that meal preparation and cleanup was being done with one less pair of hands. Now wasn't the time to ask questions, however. Instead, she replaced her white service apron with a brown one from a kitchen hook and began to wash the dishes.

"Here, Tessa, have a cup of tea," Dorothea said an hour later. "I appreciate your help. This sickness is making it difficult on all of us."

Tessa gratefully accepted the steaming cup and the proffered chair.

"You asked me the other day about the murdered woman," Dorothea said, joining Tessa at the table. "I've remembered something."

Tessa tensed. She had avoided asking the cook about Lupe's absence, preferring to let the woman believe that the grippe had also felled her most reliable, at least until last week, worker. Was it possible that Dorothea knew about Joaquin and Deirdre?

"There was talk of a child," Dorothea said.

"Oh, no." The groan slipped from Tessa's lips of its own accord.

"Oh, my dear," Dorothea said, placing a work-roughened hand over Tessa's soft, slender one, "there's always talk of a child when a pretty young woman is seen in the company of a handsome man."

"Was there a handsome man?" Tessa asked, not sure she wanted to hear the answer.

"In Deirdre's case, there were several. Then, one day, she left town, never came back and life here returned to normal. If she was with child, it wasn't obvious. Hiram Frye was sheriff then, so if anyone complained or wanted to look for her, nothing would have been done about it. This entire town must have been deaf, blind and dumb to elect that man."

"So he would have known her?" Tessa said.

"Sure, he knew who she was. They would've crossed paths when she came into town on errands for Mrs. McAllister. That lecher probably made a pass at her, but she wouldn't have had anything to do with him. Although, truth to tell, he kept himself better back then. When Hattie was with child, he straightened right up. Even stayed out of the saloons. Well, pretty much, at any rate."

Tessa had trouble picturing Hiram Frye in anything less than ill-fitting denim pants and stained shirts.

Dorothea looked at the kitchen clock and sighed. "One hour till the next train, Tessa. We'd both better get busy. You asked about Deirdre Sweeney, so I thought I'd tell you what I remembered."

"Thanks, Dorothea," Tessa said, although she couldn't think how any of the woman's information would help Joaquin. "Thank you for the tea, as well."

Refreshed, Tessa, too, rose from the table. She returned the kitchen apron to its hook. She noticed that her white one was no longer spotless, so she headed upstairs to find a clean one, as well as to see Lupe. As she climbed the stairs, she said a silent thank-you to Mr. Harvey for his policy of providing laundry services for all of the uniforms worn by his staff. Tessa cringed at the thought of washing and ironing six dresses and heavens knows how many aprons each week.

Tessa wasn't surprised to find the bedroom empty. Lupe's ramrod straight posture and brusque manner that morning spoke of continuing troubles. In her own uneasy frame of mind, she took a clean apron from the wardrobe and returned to the dining room to prepare for the next onslaught of ravenous travelers.

Throughout the lunch service, Tessa stole glances toward the kitchen door, hoping for a glimpse of Lupe. Her *amiga* needed this work, of that Tessa was certain. The wages were far beyond what a Mexican girl could make as a maid. Tessa's mind was so focused on her absent friend and Deirdre Sweeney's murder that she didn't hear one of the diners questioning her loudly. She looked down into a pair of pale blue eyes, as cold as steel.

"Excuse me. I'm sorry, sir, what can I get for you?"

The man wasn't tall, but his hands were so large that the knife he held in one of them looked more like a toothpick. Surprisingly, for a man of such slight build, his voice came out deep and booming.

"Miss, I asked if you know of a young Irish woman

who came through here in the past few days. She's tiny as a minute and very pretty, with glowing red hair. Oh, and she would be speaking with an Irish brogue."

Tessa's heart skipped a beat. If he was looking for Deirdre, he was too late. Moreover, she didn't want to be the one to tell him about the tragedy.

"Sir, perhaps you should go talk to the sheriff. He knows the townsfolk and newcomers much better than I do. I see so many travelers each day, it's hard to remember one person. Most of the women are lovely and, since they are only in the dining room for thirty minutes, I'm not sure I would notice if they had red, brown or green hair."

Tessa laughed to cover her nervousness. Then she decided that she had been too hasty in referring this man to Sheriff Bowman. If he knew Deirdre, which he obviously did, then he had information about her, things that might help Tessa and Lupe, and, most importantly, Joaquin. She backtracked.

"Maybe if you tell me more about this lady you're looking for, I can help you." Tessa encouraged him with a trademark Harvey Girl smile.

"Well, she would have come from San Francisco. A couple of days ago, I talked to someone there who knew her. He told me she was bound for St. Louis."

He hesitated, as if he didn't want to say more.

"She…she was traveling with a handsome man, maybe even pretending to be his wife." He spat the words out like a sour cherry.

Tessa had been wrong about his ability to help her. The words he spoke were harmless, but the tone of his voice, as icy as a north wind in February, frightened her. Was she talking to a murderer? Her smile vanished.

"Please, sir, go talk to our sheriff. That's Sheriff Bowman, there at the counter with the blue plaid shirt."

She walked away to get more coffee. When she turned back, she saw, to her relief, that the strange man was making his way toward the lunch counter. Not only did she want this man away from her table, she also wanted the sheriff to have at least one more suspect. It was possible that this man had snuck, unseen, into Winslow last week and had ridden back to Flagstaff to board the train there. It was a good way to establish an alibi. She hoped Sheriff Bowman would think that way, too.

Chapter Ten

"Excuse me, are you Sheriff Bowman?" the stranger asked, his voice echoing across the relative quiet of the lunchroom. Diners who had been too busy eating to talk, now put down forks and spoons to listen.

"Yes, sir. That I am", Bowman answered, reluctant to let his attention stray from Dorothea's lemon pie. "What can I do for you?"

The newcomer seemed aware of all eyes in the dining room on him. The next words he spoke were barely above a whisper. "I'm looking for a friend of mine and I was told she is in Winslow. That attractive waitress over there," he pointed towards Tessa's table, "asked me, no, rather she commanded me, to come over here and talk to you about it."

"Talk to me about what?"

Bowman scooped up a forkful of pie and studied it as he listened to the stranger's tale.

"My friend was supposed to have come through

Winslow on her way east from San Francisco. She is quite attractive, with red hair, not bright red, just kind of a soft red, and curly. It's real curly, so that it puffs out of her head in all directions."

He held his hands away from his ears to indicate just how wild this hair was.

"And she wears nice dresses," he continued. "At least she used to and people who saw her in San Francisco last week told me she looks real fine. I heard that she's traveling with a man. Apparently, he dresses fancy, too, so they must have money. I don't know anything about that. I just want to find this woman."

His voice rose again to a deep timbre. Heads turned. His next words froze Bowman in mid-bite.

"She's my wife, you see."

The sheriff noted that the man would not look him in the eye, which, in his experience as a lawman, indicated that he was either lying or had something to hide.

"She's what?"

Bowman had known the man was looking for Deirdre Sweeney before he spoke his second sentence, but the mention of a wife stunned him. He needed to stall for time to compose his thoughts and hopefully gain more information about the murdered woman.

"Your wife, you say? How long has it been since you saw her? And, land sake's man, what is your wife doing in Winslow with another man?"

"Well, Sheriff...Bowman, is it?"

The sheriff nodded, his mind still reeling with this new information.

"Well, sheriff, you see, we were married when we were

young, not much more than children really. DeeDee came to America from Ireland, maybe seven or eight years ago. I met her in Chicago. She was heading west, hoping to find some of her family who had moved to Denver. We spent some time together in Chicago and it was real nice. I enjoyed showing off a pretty girl, and she liked having someone to pay for a room and grub."

He patted his pockets, found some change and put two bits on the counter.

"Can I have a beer?" he asked the bartender. He didn't speak again until he had taken a long gulp from the frothy brew.

"That's better," he said. "Well, sheriff, it just kind of happened one day with DeeDee and me. I guess I married her because, at the time, I couldn't think of any reason not to. We figured it would be good for both of us, and, for a while it was. Later, all manner of good reasons not to marry cropped up, but by then it was too late."

The man looked around the dining room, shrugged his shoulders, and continued the story.

"I'm the first to admit, sheriff, that I wasn't all that great as a husband. I like to drink and gamble, and a beautiful woman will always catch my eye. It wasn't long until we were fighting and screaming at each other. Then the neighbors at the boarding house began to complain about all the noise."

The big man quit talking for so long, the sheriff began to wonder if that was the end of the story.

"What's your name, son?" he asked, hoping to get more information out of this newcomer.

"Rockwell Smith, but everyone calls me Rocky."

"Well, Mr. Smith, what happened in Chicago that brings you out to the Arizona Territory?"

"When we weren't fighting, DeeDee and me, we would have a real fun time together, if you know what I mean."

The sheriff couldn't believe this boisterous man actually blushed.

"Anyway," he continued his tale, "the fighting got worse and worse until one morning I woke up and DeeDee was gone. She left me a letter telling me to stop my drinking and gambling if I ever wanted to see her or our child again."

"You mean she was going to have a baby? Your baby? What did you do?"

"I was flabbergasted, sheriff. I didn't know she was carrying a child. I tried real hard to find her. I went to Denver, but I couldn't find any Sweeney's up there who knew of her. Eventually, I located some of her family outside of the city, but they hadn't heard from her. I stayed there for quite awhile, hoping she would show up. She never did. So I traveled the West, picking up work where I could. Everywhere I'd go, I would ask after her. With her Irish brogue and remarkable hair, I thought it would be easy for folks to remember her."

Sheriff Bowman grew tired of this recitation. It seemed like Rocky was ready to give him a detailed account of the past half dozen years of his life. He tried to steer the man back to the present.

"So, what brings you to Winslow?"

"Well, sir, I was in San Francisco for a couple of years when, by chance, I met a man who knew of DeeDee, only now she calls herself Deirdre. I'm sure it's the same woman. I have a photograph of her and he recognized her right off, even before I mentioned her striking red hair. She certainly draws the attention of men folk!"

"And this man knew that Deirdre had come to Winslow?" the sheriff prompted.

"No, not exactly. She told him that she planned to go to St. Louis with her gentleman companion."

Bowman could see Rockwell Smith practically gag on his words.

"In fact, she told folks in San Francisco that he was her husband. Well, he can't be that, now can he, sheriff? I'm her husband and I intend to find her and lay down the law. I want to know where my child is. No one I talked to knows anything about a baby. He probably died, if indeed she was ever with child at all. That woman is a conniver and liar. However, she's still my wife. When I locate her, I'm going to take her to Denver with me. We have to meet with a lawyer there, about settling an estate. DeeDee's brother died a couple of years ago, and part of his ranch now belongs to her. I'm going to see that she gets it."

The sheriff, who was growing bored with Smith's reminiscing, sat up and took notice at this last comment. If there was land and cattle involved, and Deirdre Sweeney was set to inherit, then her husband would certainly want to get his hands on the estate. And if Miss Sweeney, or was it Mrs. Smith, was no longer among the living, wouldn't her share of any inheritance transfer to her husband?

"Mr. Smith, do you have some proof of your marriage to this woman?"

When Smith nodded, Bowman stood up and grasped the man's elbow. To a bystander, it might have looked as if he were arresting the man.

"Come with me to the jail and let's look at your pictures and documents. I may have some news for you." He paused. "And I'm afraid you won't be back on that train today."

Chapter Eleven

"Dorothea, was that today's last train?" Tessa asked, cocking her head toward the sound of the departing engine. An idea was forming in her head.

The cook nodded her assent at the same time as she raised her ample eyebrows in curiosity at the question. Tessa realized that she would think the question strange. Everyone at the Harvey House memorized the train schedules, if for no other reason than to plan their social lives.

"I'm not feeling well, but I didn't want to leave the dining room if you still needed me."

"Of course, Tessa, you may leave. You've done a lot of extra work these past few days. You deserve a break. Now get some rest. Mr. Clifton and I don't need any more sick girls around here."

Tessa felt guilty about the falsehood, especially when she

saw the droplets of sweat running down the older woman's weary face. Actually, it was hardly a lie. She did feel terrible, just not in a physical way. Her stomach knotted with worry over Lupe. The tension made her head pound with the fury of an ocean storm.

Edward Barnes seemed to be the sole proprietor of the livery these days. Most likely, Sheriff Bowman was still at the jailhouse with the stranger, the one who was searching for Deirdre Sweeney.

"I'd like to take Ben again today, Edward," she said, as, once again, she reached for the saddle blanket and reins.

Soon she was on her way to the Silver Spur. If she was going to help Joaquin, she needed to talk to him. She fully expected to find her missing roommate at Anna McAllister's ranch, as well.

Less than a mile from town, Tessa noticed a small figure trudging along the road, kicking rocks from side-to-side, leaving a scorpion tail of dust behind. Johnny McAllister was heading home from school, book strap slung over his shoulder. She urged Ben forward and soon came alongside the boy, who looked up at her with his impish grin.

"Hello, Tessa. Are you and Ben going to my mom's ranch?"

Optimism radiated from both his face and voice.

"Sure are, young man. Where's General Lee?" she asked, referring to the boy's buckskin pony.

Anna's family was from South Carolina and still fought the *War of Northern Aggression* in their own small way.

"The farrier was coming today to give him some new shoes," Johnny explained.

"Couldn't you ride another horse?"

"Most of them are with Shorty and the other hands, rounding up the cattle for Friday's drive. Mama drove the wagon into town this morning to pick up supplies, so I rode with her. I told her I'd walk home, but now I'm sorry I said that. It's much easier on a horse."

"How about you hop up here and Ben will take us both?" Tessa said.

Johnny needed no further urging. With practiced ease, he slung his legs over Ben's back and clasped his arms around Tessa's waist. The trio set off at a more rapid pace than Tessa expected of the cumbersome mule. She guessed the old steed was showing off for the young boy.

Tessa looked down at Johnny's hands around her waist and smiled.

"Do you remember the first time we rode like this, Johnny?" she asked, craning her neck around as far as she could to speak to him.

"I do, Tessa," he crowed, happy to be able to tell her. "I don't remember why I didn't ride General Lee that day, but I do remember that my shoe fell apart, and I was crying." He mumbled the last, embarrassing detail. "I didn't know how I was going to walk home without a shoe. Then you came along and helped me. We rode Ben that day, too." Johnny reached down to pat the mottled white coat of the big beast. "He's a nice animal."

"Yes, that was the first time I met you, although I'd seen you and your mother at church." Tessa paused. "Thank you."

"Thank me for what?" Johnny asked.

"For needing a ride that day so I could meet your mother. She's one of my dearest friends now, you know."

Woman and boy conversed happily about school,

annoying girls and unfair homework assignments until the gate of the Silver Spur came into view. Tessa sensed Johnny straightening behind her.

"Silver Spur Ranch," he read, his voice full of pride. "I helped my Papa make that sign, Tessa. And those," he pointed to the two shining spurs that flanked the uneven lettering, "came from a real silver mine in the New Mexico Territory."

She was happy for this young boy. She knew the sorrow that the loss of a parent brought, and his connection with the land was his connection with his father. Tessa gave Ben a kick and they galloped the final stretch to the ranch house, laughing with the exhilaration of speed and the sense of freedom that it brought.

Anna must have heard Ben's thundering hooves. She hurried out to the stable, wiping her paint stained hands on her smock.

"Well, this is a surprise. I certainly didn't expect to see you again so soon, Tessa. And just who is this young cowboy you've got there?"

Johnny laughed at his mother's attempt at humor.

"Ah, come on, Ma. You know it's me. Tessa gave me a ride on Ben. Can I go see Shorty for awhile? He said he'd let me ride the new colt. I'll get my schoolwork done. I promise. Then I'll start digging up the ground for the winter garden. Please, Ma?"

Tessa knew that Anna couldn't refuse her persuasive son. Anna had confided to Tessa how his blond hair and freckles reminded her so much of Big John that some days she could hardly bear to look at him. Tessa saw tears gather at the corners of her eyes. Anna blinked rapidly to dispel them. She obviously would not want her son to feel that somehow his presence made her unhappy. Far from it.

"Of course, Johnny. You'll find Shorty in the near pasture, tagging some of the cattle for Friday's drive. Don't you go bothering him about riding that colt, though. He's busy enough with the cattle. Tell him to bring in the ones he has rounded up. He's done enough for today. And yes, you can start turning over the soil in the garden. We need to get the beets and sweet potatoes planted by Saturday. Get to it, boy!" She gave her son a gentle pat on his rump.

She turned to Tessa, holding up her hands.

"I've been painting," she said, not so much to explain her colorful fingers, but as an apology for avoiding a hug.

"I'd like to see what you're working on," Tessa said, "but first, I need to talk to Joaquin." She looked toward the barn. "Where is he?"

"He's out with Shorty, of course." Anna's eyes held Tessa's. "What's wrong, Tessa? You act like some horse spooked by a rattler."

"Anna, can we go inside? I'd sure like a cup of coffee, if you've got some brewing."

"Won't take but a minute to heat up the pot."

She led Tessa up the porch steps into the sunny kitchen, where smells of paint mixed with the aroma of onions and peppers.

"Will you show me your latest painting, da Vinci?" Tessa teased. She knew Anna didn't like anyone to see her works-in-progress but she wasn't ready to talk about Lupe and Joaquin and murder. At least, not yet.

Anna couldn't be sidetracked, however. "I know you've got something on your mind besides my amateurish dabbling in art. So what brings you out to the Silver Spur on a day you should be serving the passengers of the great Santa Fe Railway?"

"The last train went through at noon. I've been helping out extra with this sickness going around, so Cook gave me permission to leave." She didn't bother telling Anna that the munificent cook thought Tessa was using the free time to rest.

Then she plunged into the purpose of her afternoon visit to the McAllister ranch.

"Have you seen Lupe?" she asked. "She might have come out here to talk to Joaquin. She wasn't in the kitchen at the Harvey House, nor in our room. I'm worried that she'll try to help her brother and get herself in trouble with Mr. Clifton."

Anna's face screwed up in puzzlement.

"Lupe? No, she hasn't been here since Saturday. I told you I saw her then but she didn't speak to me. If she rode out here to talk to Joaquin today, I haven't seen her, although I don't know how she'd find him without asking me. Joaquin has been out on the range all day with Shorty. They should be back here soon. Drink your coffee, Tessa dear, and don't fret. Is this about Deirdre Sweeney? Has something more happened?"

Tessa didn't think that Lupe would be so impolite as to visit the Silver Spur without paying her respects to its owner. However, that's exactly what she had done on Saturday, so maybe she'd done it again today. Tessa thought about her promise to help Lupe and Joaquin. The more she learned about her roommate's secretive behavior, the more her doubts grew, doubts about her ability to help, and, more troubling yet, doubts about Joaquin's innocence.

Anna listened attentively, her only expression an "oh" of surprise when Tessa told her that the murdered woman quite possibly was married to a different man from the one who had been her companion in Winslow.

"What worries me is her relationship with Joaquin," Tessa said. "Without some proof that Joaquin couldn't have murdered this woman, or evidence that leads to someone else, he could be in serious trouble. Now Lupe is trying to protect him, risking her job at the same time."

Unburdening herself to Anna wasn't the panacea Tessa had hoped it would be. Joaquin's predicament sounded even worse when she voiced her concerns. In addition, when she spoke of Lupe's absence, it reminded Tessa of her own deception of the afternoon. Guilt flooded over her.

When Tessa finished, Anna rose from her chair, grabbed one of Tessa's hands, pulling her up.

"Come on, Tessa, we'll talk to Joaquin. He and Shorty should have returned to the corral by now. We'll ask him if he's seen Lupe, and what he knows about Deirdre. I recall a girl with wild reddish hair who worked here, but I don't remember anything about her friends or family."

Anna tapped her index finger against pursed lips, searching her mind for details about the murdered woman. Tessa watched as Anna closed her eyes, trying, Tessa guessed, to conjure up an image from years past.

"She didn't work for me for very long and that was several years ago. One day she disappeared without telling me she was leaving, and I was in a state about it. We had extra hands here for the branding and gelding and I had to cook for all the men as well as help with the cattle."

"I can imagine how difficult that must've been, Anna,"

Tessa said. "When one of our girls quits without notice, we have to scramble to cover for her. And there's certainly more of us to pick up the work than there is of just you."

Anna nodded her agreement.

"You say she was beautiful? Well, I guess I'm not one to notice beauty much. Just whether a girl gets the work done and doesn't cause any trouble. Until she left me high and dry, that was the case with DeeDee or Deirdre, or whatever her name is...was."

Anna stopped, hand on the door handle, then turned around to face Tessa.

"Come to think of it, I do remember folks in town mentioning my pretty new maid, so she must've made that impression on a lot of people." Anna laughed ruefully. "Although it was probably mostly men who noticed."

Anna held the screened door open, then followed Tessa into the sunshine. They were approaching the corral when Johnny came running, his hands outstretched as if he were holding the Ark of the Covenant.

"Look, Mama. Look, Tessa. When I was digging the rows to plant the sweet potatoes, I came across this strange rock."

Both women stopped to listen to this news, dropping down on their knees so they could look the excited boy in the eyes. He danced with contagious enthusiasm. "What is it, Johnny?" his mother asked.

At the same time, Tessa held out her hand. "Show me what you found."

The light in his eyes dimmed for a brief second as he realized his dilemma. Tessa could see his confusion. He wanted to share this important discovery with his mother, but Tessa was a guest and he knew his manners.

"Show your mother what you have there, Johnny," she said.

Johnny brightened. He placed his treasure in his mother's outstretched hand. She turned it over several times. "This is a strange rock for sure," she said as she handed it to Tessa.

"Where did you find this, Johnny?" Tessa asked.

"In the garden." He pointed toward rows of freshly turned earth. "I was digging a new row when I saw it. I started to throw it in the rock pile until I noticed how different it was from the others. It looks like a seashell. But there's no ocean around here, Mama."

He waved his arms at the vast expanse of land surrounding the ranch.

"We studied seashells in school. They come from the ocean, like the one by California. Do you suppose somebody dropped it here?"

Tessa, who knew a lot about fossils from her travels around Arizona and New Mexico, interrupted his discourse.

"Johnny, this is a fossil. A long time ago, millions of years ago, there was an ocean where we are now. Finding this seashell fossil in the desert is like discovering a secret that the past was hiding from us. Things that we discover today are often signs of what happened many years before. When the ocean left this part of the world so long ago, it left behind clues, like this fossil, to let us know that it was once here. We just have to pay attention."

Even as she said this, something in her own words gave her pause. Yes, the present often provides clues about events of the past. If we study what occurred yesterday, we may possibly learn more about what is happening today. Even murder, perhaps. Tessa examined the fossilized seashell.

She grinned down at Johnny as she placed the treasure in his outstretched hand.

The three explorers looked up at the sound of hoof beats to see Sheriff Bowman riding up the lane. He reined Lucky in several yards from where they stood, a thoughtful gesture, meant to avoid creating unnecessary dust. He dismounted and walked rapidly toward the trio.

"Looks like I'm interrupting something important. What are you three so serious about?"

Johnny answered quickly, his voice shrill with the excitement of discovery. "I found a fossil, sheriff. Look, it came from a long time ago, when an ocean covered Arizona. Can you imagine that? An ocean, right here in the desert!"

The lanky sheriff crouched down on one knee and held out his weathered hand to receive Johnny's treasure.

"Yes indeed, Johnny. You most certainly do have a fossil of a seashell there. I've heard about the time when this entire area was covered with water. You should put that in a safe place. Someday, people, important people, might come here to study what happened millions of years ago. I'll bet they would want to see special rocks like this."

Johnny hopped from one foot to the other as the sheriff spoke, his delight at his role in such a momentous occasion evident with every bounce. He clutched the fossil in his fist, glanced around to make sure no one else might see his treasure, and ran toward the house. The fossil was destined for a secure hiding place.

Tessa watched Johnny as he disappeared into the ranch house. Then she refocused her attention on Sheriff Bowman. His wasn't an idle visit, she knew that for certain. Part of her wanted to mount Ben and ride back into town, but she sensed that it was important for her to stay at the Silver Spur to learn what the sheriff had on his mind.

It didn't take him long to come to the point.

"Mrs. McAllister, where is your ranch hand, Joaquin? I need to talk to him."

Tessa's heart sank. Had he found out about Joaquin and Deirdre?

"Well, sheriff, I expect him back here any minute now. He and Shorty are rounding up the cattle that will go to market on Friday. What do you want with Joaquin? Has he done something wrong?"

"Ma'am, I just need to talk to him. I'd like to wait here for him, if that's okay with you."

"The coffee pot is on the stove. Why don't you come inside and tell me why you need to talk to my hired help?"

Anna wasn't cowed by Bowman's stature or his position. She spoke with the authority of a ranch owner in charge of her own land. Tessa was proud of her.

Anna and her two visitors stepped gingerly across the neat rows Johnny had dug in preparation for fall planting. Obviously, his task had been close to completion when he uncovered the fossil. Knowing the young boy as she did, Tessa was certain that as soon as he had placed his newfound treasure in a safe place, he would be back in the garden, furrowing the rest of the garden plot.

With cups of steaming coffee in hand, the sheriff and the two women sat at Anna's kitchen table, surveying each other with questioning eyes. It was obvious that no one wanted to be the first to break the silence.

With a shrug of defeat, Bowman gave in. Tessa expected as much. A woman could wait out a man every time. Plus, the sheriff was a busy man and he would want to get the information he needed and get on with his business.

"Mrs. McAllister," he began. "Today, a man arrived in town who claims that he was married to the murdered woman, Deirdre Sweeney. This man, Rocky Smith, said that some folks in San Francisco knew her and that's how he traced her back to Winslow."

He swallowed some coffee, looked toward Tessa, then back at Anna.

"I assume that you are aware that she was murdered Sunday night."

He said it with such certainty that Tessa was sure he knew that she had been the one to convey the news to her friend.

"Hiram Frye told me that Miss Sweeney worked at the Silver Spur several years ago." Bowman continued his recitation. "Joaquin Castillo was working here at the same time, so I'd like to ask him, and you too, some questions about her."

"You talked to Mr. Frye yesterday?" Tessa said, before Anna could respond.

She realized she was stating the obvious, but she hoped that her question would force Bowman to disclose something of his conversation with a man, someone other than Lupe's brother, who had a connection with the murdered woman.

"Of course," Bowman said, frustration with Tessa's non sequitur creeping into his voice. "He was Winslow's sheriff back then. He claims he didn't recognize her, but that, when she told him her name, he remembered. Personally, I find that hard to believe. That woman's combination of beauty and fire would be hard to forget."

He reddened at his poor choice of words about a dead woman.

Just then, Shorty tapped lightly on Anna's door, saving Bowman from further embarrassment. "Mrs. McAllister?"

"Yes, Shorty, come on in. How is the roundup going?"

"The fifty head of cattle are in the holding pen now. I need Joaquin to help me keep an eye on things until Friday. I can't find him in the barn. Do you know where he is?"

"Where he is?" Anna echoed. "He was supposed to be with you."

Chapter Twelve

Three pair of eyes stared at Shorty. Sheriff Bowman spoke first.

"We thought he was helping you with the roundup. Isn't that right, Mrs. McAllister?"

Anna ignored Bowman and focused on her foreman. "Shorty, this morning I told Joaquin to head out to the pasture to lend a hand with the cattle. Have you seen him at all today?"

"No, ma'am. In fact, it's been a rough day, trying to round up those fifty head almost by myself. That new hand is such a greenhorn that it was more work to train him than to run the cattle myself. I was wondering why you didn't send one of the experienced hands out there. Joaquin has always been reliable, so it never occurred to me that he wouldn't have come if you had told him to help me."

The sheriff didn't wait around for further speculation.

He grabbed his Stetson, swallowed the last gulp of coffee and headed out the door. Tessa and Anna locked eyes. Tessa's were full of concern for her friend's brother. Anna's flared with anger at her ranch hand's negligence. Shorty, sensing the tension in the kitchen, plunked his weathered hat on his head, nodded at Anna and followed the sheriff out into the yard.

"Tessa," Anna began, "if Joaquin had nothing to hide, why has he gone missing? And where is Lupe?"

Anna's voice carried an edge of accusation, as if Joaquin, brother of Tessa's friend, was Tessa's responsibility.

Tessa covered her eyes with her hands, pushing hard to block out all images of Joaquin as a murderer. Worse yet, was Lupe trying to protect her brother? She knew the Castillo siblings. She loved them. Despite how bad things looked, she didn't believe that Joaquin could have killed that woman.

Now she was afraid of what Sheriff Bowman might do. Mexicans were often condemned before they had a chance to prove themselves innocent. It was an unpleasant fact of frontier life. She offered up a silent prayer that this would not be the case with Joaquin. The sheriff had his Sharp's rifle with him and he knew how to use it. The gun wasn't called "Old Reliable" for nothing.

The women sat in silence for several minutes, neither knowing what to say to the other, each with her own, yet very different, concerns. Tessa had just decided that she should ride back to town when Johnny ran in, still clutching the precious fossil. He seemed to have decided that his treasure was safer with him than in any hiding place.

"Momma, I finished digging the rows for the sweet

potatoes and beets. I was hoping to find more fossils, but I didn't." He rapidly switched his train of thought. "Now, I'm hungry. When will supper be ready?"

The eagerness in the boy's manner lightened the dark mood of the ranch kitchen like the sun rising over the eastern mountains.

"Why don't you do your schoolwork for an hour and then we'll eat? There's cookies in the jar. But, you can only have two."

That was all the growing boy needed to hear. The lid of the cookie jar clanked as he eagerly grabbed a few cookies, maybe more than two, and ran up the stairs towards his bedroom, cookies in one hand, unburied treasure in the other.

"Goodbye, Johnny," Tessa yelled after the retreating figure. "I'll see you Friday night at the roundup."

He mumbled agreement, his mouth full of gooey oatmeal cookie.

Tessa returned her attention to Anna, searching for words that would comfort both of them. Anna was justifiably angry with Joaquin for deserting her, especially at this busy time. Tessa also suspected that there was an element of fear in her anger. She must wonder if she had a murderer living on her ranch. Tessa wanted to believe Lupe's assertion that her brother had nothing to do with these murders, but she had no proof, for either herself or for Anna.

Unable to think of anything appropriate to say, Tessa scooted back her chair, gave her friend a quick hug, then hurried out to the barn and Ben. She sensed Anna's relief at her departure. The atmosphere at the Silver Spur had turned chilly. Neither woman wanted to say something that would harm their friendship.

Tessa journeyed back to town, saddened by the knowledge that something had changed in her relationship with Anna. With renewed determination to find answers to Joaquin's actions, she gave Ben his lead, using the time to organize her thoughts.

She reviewed everything she knew, beginning with Deirdre's confrontation with the criminal conductor, through the latest discovery of a long-lost husband. She had to admit to herself, and Ben, that it was possible that Joaquin was the father of the murdered woman's child, if indeed there was a child. Deirdre Sweeney was a schemer, of that Tessa was certain.

She thought about the arrival of the man claiming to be her husband. He said she was pregnant when she ran away. No, Tessa thought, that wasn't quite right. Deirdre *told* him she was pregnant. She had no child when she first came to Winslow, nor could she have been noticeably pregnant. Was this a ploy she used with all the men of her acquaintance in order to get what she wanted, whether it be money or status? How would the man, Joaquin for instance, know if she were speaking the truth? Tessa believed that most men would have accepted her claim and acted on it however they saw fit. When put in that context, it didn't bode well for Lupe's brother.

Ben jerked his head quickly, interrupting Tessa's conjectures. It was only a lizard, a very large lizard, running across the road, where he scurried up a nearby rock and began to pump his front legs rapidly up and down. Momentarily startled, Ben regained his nonchalance and lumbered on. The antics of the reptile reminded Tessa of the ever-exuberant Johnny and his new treasure. Finding one fossilized seashell was special. She hoped he wouldn't find any more. It might lessen the wonder.

However, her thoughts didn't stray far from the murder and her concern for Lupe. Where had the gentle Mexicana gone? She wasn't at the Silver Spur or the Harvey House, so where could she be? Might she and Joaquin have planned to return to Mexico to escape punishment for a crime they may or may not have committed?

It didn't seem possible that Lupe, devoted as she was to her mother and sisters, would leave the Territory. There was nothing in Mexico to draw her back there. Her entire family lived in America now. Certainly, Lupe would never, ever, abandon her mother. No, her friend was nearby. Tessa was sure of that. In regards to Joaquin, she was not nearly so positive.

Now another worry weighed on her mind. Of course, she was concerned about Lupe and Joaquin. However, Anna McAllister was also her close friend, a woman she admired and respected. Right now, she and Anna held differing opinions regarding Lupe and Joaquin. Anna had a ranch to run and she needed dependable help. Understandably, she had no time for cowboys who shirked their duties. If Lupe was somehow involved in Joaquin's disappearance or, worse yet, in the murder of Deirdre Sweeney, then Tessa could no longer protect either the hard working Mexican girl or her brother.

At the livery, Tessa stroked Ben's mane in farewell and turned reluctantly toward the Harvey House. She decided to walk down a nearby alley, avoiding busy Second Street, for fear of encountering either Frank Clifton or Dorothea Parks. As she entered the sheltered alley, she let down her guard, lost in thought. Favoring her weak leg, she limped along, letting her stronger leg carry most of her weight. It required less concentration, giving her mind free rein to focus on the many whys and wherefores of murder and murderers that bounced around in her thoughts.

Her evasive action was in vain, however. She rounded the corner behind the Harvey House and froze. Frank Clifton waited by the back gate, hands tucked across his ample girth, watching as she approached. Tessa had the fleeting thought that he was sampling far too much of the Harvey House's delicious food.

She found some measure of comfort in his noncommittal expression. Perhaps he had not noticed her limp. It would be far easier to explain her unscheduled absence. She straightened her posture and evened her gait.

"I hope you are feeling better, Miss Crane. And your roommate, is she also healthy once more?"

Tessa, consumed with guilt, was certain his comments dripped with sarcasm. She ignored the sense of foreboding, however, and answered as if the questions were asked out of genuine concern for her welfare.

"Thank you, Mr. Clifton. Yes, I'm fine. I thought some fresh air would help my headache, and it has. I am sorry to have missed work this afternoon. I'll go inside now and see what I can do to help Dorothea." She avoided any mention of Lupe.

"Fortunately, it has been a quiet afternoon, only one train, so I don't think your absence caused any trouble."

Tessa decided not to clarify the fact that she didn't leave until after the last train had departed. The less said, the better. She started to maneuver around him toward the kitchen.

He wasn't to be dissuaded from the topic of Guadalupe Castillo, however.

"Where is your roommate, Miss Crane?"

The friendly tone vanished from his voice, replaced with harshness. Tessa shuddered.

"I understand she has missed curfew a couple of times in the past week. Then today she is neither at her workstation nor in her room. I know you two are friends. If you want to help her, you'd best tell her to get back to work and stay there."

There was nothing to do but tell the truth, what little of it she knew.

"I'm not sure where she is, Mr. Clifton. I'm concerned for her, as well. Lupe isn't the type of person to leave her work without some sort of explanation. I'm afraid something bad might have happened to her. Of course, when I see her, I'll tell her what you said."

Tessa prayed that would be soon.

"I don't think something bad could have happened to her, unless it is some no-account cow poke coming through town, looking for a good time. Nothing bad happens in Winslow."

Clifton winced as the words left his mouth. The look of chagrin told Tessa that he remembered that something bad, very bad, had indeed happened in their town. He hid his discomfort with mumbled words about the murdered woman not really belonging in Winslow. Then, probably because he was embarrassed by his choice of phrase, and angry with Lupe for her unexplained absence, he lashed out at Tessa, to her surprise and dismay.

"Now, Miss Crane, there's something else I need to talk

to you about. Why were you limping? And don't tell me that you weren't. This isn't the first time I've seen you this way. Mr. Harvey hires only healthy waitresses. If you are ill or hurt, you had better tell me."

Everything else seemed to be going wrong so it didn't surprise Tessa that Mr. Clifton had discovered her secret. She tried desperately to stop the tears from pooling in the corners of her eyes. She inhaled deeply in an attempt to slow her pounding heart.

She hadn't uttered a single word, however, when the kitchen door banged open and Lupe, tripping over a cat who lounged on the porch, half-fell, half-crawled down the steps. Frank Clifton managed to put up his arms to catch her before she hit the ground.

"I've been looking for you, Guadalupe."

Clifton's voice was stern, although Tessa could hardly keep from laughing at the comical tableau in front of her. Lupe's feet were tangled with Clifton's and, as he tried to pick her up, she fell down again. Finally, she regained her footing and her composure.

Lupe gasped her apology. "I'm sorry, Mr. Clifton. I came to tell you as soon as I got back. Cook told me you were out here. There was an emergency in my family. My Tia Elena became ill and I had to care for her young son. I thought I would only be gone for an hour, but she became delirious and I couldn't leave her. Please forgive me. I'll work on my next day off."

The frantic woman's voice resonated with abject fear, fear, Tessa knew, of losing the job that provided not only for herself, but also for her family. The scene was no longer funny.

The tears Tessa had been fighting to hold back earlier during the confrontation with Clifton quickly spilled over as she was overcome with joy at her friend's return.

"Lupe, I've been so worried about you. I'm sure Mr. Clifton is as happy to have you back as I am."

It was a bold statement but Tessa sensed her boss's discomfort and took advantage of it. Moreover, if she was going to lose her position because of her weak leg, she might as well help Lupe stay employed.

Clifton attempted to keep his voice gruff, but the overtone of relief was obvious to Tessa. Whether it was for Lupe's return or because an unpleasant situation had been avoided, she couldn't tell. She had known him to be a gentleman and a fair boss, and she was relieved when his innate good nature returned.

"All right, girls. Let's get back to work. Things might have been quiet around here today, but that won't be the case tomorrow. Lupe, please go help in the kitchen. Mountains of dishes have stacked up in your absence."

His exaggeration almost made Tessa smile. When he directed his pseudo-angry gaze at her, she was grateful that she had not.

"Miss Crane, you'll need to get your station readied for tomorrow."

It didn't escape Tessa's notice that Lupe didn't warrant a "Miss Castillo" from the manager, as she did with the "Miss Crane" directed at her. This was one more upsetting thing in a day already filled with them. It had been an exhausting day, as well, both physically and emotionally. Tessa couldn't remember ever being this tired. She longed for a chair, or, better yet, a bed, upon which to rest her weary bones. She needed to talk to Lupe, too, but that would have to wait.

The pair of truants entered the kitchen, ready to wash up and begin their work. Tessa noticed that, contrary to Mr. Clifton's description, there were no dishes stacked by the sink. The succulent aromas of Dorothea's cooking reminded Tessa of how long it had been since she had last eaten.

"You two look like you could use some hot food and a quiet place in which to eat it."

The denizen of the kitchen nodded at the women, her voice soft with sympathy. She quickly filled two plates with crispy roast chicken, potatoes redolent with rosemary and sweet butter, and green beans sautéed in bacon drippings. She carried the feast to her worktable in the far corner of the kitchen, indicating with a jerk of her head that Tessa and Lupe were to follow. Wordlessly, she cleared recipes, invoices and other assorted papers off of two chairs and motioned the girls to sit down.

"Thank you, Dorothea," Tessa said, a slight quiver in her voice.

The cook's kindness touched her. She didn't appear to be angry with either one of them. Her next words validated Tessa's thoughts.

"You two are both good workers. I hope neither of you are involved in something as serious as murder. You wouldn't be sitting in my kitchen, eating my food, if I thought that was true."

She began to walk away, then looked back, raising a finger in warning. "Just remember that Mr. Clifton is the boss and he might not be as generous as I am."

Once Tessa prepared her tables for the following morning, she trudged up the stairs to her room, each step a mountain to climb. She was glad to find Lupe already there, sitting upright in bed, obviously waiting for her roommate, and apparently ready and willing to talk.

Tessa collapsed on her bed, groaning when her hip landed on top of her hairbrush. She sat up, tugged it from underneath her leg, and began to comb out her chignon. She couldn't do much about the color of her hair, but she could, and did, brush it to a gleaming shine every day. She had her mother's coloring and she thought of her mother as beautiful. Perhaps brown hair wasn't so bad after all. She continued to brush as she talked.

"Amiga, I thought we were both going to lose our jobs today. Mr. Clifton was so angry with you for disappearing. Then he told me that he knows about my leg. You tumbled out of that kitchen door just at the right time." She chuckled at the memory of Lupe falling into Mr. Clifton's arms.

"Maybe he'll forget about his accusations." She shook her head, realizing how illogical that statement sounded. "Well, I don't really believe he'll forget, but maybe, if I don't make him so angry again, he won't mention it. He thought I was protecting you. He wouldn't believe me when I told him that I didn't know where you were."

She looked Lupe straight in the eye, her own face a mask of seriousness. "So, my friend, now I want to know. Where did you go? And where is Joaquin?"

Lupe had listened to Tessa's discourse with an expression of mild concern on her face, ready to provide words of encouragement. When Tessa asked the last question, however, her eyes widened and her face paled.

"What do you mean, 'where is Joaquin'? He is out at the Silver Spur until Friday night, when he'll bring Señora McAllister's cattle to town."

"No, Lupe, he isn't there," Tessa replied, in a tone that implied Lupe already knew. "I was at the Silver Spur this afternoon, looking for you. Anna thought he was helping Shorty with the roundup, until Shorty came in to the ranch house complaining because he had to do all the work by himself."

"That can't be," Lupe said. "Joaquin would never shirk his duty."

"It gets worse, Lupe. The sheriff showed up at the ranch while I was there. He wanted to talk to Joaquin. When he found out that your brother had disappeared, he rode off at a gallop. I don't know where he was going, but something tells me it wasn't back to Winslow."

"Oh, no, Tessa," Lupe said. "I'm sure the sheriff thinks that Joaquin ran away because he had something to do with the murder of Deirdre Sweeney. That can't be true. My brother isn't like that."

Her voice rose in distress. She threaded her fingers together in silent prayer. When she spoke again, her voice was low and steady.

"I have more news, too, *querida*. I didn't lie to Mr. Clifton about being with Tia Elena. That's all true. She is ill, yes, but, more importantly, I found the baby."

Chapter Thirteen

Tessa dropped the brush in mid stroke. It thudded on to the wooden floor then slid under the bed. She gaped at Lupe, too astonished to pick it up.

"The baby? Joaquin's baby?"

"Yes, Tessa. I have always wondered why Tia Elena adopted Enrique. She isn't a young woman and had already raised four other children. At the time, she said it was because she was so lonely after her husband, Rubio, died, even though she had several grandchildren by then. Everyone was happy for her and for the baby too, so no one asked any questions. It isn't easy for a Mexican orphan to find a home around here. The sisters at the mission were delighted that a good Mexican Catholic would raise the abandoned boy."

Lupe was quiet for several minutes, the ticking of the mantel clock providing the only sound in the room. Tessa could wait no longer.

"How do you know this is Joaquin's child? If you're so sure, why didn't you tell him a long time ago?" Tessa spoke quickly, hoping to spur Lupe on to a faster pace in her storytelling.

The strategy had no effect. Lupe's eyes surveyed the ceiling. When she finally spoke, the words came slowly, a ballet when Tessa wanted a barn dance.

"I was never really certain, until today. Of course, I knew what Joaquin told me about Deirdre claiming to be carrying his child. When she left town, I thought the problem had disappeared with her. There was no need to bring it up. Truthfully, I forgot about it. Enrique is a happy boy. Elena loves him and takes good care of him. Even now, I don't think that either mother or son needs to know the truth. Then, when that woman was murdered, I realized that Joaquin could be in trouble."

Another lengthy pause set Tessa's nerve's on edge.

"But, how do you know?" she urged, emphasizing the last word.

"I talked to the sisters at Madre de Dios," Lupe said. "I begged them to tell me something about Enrique. Sister Maria Josephina has lived there for more than ten years. She still remembers the night Enrique was abandoned on their doorstep. She told me that the child was only half Mexican. His hair and skin are so dark that I don't know how she knows this. She won't say. But, if what Sister says is true, then Deirdre could have been his mother. He is the correct age, after all."

"But, Lupe, Deirdre left Winslow long before the child was born. If she was well along with child, people would have noticed. Joaquin and Anna, especially."

"She could easily have hidden with a friend, or maybe gone to Flagstaff or Holbrook. Both of those towns are close enough that she could've brought the baby back here after he was born. And, if she was living in one of those small towns, she wouldn't have wanted to give up her child there."

Tessa was skeptical of Lupe's assertions, but she had no facts to argue otherwise. Plus, she was interested in what her friend had to say.

"Tessa, if I figured this out, Joaquin must know too. Now you tell me that he has run away. If the sheriff finds out about the child, he'll presume that Joaquin killed Deirdre, and we won't be able to save him. What am I going to do?"

Tessa tried to comfort her friend. "Tonight, we do nothing. Tomorrow we must both pay extra attention to our work so Mr. Clifton has no more cause to be angry with us. We'll pray that Joaquin is safe and that the sheriff discovers who the real killer is before he finds your brother."

Tessa extinguished the lamp. She lay in the darkness, worry crowding her mind. By the frequent rustle of sheets and heavy sighs from across the room, she knew that Lupe, too, slept fitfully or not at all. Finally, after the clock chimed twice, she drifted into a troubled sleep.

Chapter Fourteen

Eighty miles to the north, near the Hubbell Trading Post, the soldiers from Ft. Apache pitched their tents in the semi-darkness. The stars shone with selfish brilliance in the moonless sky. Colonel Crane thought of that long ago, far away star that guided men to peace on earth. He had seen the terrors of a war where brother killed brother. He recoiled at the memory of the unspeakable atrocities committed by both sides in the Indian wars. As he glanced at the night sky, he offered a prayer that someday, somehow, there would be peace.

The men built a campfire over which to cook a meager meal and to provide some warmth against the chill autumn air. None of them knew what tomorrow would bring. Tonight, however, the distant howl of coyotes and the whisper of the night breeze through the sagebrush were as comforting as a mother's lullaby.

* * *

"Let's go, men." Colonel Crane woke his sleeping soldiers the next morning. "Keep it quiet, though. Those deserters may be hiding in one of these canyons, and you know how sound travels like a rifle shot here on the high plateau."

The men kept alert as they rode across the rocky terrain toward Hubbell's Trading Post. John Lorenzo Hubbell, Lorenzo, to all who knew him, purchased the trading post in 1878. Immediately, the adobe brick structure, located near the town of Ganado on the Indian Reservation, became a gathering place for the Navajo. Here Hubbell acted not only as a merchant, but also as a liaison with the outside world. He wrote letters, settled arguments and explained US Government policy--never an easy task--to the Indians, quickly earning their trust. He garnered saintly status when, during the smallpox epidemic of 1886, he worked day and night to care for the sick and dying. The Trading Post became a hospital and its owner a god.

The sun peaked over the eastern plateau, blinding the cavalry party as they neared the mud buildings. Colonel Crane signaled for his men to dismount and proceed on foot. The two horses tied up outside the building concerned him. It appeared that Lorenzo Hubbell had early morning guests.

The colonel waived his hand to the left. Lieutenant Longbridge circled toward the back of the Trading Post, followed by Private Dennison. Eustace Hobbs, the newest recruit at Ft. Apache, ran toward his commanding officer, rifle at the ready. The colonel remembered his own naïve excitement as a young soldier, as yet unaware of the horrors of battle.

Tall windows bracketed the front door, so Colonel Crane, followed closely by Hobbs, belly-crawled across the dusty yard. When the two men reached the protection afforded by the door's thick wood, they stood, listening for any sign of a disturbance inside. The colonel wanted to give his lieutenant enough time to get in place at the rear, so he motioned for Hobbs to stay by the door and wait for his signal to enter.

Without warning, loud voices burst like cannon fire from inside the trading post. Crane recognized Hubbell's sonorous voice, raised in anger. Fearing for the good man's safety, he kicked open the door and rushed inside, hoping that Longbridge and Dennison would hear the commotion and move in from the back. His rifle was cocked and ready in his hand.

Two men towered over Hubbell, long bore Winchesters aimed at his chest. The trader's ankles and wrists were bound with thick rope. A dirty bandana hung loosely below his mouth, an indication, Crane thought, that the intruders had gagged him at some point, then thought better of it. Perhaps they had attempted to elicit information about a safe or certain valuables items from the venerable old man.

Despite the shackles, Hubbell sat straight and proud in a weathered chair, whose spindly legs wobbled under his weight. The cast iron stove in the middle of the main trading area sputtered hungrily to life as dry piñon branches caught fire.

Colonel Crane immediately recognized the lanky deserter from Ft. Apache. His stocky, much shorter companion stood beside him. Crane raised his weapon, firing quickly before Hubbell's captors could react. The bullet tore into the deserter's shoulder. His companion took quick aim and Pvt. Hobbs fell to the floor with a sickening thud.

Longbridge and Dennison rushed through the back door, fixed their weapons on the two outlaws and fired. The short man fell immediately, a dark red stain spreading across his chest. The deserter, blood already dripping from his shoulder wound, grabbed his other arm and fell to the floor, writhing in agony.

The skirmish ended almost before it started. The soldiers rushed to their fallen comrade, removing their own kerchiefs to staunch the flow of blood from his chest. Even the fragrant piñon wood couldn't mask the odor of fear and death that permeated the room. Crane quickly untied Hubbell, who rushed out of the room, rubbing his wrists as he went.

"This one's a goner, sir," said Longbridge, as he rose from the body of one outlaw. "The other will probably live. Maybe we should gag him so he'll shut up."

"First, let's see to Private Hobbs," Crane said. "He doesn't look good."

Crane hurried over to help Hubbell, who had returned to the room carrying a basin of water and several ragged shirts. As he lifted the heavy basin from the older man's grasp, he asked, "Is there a doctor anywhere near here?"

"I'm as close to a white man's doctor as we have. However, there is a medicine man on the reservation. I'll send one of my boys to fetch him. The two of them were tied up in the other room. They'll be so anxious for action that they'll probably fight over who gets to go."

The colonel started to protest, but Hubbell had left the room once again. Soon the loud thundering of a horse at full gallop echoed through the trading post.

He turned to his men. "Help me make Hobbs comfortable, and see to this man, as well. He's the deserter we've been searching for. Might as well fix him up so we can hang him."

Within the hour, an ancient Navajo arrived. His already substantial height was augmented by a stovepipe hat. It put Colonel Crane in mind of Abe Lincoln. He liked the old Indian immediately. The man had to bend his head to avoid hitting the doorframe. As he did, something sparkled. A bag tied to a thin black cord swung from his neck. Its brightly colored beads caught the sunlight, a glimmer of hope in the dreary room.

Nodding to Hubbell, he knelt beside Private Hobbs. He uttered a few words in Navajo, which Hubbell seemed to understand. He deftly lifted the pouch from around his neck with one hand, while covering the soldier's wound with the other. His words had the rhythm of a chant. He spoke them so softly that Colonel Crane, who knew a smattering of the very difficult Navajo language, didn't recognize a single word.

The Medicine Man quickly, yet gently, maneuvered the soldier's blood-soaked uniform over his head. He opened the pouch, exploring inside it with long, bony fingers and pulled out a stringy black substance. He packed the concoction into the wound, then covered it with strips from the shirts Hubbell provided. The trader and the medicine man conversed in rapid Navajo, concern lining their faces.

Hubbell held up a hand, signaling the Navajo to silence. He faced Crane, lips drawn into a tight line.

"Sichei'i says that this man should see a doctor very soon. He's lost a lot of blood and, obviously, the bullet needs to be removed. He packed the wound with medicinal herbs to keep out infection and stop the bleeding. You need to get him into Winslow to the doctor right away."

Hubbell noticed Crane's skeptical look, and quickly

continued. "Take one of my wagons to transport him. He's in no shape to ride a horse. That way, you can also take the body of this man." He pointed disgustedly toward the dead intruder. "This other wounded one, too. Someone can bring the wagon back to the Trading Post after these men are cared for."

Colonel Crane accepted the offer gratefully. He had lost men under his command a few times in the past. He didn't want to add one more to the count today. It was the one part of Army life he didn't love. He took his job as commanding officer seriously. Anything that could possibly save a life was worth whatever inconvenience came along with it.

"Thank you, Mr. Hubbell. You can rest assured that the US Army will return your wagon. You are most kind."

"You are the kind one, sir. I do believe you saved my life this morning. I don't know how those men knew that I had received a tidy sum of money from the government yesterday. Thanks to you, that money will find its way into the hands of the Navajo, for whom it was intended."

He gave a mock salute to Colonel Crane. "Now, you had best get moving. These men need to see a doctor, the sooner, the better."

"I had another reason to ride out here today," Crane said. "Do you remember the man who was buying some of your rugs when we rode through here a couple of days ago?" The words tumbled from his mouth in his haste to get his soldier to a doctor.

"Of course," Hubbell said. "That was Mr. Stanton. He said he had planned to get married and now he wasn't going to, so he had extra money. He bought two rugs from me and several pieces of turquoise jewelry to sell back east."

"Are you sure his name was Stanton? We're looking for a Mr. Perry."

"Wait, colonel," Hubbell said. "You're right. Stanton was his given name. Surname was Perry. I remember thinking that his names were the reverse of what they should be. Guess that's why I got it confused."

"He was heading for St. Louis when he left here?" Crane asked.

"Come to think of it, Colonel Crane, he started out riding west. That is strange."

"Strange, indeed," Crane said.

At the door, he turned and bowed low to the old Navajo who stood as if carved in stone.

"Thank you, Grandfather," he said in Navajo, using the term of respect that Hubbell had spoken earlier. He hoped his pronunciation was good enough to convey his gratitude.

"One more thing, Mr. Hubbell, if you see Mr. Stanton Perry again, can you get word to the sheriff in Winslow?"

"I'll certainly try. You ride safe now, son, you hear?"

It had been a long time since anyone had called him son. Crane smiled, however briefly, then hurried to the wagon and the wounded men.

They rode hard all day, pushing the cavalry-trained men and horses to their limits. Night had fallen by the time the weary band entered Winslow. Colonel Crane visibly brightened when he saw a faint light from inside the doctor's surgery as the wagon, bearing its sad cargo, pulled up in front.

His fierce pounding brought Mary Kingsley, the schoolteacher who shared a home with Dr. Dahlgren, to the door.

"I'm sorry, colonel," she said after he introduced himself and explained the situation. "The doctor was called away to the Jameson ranch. Mrs. Jameson was having a difficult time delivering twins."

"Can you help these men?" he asked, indicating the blanketed mounds in the back of the wagon.

Even in the night darkness, Crane saw her blanch.

"I'm not a trained nurse, but old Doc Benton lives nearby, just outside of town. He could help you, I'm sure."

"Help me get these wounded men inside and comfortable. Then tell me where to find Benton. I think I remember him. Wasn't he going blind, that's why he had to give up his medical practice?"

"Well, it is a little difficult for him to see. But, he knows his business, at least as far as bullet wounds are concerned."

The tone of Miss Kingsley's praise for the old doctor gave Colonel Crane pause, but he wasn't going to pursue it right now. When she resumed speaking, her voice was more encouraging.

"He could probably fix up these men blindfolded. Now, let me tell you how to find him." She gave succinct directions. "Will you send one of your men out there?"

"What's going on here?" a voice said from the door. The sheriff's tall frame was silhouetted against the streetlamp outside. "I saw the cavalry horses hitched to the wagon outside. Is there a problem?"

Colonel Crane stepped forward to answer the lawman. "Yes, you could say that. One of my men is leaving now to fetch Doc Benton. We had a little trouble with a deserter and his outlaw friend at Hubbell's Trading Post this morning."

He raised his eyebrows to Dennison, jerking his head

toward the door. "Get going, Private. Bring that doctor back here as quickly as you can."

"Yes, sir. I'm on my way," he called over his shoulder as he rushed toward his horse.

The colonel returned his attention to the sheriff. "As soon as we get this one patched up, we need to lock him in your jail. His wounds aren't serious. First, I want the doctor to look at my soldier. He's in bad shape. There's also a dead body here. It's the other outlaw."

"I'll tell you what, colonel. Since this one isn't hurt too badly," he signaled toward the injured deserter, "I'll just take him along to the jail now. The doctor can come down there and patch him up when he's done taking care of your man. That way, you don't have to keep an eye on him."

"Okay, sheriff. You got yourself a deal. I'll bring the doctor along as soon as I can. And, thank you for your help. I guess we shouldn't be too concerned about fixing that one up. He's got a necktie party in his future anyway."

He glared at the soldier-turned-runaway and saw, with satisfaction, a look of terror in the wounded man's eyes. Wars and hardships had toughened the colonel, however, and all he could feel was disgust for a man who would turn his back on his country and his fellow soldiers.

"Take him away."

Chapter Fifteen

S heriff Bowman pushed and prodded the wounded deserter up the steps to the jail, using more force than was necessary. He, too, had served in the US Army and had no sympathy for men like this coward.

He was so intent on his human cargo that at first he didn't notice tiny Agnes Frye sitting on a bench outside the door. She swung her stylish little shoes back and forth in some imagined rhythm. She looked up at the sound of boots on the steps and her short legs stopped in mid-stride. She stared at the two men as if she had never seen such strange creatures.

"What are you doing here, young Miss Frye?"

The sheriff fervently hoped he wasn't going to have to find someone to take care of the girl. The day had been busy enough without that problem to worry him.

"Waiting for my momma and papa. My daddy's locked

up in your jail, sheriff. Please let him out." She said these words without whining or pleading. It was a matter-of-fact request, as if she were asking for a penny candy.

That Hiram Frye was sitting behind bars was no surprise to Bowman. Drunk again, he thought, hoping that no one had been hurt in what was probably an all-out brawl. The man spent more time in the jail now than he did when he was the sheriff, albeit on the other side of the bars. Bowman shook his head in disbelief.

"I'll have your momma come out and take you home, Agnes. Sit here for a few more minutes, okay?"

When Bowman entered the jail, he saw Edward Barnes perched on the edge of his desk, eyes wide with fright. He had to restrain a hearty laugh when he saw the cause of his deputy's terror. Hattie Frye loomed over him, poking him in the chest with a stubby finger, each jab accented by an angry word. Relief flooded over Barnes' boyish face when he saw the sheriff. Bowman could contain himself no longer and erupted with a deep guffaw. Not many men were a match for this fireball, and certainly not quiet Edward, who would rather be back in the livery with only the horses and a barn cat for company.

"Sorry, Ed." Bowman attempted a serious tone, although his eyes still twinkled. "I guess you got more than you bargained for tonight. Tell me what got ol' Frye tossed in my jail, then you can go home."

"I'll tell you what happened," Hattie bellowed, turning her fury on the sheriff. "That no-account saloon keeper…"

"Mrs. Frye, you can answer when I ask you a question." Bowman's stern voice made it clear he was in charge of the conversation. He nodded at his deputy to speak.

"Well, sheriff," Barnes said. He paused, glancing nervously at Hattie, whose finger again pointed in his direction, as threatening as if it were an actual gun.

Barnes took a deep breath, then began again. "Jacob, you know, Jacob Morris, over at the saloon? Well, he came to the livery dragging Frye behind him like a sack of potatoes. He was spitting angry, too. Apparently, Hiram lost all his money at the poker table. Didn't bother to save out enough to pay for his drinks. When Jake threatened him, Hiram started swinging. Not only did he give the bartender a black eye and busted lip, but he broke a full bottle of whiskey."

Bowman chuckled again. Hiram Frye was an entertaining prisoner.

"Guess we're lucky Morris didn't decide to introduce him to his other business," he said, referring to the fact that Jacob Morris was also Winslow's undertaker.

Hattie listened to this exchange, angry eyes mere pinpoints on her rapidly reddening face. The effort to remain quiet had her rocking back and forth on the balls of her feet. Bowman sensed the volcano about to erupt, so he turned quickly toward the jail cells. He wanted to get the deserter onto a bunk, not so much for the rascal's comfort, but it was as good a way as any to forestall the firestorm that was Hattie Frye.

He took his time removing the man's boots, adjusting a blanket and offering water. When he could delay no longer, he returned to the office area where trouble waited. Hattie had her back to him now, and she was staring at the picture of the murdered woman that Bowman had placed on the wall with a plea for anyone with information about Miss Deirdre Sweeney to please step forward. The photograph was the one that Rocky had given the sheriff. It showed Deirdre in a long, pale dress. Her wedding gown, Bowman guessed. He hadn't pressed the husband for details.

"Now, Mrs. Frye, don't start yelling at poor Ed. He was helping out here while I've been looking for Joaquin Castillo."

As soon as he said the name, he realized his mistake. It had been a long, tiring day and he was neither thinking nor behaving like a sheriff. He mentally slapped himself awake. Murder in Winslow seemed an improbability when he accepted the job as sheriff, but now it had happened and he was a man who took his commitments seriously. He wouldn't allow such a mistake again.

Hattie pulled the picture from the wall, ripping a slash where the nail had held it in place. Despite the large black lettering, she held the paper only inches from her nose. The anger that had turned her eyes to stone gave way to teary pools. She plopped the paper down on to the sheriff's desk, although she continued to stare at it even as she spoke to Bowman.

"Has anyone come forward with information about this poor girl? It seems like she appeared out of nowhere and ended up getting herself killed in a town where no one knew her. It just goes to show you that expensive jewelry," she pointed to the woman's sparkling diamond ring and delicate necklace, "doesn't mean a thing. Not when it comes to life and death. What have you found out about her, sheriff?"

Bowman wasn't going to let his tongue slip again. He ignored the woman's question and returned to the reason she was there in the first place.

"Your daughter is outside, Mrs. Frye. Don't you think it's time she went home to bed?"

Hattie's anger returned. Nostrils flared and dark eyes flashed daggers at the sheriff. Spittle rained from her mouth

"Don't you go telling me how to raise my child, Sheriff Bowman. Every one in this town thinks they know better than me. Now, let Hiram out of here so I can take him home, too, and then the entire Frye family will be out of your hair."

"Now, ma'am, I didn't mean anything of the sort. I'm sure you're a fine mother to that pretty girl. I'm just saying that it's late and she's bound to be tired." He softened his voice in an effort to calm the woman down.

"And, I think it's best if we keep your husband here overnight. It's obvious that he's had too much to drink. He'll have to work something out with Mr. Morris to pay for damages. I'll talk to the barkeeper in the morning. Right now I've got a wounded man to worry about."

Chapter Sixteen

After what seemed an eternity, the last of the day's train passengers departed. Tessa was daydreaming about supper and bed when she overheard snippets of a conversation among several of the local men who were whiling away the evening hours at the lunch counter.

"Well, it was cavalry men all right, but they were in a wagon. They definitely had a wounded man with them. Maybe even two or three."

Tessa's heart pounded. Were they talking about her father? She rushed over to the horseshoe bar, raising her voice to get their attention.

"Excuse me. Do you know who the wounded men were? How bad are they hurt? Where are they?" She ran out of questions and breath at the same time.

At that minute, Lupe came through the kitchen door, ready to clear the dishes from the bar. She almost collided with Tessa, who was gasping for air, and trying to talk. Her words were unintelligible.

"Tessa, what's wrong? You look about to faint. Sit down here and tell me what happened."

"No, *amiga,* I'm fine, but I heard these men talking about wounded soldiers."

"Is it your father?" Lupe asked.

"I don't know." Tessa could feel the hysteria rising in her chest. With great effort, she forced herself to remain calm, at least on the surface. Her insides told a different story.

"Ma'am," began one of the men. His eyes softened as he looked at the distraught woman. "I don't know how many men are hurt, or who they are. I just know that it was cavalry uniforms I saw on that wagon."

Another one of the locals chimed in. "The sheriff was helping one of the injured men. They headed toward the jail. Maybe you could find out from Sheriff Bowman what's going on."

Tessa nodded her thanks. Her shoes clicked double time as she hurried towards the door. Out on the street, she heard Lupe behind her, but didn't slow down. Her mind was focused on her father. They had almost reached the sheriff's office when Lupe got close enough to grab her friend's hand and give it a supportive squeeze. Tessa returned the pressure, acknowledging the kindness.

"I am praying for your father," Lupe said. "It will be all right. I know how much you adore him. He will be safe, *amiga.* I'll keep praying."

Tessa reached for the jailhouse door at the instant it was opened from within. Edward Barnes rushed past them with such speed that Tessa expected to see someone chasing him. She panicked as she realized that he might be running for help instead. When he turned around to apologize for his haste, he grinned sheepishly, giving the impression of a comedy unfolding inside. He tipped his hat to the two women, and rushed into the night without saying a word. Tessa stared after him in total confusion.

The shrill voice of Hattie Frye reached Tessa's ears. The woman was obviously angry with someone, probably the sheriff. Tessa then realized that she had seen Agnes outside. What was the young girl doing in front of the jail so late in the evening?

She wasn't going to waste time worrying about that. She stepped between Bowman and the tempestuous Mrs. Frye.

"Sheriff, I've been told that you have a wounded soldier here in the jail. Is it my father?"

Bowman put up his hand to silence Hattie's ranting, then addressed the distraught Tessa.

"No, Miss Crane. Your father stayed at Doctor Dahlgren's surgery with one of his soldiers who got shot up pretty bad. The man here is only slightly wounded. The cavalry patrol caught up with him at Hubbell's. He's the deserter they'd been looking for. Your father," he continued, then stopped as the door banged open again.

Doc Benton's substantial figure was framed by the night sky. He looked at the sheriff with eyes so cloudy it was a wonder he could focus at all. He blinked several times, then pulled out a kerchief. After he wiped away the moisture that pooled in the corner of his eyes, some of the cloudiness disappeared. He strode into the jail with a firm step. Despite his age, he held himself erect. An air of confidence filled the room. Even Hattie Frye shrunk back, letting the newcomer take over.

142 // Susan Tornga

"I've just come from Doctor Dahlgren's. The private will be fine. He should rest for a few days, so I told Colonel Crane to leave him right there. No reason to subject the poor man to a horse ride into the mountains toward Ft. Apache tonight. When the doctor gets back, she'll take over and I expect she will tell the colonel the same thing."

The old man rubbed at the stubble on his chin, let his fingers move up to his temples where he seemed to be massaging away a headache.

"For now, the young man is asleep," Benton continued. "He was a lucky one, for sure. Crane told me you've got another wounded one here, locked up. Must've been some kind of shoot-out. We don't have that kind of excitement around here much anymore."

"He's back in one of the cells, Doc," the sheriff said. "Let me get the key and we'll go on back."

Bowman gave Hattie a puzzled frown.

"What are you doing here, Mrs. Frye?" he asked.

Before she could answer, he slapped his head and said in a curt tone that booked no further argument, "oh yes, your husband. I forgot, but I haven't forgotten that your daughter is sitting outside my jail. Get going and take care of her. I'll see you tomorrow morning. We'll sort out this trouble with your husband then. Right now, I've got more important matters to tend to."

He reached across his desk to grab the heavy key ring, knocking papers on the floor in his haste. Doc Benton bent over to retrieve them, then rose very slowly as he stared at the picture in his hand.

"I know this woman, sheriff." He held the paper closer to his watery eyes, again blinking rapidly. "I'm sure of it. If I could just remember when I met her."

His head moved quickly back and forth as he read the brief message below the photograph. Slowly, he laid it back down on the desk, a puzzled frown distorting his face.

"Well, let's go see to this prisoner. I'll remember about that young woman. Just need to think on it for awhile." He followed Bowman toward the cells mumbling, "perhaps in one of the files I kept…"

Tessa's eyes followed the two men as they headed toward the cold, Spartan cells. The loud thud of the front door slamming drew her attention back to the office. She was surprised to find herself alone there. Both Hattie Frye and Lupe had disappeared. Now that Lupe knew Tessa's father was not among the injured, she was probably hurrying back to finish her chores. Tessa could forgive her absence. Lupe's position was at stake. In fact, so was her own. She knew she needed to get back to work, too. Her absence the previous day had already created enough problems with Mr. Clifton. First, however, she would go to the surgery to see for herself that her father wasn't one of the wounded soldiers.

Chapter Seventeen

Tessa sat by the injured soldier's bed, watching her father pace across the surgery's immaculate floor. Colonel Crane was obviously impatient to move on. He wasn't a man who sat still very often, nor very well. At the first sound of the door opening, Crane rushed over to meet Dr. Dahlgren, explaining, all too rapidly Tessa thought, about his wounded soldier.

The doctor's blond hair had escaped from its carefully constructed chignon and her eyelids drooped. Her clothes were soiled and wrinkled. Tessa had some experience with delivering babies, and she knew the birth of twins was especially challenging. The bedraggled doctor obviously needed a bath and sleep.

"Colonel Crane," she said, "we meet again, and so soon. Let's see what we have here."

Tessa marveled at the doctor's resilience. She was the

embodiment of the Hippocratic Oath. As she walked to Private Hobbs' bedside, she shrugged her shoulders, as if shedding a heavy cape on a hot night and her exhaustion with it. Her step quickened and her voice lightened. She spent a half hour examining the young soldier, then pronounced him well on the way to recovery.

"Doc Benton is a good man and an excellent doctor. Your soldier was in capable hands," she assured the colonel.

"It's a pity about his sight, though, doctor," Crane said, inclining his head toward the street, so Doctor Dahlgren would know he was referring to Benton and not the wounded soldier.

"I have asked him many times to go to San Francisco, to the hospital there. They are developing new procedures all the time to help people like him. He's as stubborn as they come, however. Won't consider having another doctor look at him."

Tessa joined the conversation. "I saw Doc Benton at the jail when I was there looking for you, Father. He seemed to know something about Deirdre Sweeney and was trying to remember exactly why her face was so familiar to him. He said he would look through some of the old records that he keeps at his ranch. What you say about his sight makes me wonder if he'll even be able to read them."

Tessa would have loved to stay and talk more with her father, but she couldn't forget her precarious status with Mr. Clifton. She bade her father and the doctor good night, giving each a quick hug.

It had been a long day of work and worry, but Tessa felt like she was walking on air as she hurried back to the Harvey House. Seeing her father unscathed was better than any elixir hawked from one of the healers who frequently traveled through Winslow.

And, she was hungry. The aromas of the evening's dinner still hung in the heavy air of the kitchen: lamb steak with a dark, rich sauce, roasted baby potatoes and string beans. There had been mince pie, too. Tessa, well aware of the Harvey House proportions, knew a slice of that would suffice. Dorothea was happy to oblige.

The cook was sitting at the kitchen table talking with Ardella Gibson. Tessa was surprised to see the housekeeper in the kitchen this late. Because she rose so early, Mrs. Gibson usually went to her room immediately after dinner, making herself available there if any of her girls wanted a private conversation. There always seemed to be man trouble, female problems or just loneliness that needed the wisdom of a surrogate mother.

"Where's Lupe?" asked Mrs. Gibson. "She had best not miss curfew again."

Tessa knew the housekeeper liked her roommate, so the sharp edge of anger in the woman's voice startled her.

Not again, Tessa thought, but did not say aloud.

Tessa stalled, trying to find a reply that wouldn't get Lupe into further trouble, yet would also not be a lie. She was growing tired of making excuses for her roommate. Nevertheless, she did her best to protect her.

"I expect her here soon. She was worried about me because we thought my father had been shot. We've been at the jail with old Doc Benton. I'm sure she'll return before curfew."

The hinges of the kitchen door creaked, startling the three women. Lupe's petite frame was silhouetted in the doorway. She hugged her arms around her, a human jacket to ward off the chill of the autumn evening.

"Brrr. It is getting cold out there. Winter isn't far off." Lupe seemed oblivious to the women's stares. She continued to rub her arms, which, in the heat of the kitchen, seemed a gesture more of nervousness than a desire for warmth.

"Putting your hands in some hot, soapy water will fix you right up." Anger still lingered in Mrs. Gibson's voice.

It surprised Tessa that Lupe offered neither an apology nor an explanation. She quietly said, "yes, ma'am", reached for an apron and began scrubbing at a blackened pot, her elbows disappearing into the sudsy water.

Tessa very much wanted to know where her friend had been since she left the jail. She reached for a towel and began to dry the dishes. The sooner they finished their chores, the sooner they could be alone in their room. Maybe then, Tessa would get some answers from her uncommunicative roommate.

"I went to Dr. Dahlgren's surgery to see my father after I left the jail. You left there earlier than I did, so why weren't you here when I got back? Mrs. Gibson is very angry with you, Lupe."

Tessa could barely contain her own temper and her voice cracked with the effort. The two women were alone in their room. Tessa lounged on her bed surrounded by several magazines and books that had arrived from cousin Sarah in yesterday's mail pouch, while Lupe sat in the middle of her neatly made bed, legs tucked up, with not a hair out of place.

"I'm sorry, *amiga.* I didn't mean to worry you. And I certainly don't need Mrs. Gibson mad at me. I know I'm in enough trouble with Mr. Clifton as it is. Things are such a muddle now, I don't know what to do. I went to check up on Tia Elena to see how she is doing and to make sure that Enrique is all right. We talked about Joaquin. She is as worried as I am."

Lupe ran her fingers through her hair, raising the shining black tresses high above her head. When she let them fall, then landed neatly in place. Tessa marveled, then turned her attention back to what her friend was saying.

"I wanted to ask her about Enrique," Lupe continued, "but I was afraid to. The poor woman is still very sick and I don't want to make things worse for her. If she knows that Enrique is Joaquin's son, she must have decided to keep it a secret. If she doesn't know, I don't want to be the one to tell her. "

"Do you have any idea where Joaquin might be? Do you think he has gone back to Mexico?"

"Honestly, Tessa, I don't know and I am afraid for him. I'm sure he had nothing to do with Deirdre's death, so I don't understand why he would run away."

Lupe bit her lip to steady the quiver in her voice. A tiny drop of blood appeared on her mouth, testimony to the fear and worry that were eating away at her.

Tessa decided that she would get no answers to her questions tonight. She wrapped her arms around her friend and was gratified by the fervor with which Lupe returned the gesture.

* * *

The next morning, Tessa awoke early, but refreshed. Despite the trauma of the previous day and her concern for Joaquin, she had slept soundly. She hoped the same had been true for her distraught roommate. She made an effort to stay quiet while Lupe slumbered on. She was fumbling through a pile of clothes, looking for her petticoat, when Ardella Gibson pounded at the door.

"Miss Castillo? Lupe, are you awake?"

Tessa glanced at the mantle clock, wondering if it had stopped. She pulled a blanket across her bare chest and opened the door to admit the excited woman.

"Mrs. Gibson, what's going on? We're not late, are we?"

"No, the sheriff is downstairs and he wants to talk to Guadalupe right now."

She hurried over to the form lying inert in the other bed and poked at the mound. "Get up, Lupe, and get dressed quickly. I've never seen the sheriff this rattled. Something has happened, but he wouldn't tell me what. Just yelled at me to get you down there right now."

The housekeeper jerked the blanket off with one angry tug. Lupe was now wide-awake, her dark eyes staring at Mrs. Gibson, her lips a tight line. She opened her mouth to speak, but the only sound that came out was a weak "oh."

The housekeeper, acting in her role as substitute mother, pulled Lupe's uniform from its hanger, handing it to her with one hand while bending over to retrieve stockings and shoes with the other.

"Get your clothes on and come downstairs. I'll give the sheriff a cup of Dorothea's coffee while he's waiting. Maybe that will calm him down."

Both women were dressed, with their hair combed, in a matter of minutes. Tessa followed Lupe down the carpeted stairs, wondering what could have happened so early in the morning. She was sure it had to do with Deirdre Sweeney's murder and the subsequent disappearance of Lupe's brother, a coincidence that seemed fixed in the sheriff's mind. Couldn't he wait until after breakfast? Lupe had supported her last night when she thought her father had been wounded. Now, it was her turn to be the shoulder to lean on.

Jed Bowman was pacing across the kitchen floor, steaming coffee cup in one hand, when Lupe entered the room, Tessa close on her heels. The rich Harvey House coffee had not had the desired effect. The firm set of his mouth, narrowed eyelids and flexing jaw were clear indications of a seething anger. The pacing stopped. He glowered at Lupe, his dark eyes tiny black dots that drilled right through her.

Without preamble, he asked, "Where is your brother, Miss Castillo? And don't tell me you don't know."

Red blotches appeared on Lupe's cheeks. Her eyes avoided his. Tessa held her breath, wondering how Lupe would answer the sheriff's question. A week earlier, Deirdre Sweeney had arrived in Winslow, disturbing the peaceful rhythm of the Harvey House. When she first saw the newcomer, Lupe had become distraught. Every day since had brought more trouble. Now Tessa watched as her friend knitted her fingers together, sucked in a deep breath and looked directly at the sheriff. Tears leaked from the corners of her eyes, but she did not whimper.

"Sheriff Bowman, what can I say to you? I really don't know where Joaquin is."

She untangled her hands and began pounding one fist

into the other palm, emphasizing each word. Her tears vanished as quickly as they had appeared, replaced with a piercing stare of righteous indignation.

"What I do know is that he had nothing to do with that woman's murder. Joaquin may be headstrong and temperamental, but he is not a killer."

The words, spoken in haste and agitation, were heavily accented. Lupe seemed to recognize this. When she continued her diatribe, she spoke slowly and distinctly, eyes still ablaze.

"Why are you here so early in the morning to ask me these questions? I don't know any more about my brother today than I knew yesterday. Please, may I get to work?"

Her words did nothing to lessen the sheriff's anger. Quite the contrary. The lawman towered over Lupe, his gray eyes as cold as a January snowstorm. His next words, spoken through a jaw clenched as tightly as his fists, shocked the entire room.

"Doc Benton was murdered last night. Shot off his horse as he was riding back to his ranch after treating the two wounded men here in town. He knew something about Miss Sweeney. You, Miss Castillo, were in the jail when Doc said he had files at his home that would tell me something about her. Did you go to your brother in his hiding place and tell him?" He unclenched his fists to point an accusing finger at the trembling Mexicana.

A loud crash made them all turn towards the stove, where Dorothea Parks had dropped the pot of water she had been carrying. Her knees buckled and she folded to the cold kitchen floor, cradling her head in her shaking hands.

"Not Doc Benton," she cried. "He was such a wonderful

man. Many of us here owe him our health, maybe even our lives."

Her face was a mask of grief, eyes brimming with tears, skin ashen. Her lips trembled, yet she raised her voice in anger as she lashed out at Lupe.

"You had better tell the sheriff where your murdering brother is. Then get out of my kitchen. I can't look at you without thinking about the murder of a good doctor. Go, get out!"

The outburst was so sudden and so out of character for the tenderhearted cook that Tessa and Lupe froze in confusion. Dorothea's eyes spewed anger and hatred. Lupe burst into tears and ran from the room. Mrs. Gibson raised her hand as Tessa attempted to follow her friend.

"I'll take care of Lupe, Tessa. You'd best get to work. It looks like the kitchen will be short staffed again today, so we all need to pitch in. I'll see if any of the girls who are off today can help. Mr. Clifton will be here soon, too. I suppose it will be my job to tell him what has happened."

With that matter-of-fact statement, she hurriedly followed Lupe up the stairs.

"I'll come back, Miss Crane," Sheriff Bowman said, "and when I do, I expect that you and Miss Castillo will be here and you'll have something to tell me."

He turned on one heel and was gone.

Tessa did as Mrs. Gibson requested, helping out in the kitchen as well as running her own workstation in the dining room. She was grateful that only two trains would arrive today. Lupe didn't return to the kitchen. Tessa supposed that her friend was hiding out in their room, afraid of the cook, the sheriff and Frank Clifton.

When the Harvey House manager was told of all that had happened, he fixed a tired gaze on Tessa. With a soft shrug of his shoulders, he seemed to be saying, "See, Miss Crane, I told you that your Mexican friend was trouble."

Tessa didn't believe any of what was being said about Lupe, whether by words or gestures. For the past week, she'd known that Lupe was hiding something, but she was convinced that her friend did not know where her brother was. Lupe was adamant about that, even under the sheriff's forceful questioning, and had put herself in grave trouble by maintaining her ignorance.

"Are you all right, my dear?"

The quiet words startled Tessa out of her musings. She hadn't heard her father approach. Now, he stood behind her, his military stature sagging only slightly from a night with little or no sleep. He fixed steely eyes on his daughter.

Tessa had years of experience with that look, which, coupled with his grave countenance, warned Tessa that he expected to receive a truthful answer.

"Papacita." Tessa melted into her father's arms, unconsciously reverting to the endearment she used for him when she was a child.

Her tears quickly dampened his shirt. He pulled the yellow kerchief from around his neck, handing it to her to dry her eyes.

"I've just heard about Doctor Benton," the colonel said. "I feel responsible for this terrible murder. I'm the one who asked him to come into town and now he's dead. That's all anyone is talking about this morning. He was much loved."

"Oh, Papa," Tessa said through sniffles, "the sheriff thinks that Joaquin Castillo was involved in his death, as well as Deirdre Sweeney's murder. And now, Joaquin is missing. People are blaming Lupe, too. For what, I'm not sure, but she is afraid to come out of our room. I want to help her, but I don't know how."

"Tessa," Colonel Crane's tone was severe, "you must be careful. There is a murderer in this town. Maybe more than one. If Lupe tells you anything, anything at all, about her brother, you must go straight to the sheriff. I hate to leave you but I have to return to Ft. Apache today. Please, promise me you'll be careful."

Tessa dried her tears. She didn't cry often and was embarrassed by this show of weakness. She nodded at her father and managed a feeble smile.

"Don't worry about me, Papa. I'll be fine, and yes, I promise I'll be careful. Don't you be so hard on yourself about Doc Benton. You did what you had to do to take care of your men. The person who killed him is to blame, not you. Whoever that is will be found and punished." Tessa fervently hoped she wasn't talking about Joaquin Castillo.

Chapter Eighteen

Tessa studied her reflection in one of the two coffee urns that gleamed on the sideboard. She had polished them until her arms ached, then stacked snow-white cups and saucers in a neat pile by their side. Sugar cubes formed a perfect pyramid atop a small dish and the cream pitcher stood ready for filling. Her leg throbbed, reminding her of how long she had been standing, but she would allow herself no thoughts of rest.

She limped into the kitchen, not caring at this point whether Mr. Clifton saw her or not. She yanked the starched white pinafore over her head, marveling that it had stayed clean all morning, and replaced it with one of the service aprons from the hook by the stove. Rolling up the sleeves of her dark dress, she plunged her hands into the hot, soapy water and began to scrub pots, her thoughts and arms maintaining a staccato rhythm.

"Hi, Tess…uh, Miss Crane. We're here for the roundup."

Johnny's cheerful voice broke through the gloom of the steamy kitchen. His boyish wonder was the perfect panacea for Tessa's despair.

"Oh, my goodness. I forgot what day it was. What are you doing here by yourself? Where's your mother?"

"She should be here in a few minutes. She stopped to talk to the sheriff. She told me to come here and wait for her. Are there any cookies in this kitchen?"

"I think I can find one or two, Mr. Johnny. Here, take this towel and dry these pots while I scrounge up a treat for you. How about some milk to go with them?"

It felt good to talk about something besides murder.

"I brought my seashell fossil to school today to show Miss Kingsley."

The boy reached into his overall pocket and extracted the etched rock as slowly and carefully as if reaching for a butterfly.

"She told us that next month our class is going to study how the desert here used to be an ocean and that my fossil is a very important discovery. I want to find more, so I told Momma that I would start digging next spring's garden right now."

"I think I've got a budding archeologist on my hands."

Tessa and Johnny looked up at the sound of Anna's voice. She strode into the Harvey House kitchen, smiling at her son.

She wore a modest cotton dress that flowed softly from her shoulders, adding a feminine touch to her sturdy build. Its deep green color turned her hazel eyes into emerald pools.

Tessa opened her mouth to comment on their chameleon characteristics when she realized that what caught her attention in Anna's eyes wasn't their startling color. Instead, they reflected trouble, or anger, or maybe sadness. Perhaps all three. She cocked her head, puzzled, trying to assess Anna's mood, when the ranch woman's words shot through the air, landing with an unwelcome thud in her heart.

"Joaquin Castillo has been arrested. The sheriff found him at his aunt's house. At least I think she is his aunt. He is always calling her 'Tia Elena,' but local gossip is that they aren't related. That's not important. What is important is that Sheriff Bowman just now locked him up in the jail and there's talk of a hanging."

Despite Anna's sobering words, Tessa was gratified by the gentle tone in which they were spoken. Anna's sympathetic eyes told Tessa that the hard feelings between the two of them were forgotten.

"Oh, no. Poor Lupe."

Tessa knew she would have to go upstairs soon and break the bad news to Lupe before she learned about her brother's arrest from a stranger.

"There are folks here in town who want to lynch Joaquin right now," Anna continued. "No one cared that much about that poor girl from San Francisco. But, old Doc Benton. That's something altogether different. The folks around here liked and respected him. He certainly didn't deserve to die."

"But, why would Joaquin kill the doctor?" Tessa couldn't make any sense of Anna's words.

"Joaquin wouldn't hurt anyone. He always takes good care of the horses," a tiny voice said.

The women had forgotten about Johnny, who was sitting at the kitchen table, glass of milk in one hand and a half-eaten cookie in the other. His eyes were as wide as the plate set before him. He looked at his mother and Tessa with an expression that begged them to tell him that his friend, the trusted ranch hand, was not in trouble after all.

"Johnny," Anna said, "please go outside for a few minutes. I think Miss Parks would like you to find some ripe tomatoes hidden in those scraggly vines in the garden."

The kitchen door slammed, emphasizing Johnny's reluctance to obey his mother. Anna kept her voice low, barely above a whisper, aware that her son might still be listening.

"The sheriff told me that Joaquin is maintaining his innocence for both murders. He admitted to him that he had known Deirdre Sweeney many years ago, but he wasn't aware that she had returned to Winslow until after she was murdered."

"And what reason would he have to harm Doc Benton?" Tessa said.

"That's what Joaquin said, too, Tessa," Anna said. "He told the sheriff that he never had occasion to consult Doc, even though all the other cowpokes sang his praises. In fact, I remember that once, when he stitched up Shorty's scalp after he had misjudged the height of some barbed wire, Joaquin praised Doc for helping his friend. I let the sheriff know about that, too."

"I'm going to have to tell Lupe," Tessa said in a tone that made it clear she would rather face a nest of rattlesnakes. "I'd better do it now before someone else does." However, she remained seated, feet as leaden as her heavy heart.

"John always asked my opinion when it came to hiring the ranch hands," Anna said. "He said I was a good judge of character. I wonder what he would say if he were here today.

Was I wrong about Joaquin? He impressed me from the first time I met him. He's a hard worker and has been a friend to Johnny."

"Don't hang him yet, Anna," Tessa said. "Even though I don't know Joaquin as well as you do, I can't picture him as a murderer."

"That's another thing," Anna said. "The sheriff made it known that he was looking for Joaquin before Doc was murdered. I think a few people remembered Deirdre from five years ago and they spread the rumor that she and Joaquin were acquainted back then."

"And, of course," Tessa said, "whenever a young man and a pretty girl are seen together, people talk about them."

Anna picked up Tessa's train of thought. "Yes, and often the talk becomes malicious gossip. I never heard rumors about a baby until today. I think people are making up stories to justify their rage toward Joaquin. Deirdre worked for me, Tessa. Believe me, if she was with child, she wasn't having it any time soon. Whether the talk comes from knowledge or speculation, I don't know. What I do know, though, is that it will be difficult, if not impossible, for Joaquin to have a fair trial."

"There must be something else going on that we don't see, Anna. I think you were right when you hired Joaquin. Lupe insists that Joaquin wouldn't kill anyone and I believe her. And again, I have to ask why would he kill the doctor?"

Anna stood up. Seated, the women were eye level with each other. Standing, Anna towered over Tessa.

"The sheriff told me that Doc Benton knew something about the murdered woman," Anna said, looking down at Tessa. "He was determined to ride back to his ranch last night to review his files. He was sure those files would refresh his memory."

Tessa, tired of crooking her neck to look up at Anna, stood as well. Anna continued to speak.

"That's where he was headed when he was shot. Another thing the sheriff said was that Lupe heard the doctor talk about Deirdre, how her face was familiar to him. So, he thinks Lupe told Joaquin about it. Do you think Lupe knew where Joaquin was all along?"

"No, no, no." Tessa shook her head with such vehemence that a few loose curls whipped at her cheeks. "She's been as worried as any of us about his disappearance. She thought he might have gone back to Mexico because that's what he had planned to do years ago when Deirdre Sweeney threatened him. You can't blame Lupe for any of this."

Once again, Tessa sensed the tension between the two of them, fueled by her loyalty to Lupe and Anna's anger at Joaquin.

Anna walked to the door, paused with her hand on the knob. She leveled her gaze at Tessa. Then she did something so surprising that Tessa was too startled to respond. She winked.

"I need to check that my cattle are safely corralled, Tessa. Will you be at the roundup this evening? I doubt anyone will feel much like celebrating, but I have prepared baskets of food, and the boys deserve a little fun after all of their hard work. The money these cattle bring in will get Johnny and me through the winter so this is an important day for the Silver Spur. Please come."

"Of course, I will," Tessa said.

She read kindness into the invitation, a willingness on

Anna's part to overlook their opposing sentiments regarding murder and murderers, and to remain friends. Tessa smiled with relief.

"I know how hard you and your cowhands work. Everyone needs some relaxation. Go on, now. I have to talk to Lupe and finish my chores here. I'll come to the corral as soon as I can."

Tessa's anxiety increased with each step on the stairs. She dreaded facing Lupe with the horrible news. She was right to be concerned. Lupe's reaction was even worse than she expected.

"The sheriff is wrong about this," Lupe wailed after Tessa broke the news of Joaquin's arrest.

The distraught girl hugged her arms around her waist, rocking back and forth on the edge of her bed. Her eyes watered with tears, yet she made no effort to wipe them away. Tessa excavated a clean handkerchief from a stack of unfolded linens and handed it to her friend.

"Lupe, we have to talk to Joaquin. And the sheriff, too. Anna told me that he found your brother at Elena's house. Did you know that he was there when you visited her last night?"

"Of course not, Tessa. If I knew my brother was hiding out there, I would have convinced him to go to the sheriff. He's not a murderer, but someone is. You have to help me find out who did this before Joaquin is tried and convicted. From what you say, this town has already decided he is guilty. You heard the way Miss Parks talked to me this morning. I might as well be on trial too."

As much as Tessa wanted it to be otherwise, Lupe's words rang true. A Mexican boy was in jail and he needed

162 // Susan Tornga

help, guilty or not. Prejudice could rear its ugly head at any time. Lynching parties took on a life of their own. Even the fiercest of lawmen would have a difficult time restraining them. Jed Bowman's stature and deep voice gave him a commanding presence, but he had yet to be tested against an angry mob.

Doubt crept unbidden into Tessa's mind. Right now, she needed to assure herself that Joaquin was as innocent as Lupe insisted he was. Someone, somewhere in this town must know more than they were telling. Like Johnny's fossil, the past held clues to the present. Also, like the ancient rock, those clues might be disguised as something they aren't. She needed information, and Anna McAllister's roundup was as good a place as any to start digging.

The October chill coated the evening air. Although the early fall days were summertime warm, the temperature dropped rapidly once the sun dipped below the western horizon. To ward off the cold, Tessa donned a heavy suede blouse and a beautiful shawl knitted by her last Mexican nana.

She fingered the soft shirt, remembering how delighted George had been in his choice of a gift for his fiancé. The cavalry patrol had ridden all the way to Albuquerque, chasing a party of renegades who were terrorizing the settlers. Their mission was unsuccessful, but he returned with a blouse the color of the first luscious strawberries of spring.

"It's sort of an engagement gift," he had said over her protestations of the expense. One month later, he was killed, perhaps by one of those very renegades, leaving Tessa to reevaluate her life.

"Oh, George," she said to the mirror, "this shirt wraps me in your love, but I still miss you so much."

Tessa pulled the sunset-colored shawl tight around her shoulders, feeling her nana's presence as well. The shirt and shawl warmed her heart as well as her body. The glow was short-lived however. As she walked down the dusty street toward the rail-side corral, she heard snippets of conversation from passersby.

"I knew that Mexican was trouble when I first saw him."

"I don't know why Mrs. McAllister employs *those* people. There are plenty of us who need work."

She was glad that Lupe hadn't accompanied her.

The indignant voices were soon overtaken by the mournful lowing of Anna's fifty head of cattle. Tomorrow, they would be herded into cattle cars for the one-way trip to the stockyards in Kansas City. Just as they were protesting their fate, Tessa wanted to do the same for Joaquin. He had a right to a fair trial. Right now, she was wondering if he would get it.

Tessa had attended several festive roundups since she arrived in Winslow. These events, complete with lively music, singing and dancing, were social highlights for many of the townspeople, as well as folks from all the nearby ranches.

Often one of the local cowhands, feeling the effects of too much whiskey, would read a heart-felt poem about life on the range. Often, in the midst of the gaiety, folks would be moved to tears by these poignant, emotional recitations.

Tessa recalled one such poem from an earlier roundup. The trail-hardened poet compared the beauty of the West to the love of a good woman. Truly blessed was the man who shared his life with both. The romanticism of the rugged man had touched Tessa and she wished that she could recall his exact words. Perhaps he would be at the roundup this evening.

The night air bore the sounds of chatter and subdued laughter, but the normally raucous atmosphere was missing. Even the heartiest partiers felt the pall cast by two murders and the arrest of Joaquin Castillo. He was, after all, one of the close-knit group of ranch hands and he had numerous friends among the attendees at tonight's fiesta.

Tessa knew that Joaquin loved his life at the Silver Spur, and that Anna McAllister was a fair and generous employer. She also knew how quickly such comforts could be snatched away. The desire to find the real killer, to see justice done not only for the two murdered victims but also for a falsely accused man, burned deep inside her.

By the time Tessa arrived at the corral, many of Mr. Harvey's *girls* were gathered around the campfire, attempting to remember the words to a popular new tune, and failing miserably. Each mistake of wording would send them into fits of childish giggles. Tessa envied them their naïveté. Many of them were older than she was, but the absence of a mother in her life and the loss of her fiancé had given her a maturity beyond her years.

She recognized Beryl Turner, who was perched on the fence by the corral. On the walk through town, Tessa had decided that she would talk to anyone who might know something about Deirdre Sweeney or Doc Benton. She hadn't learned much from Beryl when she questioned her early in the week, but she was hoping that the girl might have remembered something else, anything that would help Joaquin.

She threaded her way through the still-giggling girls

toward her co-worker, who was busy batting her wide eyes at Lucas Carr, another of Anna's cowhands. When Tessa sat down beside her, Lucas excused himself, with what Tessa thought was a grateful nod in her direction.

"Good evening, Beryl," Tessa said. "I'm surprised to see you here. Isn't this the first time you've come to a roundup?"

"You're right, Tessa. Since I'm working tomorrow, I didn't go home tonight. Isn't this exciting?"

She didn't wait for an answer, just pointed a slender finger at Lucas' retreating back.

"Lucas just told me about Lupe's brother, Joaquin."

"Yes," Tessa said. "Of course, Lupe is upset."

Beryl looked at Tessa, her eyes suddenly hard and unblinking.

"I know Lupe is your friend, Tessa, and I'm sorry for her, but her brother killed good Doc Benton. He should hang."

The words stung Tessa. She had never heard Beryl raise her voice in anger before now. If this good-hearted woman had already tried and convicted Joaquin, what chance did the young man have against the fury of Winslow's townsmen?

"I don't believe that, Beryl, and I need you to help me prove it."

"Me?" Beryl said, tapping her chest with one finger. "I don't know anything that would point to his innocence."

"You were the only person who served Deirdre Sweeney the day she arrived. Have you remembered anything more that she might have said?"

Beryl sighed, obviously exasperated with Tessa's questions. Before she answered, Tessa saw her search the crowd, looking, Tessa guessed, to be sure Lucas Carr had not settled next to another girl. Seeing him talking to several

166 // Susan Tornga

other cowboys seemed to be all the assurance she needed, so she turned back toward Tessa and answered the question.

"I already told you everything I remember. This woman, Deirdre Sweeney, was very upset the day she arrived. She told the man she was with that he didn't understand why she had to fix the things that happened in the past. She couldn't go on to St. Louis without knowing what had happened here in Winslow."

"Wait, Beryl. What are you talking about? What things happened?"

"Tessa, I'm just telling you what I heard her say. I don't know what she meant, but I do know that she was very upset with this man. He wanted her to let go of the past. They were to be married in St. Louis. Or so he said, but then that other man came to the dining room several days later and he said that she was already married to him." Her voice trailed off, now uninterested in the conversation with Tessa.

Tessa saw Beryl's eyes wander once again toward Lucas Carr. He was handsome, Tessa admitted, but very young. Now, he was leading several Silver Spur cattle across the railroad tracks and into the pen.

"Let's enjoy the roundup, Tessa. This is my first one and I want to have some fun. See Lucas Carr over there?" Beryl pointed to the cowboy who seemed to be corralling her emotions as well as Mrs. McAllister's cattle. "Isn't he just the most handsome man you've ever seen?"

Tessa realized that she would get no more information out of the love-struck woman this night. Resolved to continue her quest, she left the corral area and went in search of Anna and Johnny. If nothing else, those two would provide her with the comfort of good friends and delicious food.

Anna had set up a table laden with her famous cooking. There were warm, flaky rolls and tender beef in a rich, tangy sauce, made from a recipe her mother had brought west from South Carolina. She arranged corn, tomatoes and peaches that she had canned over the summer in an edible rainbow across the white cloth. Tessa thought she had no appetite until the aroma of the simmering beef reached her nose. Then, she could hardly wait to get a plate and dig into this succulent chuck wagon supper.

She had devoured two helpings of everything when Anna at last broke free from her hostess duties and joined her, looking both excited and harried. The women chose to sit on a blanket away from the smoke of the cooking fire and the dust the restless cattle were kicking up in the corral. A guitar played in the background, its soft notes carried skyward on the evening breeze. The camaraderie of the cowboys and town folks, the sumptuous feast and the plaintive western ballads punctuated the roundup tradition, a part of life in the American West that Tessa so loved. The tone of Anna's words snapped her out of her reverie.

"Tessa, I need to talk to you. I was very angry with you when you came to the ranch Wednesday and I'm sorry. It isn't your fault that Joaquin is in all this trouble. It isn't Lupe's fault either. I was well aware that running the ranch alone after John died wouldn't be easy for me. Truthfully, things have gone more smoothly than I expected. I suppose that I worry most about working with all those men. If one, like Joaquin, is bad, then perhaps I should be afraid of all the men here." She waved her arms toward the campfire. "And what of Johnny? I can't risk a killer, or even a thief, living so close to my son. Do you know what I'm trying to say?"

"You don't owe me an apology, if that's what this is all about," Tessa said. "I know that you have to be careful about who is working for you. What I don't understand is why everyone, including you, has already decided that Joaquin is a murderer."

Tessa could hear her voice rise with indignation. She stopped speaking for a few seconds in an attempt to get her emotions under control. Anna had been gracious enough to apologize and Tessa had no desire to undo the goodwill her friend had created. With a deep breath, she was able to summon a genuine smile to her lips, but it faded quickly as she thought about the situation that had generated this conversation.

"I've seen the way many of the townspeople treat Lupe," Tessa began. "She might as well be on trial, too. Yesterday, I was walking through the dining room and I heard someone, I don't know who, call me a 'Mexican Lover.' I suppose that's true, but why should it be a crime?"

Anger welled inside her at the memory. Tessa was mad at herself for the feeling of humiliation that the words created, and even angrier with the insensitive person who uttered them. Once again, her voice rose to a fevered pitch and she knew her face was as red as one of cook's autumn peppers. She took another deep breath. Anna was a good friend and it would do no good to argue about things neither one of them knew to be true, or false, for that matter. She covered Anna's hand with her own.

"Anna, please believe that I'm not mad at you. I'm upset by the treatment of Lupe and, yes, Joaquin, too. I feel deep inside me that he had nothing to do with either of these ghastly murders."

She gave Anna's hand a stronger squeeze. "You have done a wonderful job with this food. Someday I'd like to learn to cook like you do, especially that wonderful sauce that's on the meat."

Anna acknowledged the compliment with a nod. "Here is your first lesson, Tessa. It's not only the sauce that makes this so good. You have to make sure the beef and pork are always under the brine and that the brine is sweet and clean."

"Save your cooking lessons until I actually have a kitchen of my own," Tessa said.

A glimpse of the home she had hoped to share with George flashed through her mind. She pushed it aside before sentimentality took root.

"Now, I'm going to go get a slice of that chocolate cake I saw on the table. Can I bring you some?"

Beryl was cutting a generous slice of the dark, gooey cake when Tessa returned to the food table in search of the same thing. "That looks delicious. Do you bake a lot, Beryl?"

"When I'm home I do a lot of the cooking, but I never have enough time or the appropriate ingredients to bake cakes. Certainly never anything as wonderful as this. I think I'll take a piece to Lucas." She cut an even larger slice for the unsuspecting ranch hand.

Tessa could see that the girl's sole focus was her cowboy. She figured the only way she was going to get any further information from her would be to play along.

"Why don't you eat yours first? Then, when you take the cake over to Lucas, you both won't be eating at the same time. You can talk to him while his mouth is full and he'll have to listen to you."

Beryl blushed and giggled, making her seem younger than the nineteen that she claimed to be. It made Tessa wonder if perhaps the girl had stretched the truth somewhat in order to obtain her position as a Harvey Girl. It hardly mattered at this point. She had proven her ability to handle the job.

"You're right, Tessa. Would you hold this while I eat my cake?"

As Tessa reached for the cake-laden plate, she studied Beryl, still wondering about her exact age.

"Isn't Lucas just the best cowboy? He really knows how to get those cattle to do what he wants them to do," Beryl said.

The girl was besotted. Tessa was ready to give up on ever learning anything else about Deirdre Sweeney when Beryl's next words caught her attention.

"If he would ask me to marry him, I'd say yes in a heartbeat. And if I had his children, I certainly wouldn't go giving them away like that stupid woman did."

"Are you talking about Deirdre Sweeney, Beryl? What do you mean, 'give away a child'?"

"Didn't I tell you that, Tessa? I thought I told you everything that I told the sheriff. That's what she said to that man at my table that day. 'I should never have given away my baby.' Then she ran out of the dining room, crying. And later we find out that she already had a husband. Why didn't she go back to him and give that child a proper family?"

Not only had Tessa grown up without a mother, she had lived on several Army posts where there were always unusual family circumstances. Of course, Beryl didn't share Tessa's perspective. She'll learn that life isn't always so predictable, thought Tessa, returning her attention to Beryl's revealing story.

If Deirdre was in Winslow to find her child, maybe she had confronted Joaquin. Even after five years, she might still have hoped for some monetary gain in exchange for her silence. Tessa had begun the evening in search of evidence that would help her friend. So far, the only information she had obtained had the opposite effect.

Chapter Nineteen

Beryl's words dampened what little enthusiasm Tessa had mustered for the roundup. She decided to return to her room, even though she dreaded telling Lupe about Beryl's disturbing revelation. She said her farewells to Anna and Johnny. The boy, although obviously tired, was busy counting cattle and eating cake. She hugged Anna with deep emotion. Her spoken thanks for the good food included unspoken gratitude for Anna's continuing friendship.

Tessa walked down the street toward the Harvey House, deep in thought. The chorus of a raucous popular song faded behind her. Was Joaquin Castillo really a cold-blooded killer? Many townsfolk thought so. Or, did they prefer to blame a poor Mexican ranch hand as an easy solution to a crime no one cared to examine further? Her heart and mind battled, with no clear winner.

Loneliness overcame her. Her father was far away and

she couldn't discuss any of this with Lupe. She shivered, not only from the cold. Tears pricked at the corners of her eyes. Tonight she missed George deeply. Last week she thought she had recovered from the loss. Now she knew she hadn't.

"Where are you, my love?" she whispered into the starry night. The only answer was the symphony of crickets that accompanied her down the dusty street toward a conversation she didn't want to have.

"What is it, Tessa? What happened?" Lupe jumped from the chair. She wiped at Tessa's tears with the soft touch of her fingers.

Tessa sat down gingerly on the edge of her bed, mindful of the freshly pressed uniform that Mrs. Gibson had laid out for the morrow. Often she would return to her room to find the dress and pinafore so carefully positioned that it appeared to be the ghost of a Harvey Girl, napping on the spread. The sight usually made her laugh. Not tonight.

"I think the sheriff knows about the baby."

Lupe's eyes widened. "The baby? Deirdre's baby? How did he find out?"

She brought her hands up to her mouth, and closed her eyes, a silent supplication to her God.

Tessa smoothed invisible wrinkles from the uniform, talking to Lupe as she did so. The gesture had a calming effect, like petting a cat. She told her about what she had learned at the roundup, omitting any mention of the angry undercurrent running through town as people proclaimed Joaquin's guilt.

"Beryl Turner heard Deirdre tell the man with her that she gave away her baby. And he knows that she and Joaquin were *friends,*" she said, stressing the last word. "Sheriff

Bowman may not have any notches on his gun handle, but he's a smart man. He knows that both Deirdre and Joaquin worked at the Silver Spur at that time. Then your brother disappeared just when the sheriff wanted to talk to him about her. Today, he found Joaquin at Tia Elena's. Worse yet, she's the woman who adopted Enrique, who is very possibly his son. If he's innocent, why does he act like a guilty man?"

Behind splayed fingers, Lupe gritted her teeth.

"Why Joaquin?"

Her lips trembled and she said no more, leaving Tessa to wonder if the question were asked of Joaquin or God.

The young women spoke no more that night, nor did they sleep. Lupe's constant thrashing unnerved Tessa, who wished for words to comfort her friend, but could find none. Joaquin's behavior made it difficult for her to offer encouragement. Two people were dead. Oh, how she wanted to talk to her father about the events of the past week, but he was a hundred miles away. The sleep she craved eluded her. When the clock chimed three times, she resigned herself to the day ahead, one she knew would be tiring and, most likely, tiresome as well. She began polishing silver in her head, and soon drifted off in a dreamless slumber that ended all too soon with Ardella Gibson's "wake up, girls!" booming voice.

"She's worse than reveille on an Army post," Tessa grumbled.

Tessa wasn't hungry after the roundup feast the previous night, but she knew it would be a long time before she would be able to eat again. One of Oswald's cinnamon buns would be just the thing to get her through the morning. She entered the kitchen, mouth watering. The change in the atmosphere was instantaneous.

Where girlish chatter usually filled the air, today there was only silence. Even the requisite clatter of pots and pans seemed muted. No one greeted her. She smiled tentatively at Dorothea, but the cook merely nodded once and returned to the fascinating array of pots and pans on the stove. This cool reception unnerved Tessa. She had never felt like such a pariah. What must it be like for poor Lupe? She wished she could warn her friend before she walked through the door.

Tessa decided the best course of action would be to ignore the snubs from the others. She chirped a pleasant "good morning," ate her toast quickly--no sweet, sticky rolls in sight--and rushed into the dining room, praying that the icy air of the kitchen wouldn't follow her. Most of all, she hoped Dorothea's attitude toward Joaquin's sister had softened over the past 24 hours. She met Lupe at the foot of the stairs.

"Amiga, please be strong."

"What has happened now, Tessa? I don't think I can take one more piece of bad news."

"It's not that. Nothing else has happened. However, the entire town must now know of your brother's arrest, and most of them have decided that he is guilty. I'm afraid it will be hard on you for a while. You know I'm your friend. Remember that when you think that you don't have one."

With a heavy heart, Tessa walked toward the dining room. She had just experienced the animosity that Lupe would face when she entered the tomb-like atmosphere of the kitchen. Last night she had wavered in her belief of Joaquin's innocence. Nevertheless, he deserved a fair trial, just as any other man would. That thought strengthened her resolve. She would continue her efforts to put a name to the murderer of Deirdre Sweeney and Doc Benton, whoever it might be.

Luck was with Tessa that Saturday. Heaven knows, there had been little enough of that lately. She had been surprised, and more than a little grateful, to find that Mr. Clifton had assigned her to work the lunch counter on a day when she usually worked two of the large dining room tables. Was this his apology for the uncomfortable confrontation in the alley?

When the sheriff strode in and took a stool next to Hiram Frye, she was doubly grateful for the change of plans. The lawman was just the person she needed to talk to about Joaquin Castillo. She knew that she would have to choose her words, and their timing, with care. She smiled sweetly at Bowman, hoping her dimples might work a little magic, and asked him for his order.

When she returned to the counter with the aromatic butternut squash soup that Dorothea had created, the sheriff and Hiram Frye had their heads together, deep in serious conversation. The old sot actually appeared to be sober today, and the usual nauseating smell of sweat and cigars didn't cling to him. The words he spoke were crisp and his tone serious. Unfortunately, he spoke too softly for Tessa to understand them. She leaned closer. Surely, the counter needed cleaning there.

"You know, sheriff, I think babies are a wonderful thing. I probably haven't been the best father to Agnes, but I love that little girl. And when I hear about somebody giving up their child, just giving it away like a Christmas gift, I get real mad. Hattie and me, we've had our troubles. I'm sure the whole town knows about that."

The man actually blushed. "But, when Hattie told me

she was expecting a child, our child, after all those years, well, we just decided to let bygones be bygones. I'll never be the perfect husband, but then Hattie sure as shootin' isn't the perfect wife. But, give away a baby? No, sir. You need to see to punishing that Mexican for getting that poor girl in a situation where she had no other choice."

Tessa cringed. From the gossip she heard around town, Hiram Frye himself might have a few more babies scattered around the area. He was hardly the person to be Joaquin's judge and jury. However, Tessa had learned enough about people from her Army life to know that those who had the least right to accuse others were usually the ones who condemned the loudest.

She breathed a sigh of relief when Frye left the counter as soon as she placed the sheriff's meat and potatoes down. She picked up the nickel Frye left her with a shrug of resignation. Oh well, some people didn't leave her anything. At least this was some recognition, however small, of her service.

She placed the steaming plate of thinly sliced beef and snowy potatoes, all covered in a rich brown gravy, in front of Bowman. With an effort, she released her grip on the platter. The enticing aroma reminded her of the hours that had passed since her meager breakfast.

"Sheriff, can I talk to you while you eat?"

"Miss Crane, you've been a big help to me this past week, given me a lot of information. So, say what you will. I have an inkling that this has something to do with the Mexican boy who is sitting in my jail right now."

"Yes. I suppose you know that his sister is my roommate. Actually, we're good friends."

It felt good to Tessa to say that. How could she condemn

the people of Winslow for their treatment of Joaquin when she was afraid to admit to a close friendship with his sister? She had decided that she might as well come right out and ask the questions she wanted answered. This wasn't the time to beat around the bush.

She was aware that other customers required her attention and she owed Mr. Clifton her best effort. However, she owed Lupe that much, as well. If her mind kept up this muddled thinking, she wouldn't be of help to anyone. She shook her head in an attempt to expel all the conflicting emotions raging there.

Looking pointedly at the sheriff she asked, "Why do you think Joaquin killed that woman and Doc Benton?"

Bowman's fork halted abruptly. His mouth, ready to receive the delicious food, stayed open in surprise.

"Well, Miss Crane, you certainly get right to the point," he said as he placed his fork down on his plate. "If I wasn't looking directly at you, I would think I was talking to your father. He's a man who speaks his mind and I can see that there's no doubt you're his daughter. You know that I can't answer that question. However, I like you and I respect your father, so I'll tell you what I can."

Tessa couldn't believe her good fortune. Would the sheriff tell her what he knew that had resulted in Joaquin's arrest?

"Joaquin Castillo was hiding from the law," Bowman said. "That alone makes him guilty of something. I also have reason to believe that he was acquainted with Deirdre Sweeney several years ago. I think you know that, too, because you and Mrs. McAllister are friends. I know what the town is saying about Castillo, but I'm the sheriff here and I'll see to it that the law is obeyed."

When Jed Bowman stood up, he towered over Tessa. She didn't know whether he was trying to impress her or simply convince her that he meant what he said.

"My father was a newspaper man in Tucson, over thirty years ago," Bowman said. "I was raised with Chinamen, Negroes and Mexicans, or *Norteños,* as we call them here. I don't see color, Miss Crane. I see human beings."

His indignation rose along with his temper. "Did it ever occur to you that maybe, just maybe, I put Joaquin Castillo behind the bars of my jail for his own protection?"

Bowman sat back down with a thud. He looked at the fork full of food, seemingly surprised to find it there, shrugged and raised it to his mouth. He swallowed, wiped his mouth with his napkin, and looked her straight in the eye. Tessa wasn't a woman who was easily intimidated, but his steely gaze succeeded in doing just that. His words had unnerved her. She hadn't thought that perhaps Joaquin was safer in jail, accused of murder, than he would be on the streets of Winslow, theoretically a free man.

"It's my turn to ask you some questions, Miss Crane. Lucky for you, though, I don't have the time right now. I plan to talk to your roommate soon, too. I'll know if you give me straight answers. You can do yourself, your friend, and her brother the most good by telling the truth. Please pass that advice along to Miss Castillo and urge her to talk to her brother."

He bent his head over his plate, signaling the end of the conversation. Tessa needed to get back to work, so she was happy to oblige. Her plan to get information from the sheriff had backfired. However, Bowman's declaration comforted her. She believed that he would be fair. Right now, it was the other residents of Winslow who worried her.

Tessa welcomed the hectic diversion of the three afternoon trains. The passengers heading toward San Francisco and Los Angeles provided a continuing source of amusement, with their misconceptions of the Wild West. They were certain that the train would be robbed, or attacked by renegade Indians, or both. Many were surprised to discover the amenities of the Harvey House and to find genteel women there to serve them.

Those returning east from the California cities wanted to show-off their sophistication, dropping examples of their newly gained cultural knowledge into every conversation. Very few people asked about Winslow and the surrounding area, although Tessa would have been very proud to tell them of the wonders of the Grand Canyon and the nearby phenomenon, a recently discovered meteor crater.

She also liked to point out the marvelous turquoise and silver jewelry for sale in the gift shop adjacent to the dining room. Fred Harvey encouraged the Navajos to sell their creations in his establishments all over the West. As well as being fine jewelry artisans, the Navajo Indians were extraordinary weavers, creating the most beautiful rugs Tessa had ever seen. Their work was detailed, exquisite, breathtaking. Collectors and museums all over the world coveted these works of art. She could not imagine why they were called rugs.

Most of the Santa Fe passengers simply stepped off the train, complaining of the dust and heat. They rarely commented on the food that Tessa knew to be delicious, merely sighing with relief when the whistle blew two short blasts signaling impending departure. Today, however, the idiosyncrasies of the travelers were a pleasant distraction.

Although her mind frequently wandered back to Joaquin, she didn't have time to dwell on the weighty issue of murder.

The eastbound train delivered a large crate of fresh flowers, grown in the cool valley south of San Francisco. Tessa finished her day with the happy task of arranging bouquets for each of the large tables, and bud vases containing single blooms for the lunch counter. She marveled at the variety of flora, so many colors, sizes and smells. Perhaps when she had worked for Mr. Harvey long enough to earn a travel voucher, she would journey to California to see this place that could produce such a painter's palette of blossoms.

Tessa spent more time than needed creating the bouquets. She found it necessary to polish the silver and crystal to an exquisite shine so that the rainbow colors of the flowers would reflect off their gleaming surfaces. By the time she reached her room, Lupe was there, her uniform hanging neatly from one of the wall hooks. Tessa quickly removed hers, tossing it on the bed. Lupe laughed in spite of herself.

"It's nice to hear your laughter, *amiga,* but I have a feeling you are laughing at me."

"Tessa, you know very well that you'll be looking all over for your nightgown in a few hours, only to find it underneath your dress and apron. Why don't you just hang them up now and save yourself some aggravation later?"

Before Tessa could think of a suitable response, Lupe's tone changed.

In a voice so soft Tessa had to lean close to hear her, she said, "After I finished my work in the kitchen tonight, I visited Joaquin. He talks only of escape because he knows he won't get a fair trial. He has no way to prove his innocence. Perhaps Enrique really is his son. Joaquin can't, and won't, deny it. He has always liked the boy. Now he says, he'll take him from Tia Elena and make a run for the border."

Her voice faltered.

"Tessa, you and I both know that if my brother tries to escape, he'll be hunted down, shot and killed. Worse still, if he manages to take Enrique with him, the boy's life could be in danger as well. I tried to talk some sense into him, but he won't listen to me. Fear makes even strong men behave carelessly. I know one thing for sure. Joaquin is afraid, which makes me afraid too. Isn't there anything you can do to help us?"

Tessa hated questions she couldn't answer. This was one such question, and it upset her to see her friend hurting so badly. Even though she knew it was a mistake, she decided to tell Lupe what she had been thinking about all afternoon. She hoped she wouldn't regret the impulsive action. She limped over to Lupe's bed and sat down gently. Taking her friend's delicate hands in hers, she laid out her plan.

Chapter Twenty

"We should go now while the town sleeps." The quiver in Tessa's voice matched the shaking of her hands. "If anyone is out, the dark streets will hide us."

Lupe nodded her agreement. She quickly shed her nightgown and pulled on her split skirt. The night air would be cool, cold even, so she grabbed her wool jacket from its peg, to be put on when they were safely outside. Tessa located her gloves at the bottom of a still-neat drawer. Lupe extinguished the light and the two women waited silently, silent that is, save for the hammering of their hearts, as they allowed their eyes to adjust to the darkness before venturing into the hallway.

The Harvey House rested in its evening quiet. Fortunately, the commotion of so many trains had worn out the staff. Tessa knew that anyone with an ounce of sense would be sound asleep. Yet, here she and Lupe were, sneaking down the stairs, praying that no one would be wandering the halls in search of a drink of water or a late snack.

They reached the livery without incident. Tessa motioned for Lupe to wait outside.

"Whistle softly if you see anyone approaching," she whispered.

She clucked her tongue softly to alert Ben to her presence. The gentle mule fixed his liquid gaze on her, blinked his eyes in recognition and continued chewing a hank of hay. Tessa led him from his stall and quickly hitched the saddle over his substantial belly. The women mounted up. Lupe, who was not an experienced horsewoman, held firmly on to Tessa.

"Not so tight, *amiga,*" Tessa whispered. "I can't breathe."

"Sorry. I'm scared, that's all. We can't explain why we are riding out of town in the middle of the night. Not only are we going to break into Doctor Benton's house, but we've stolen a horse, as well. I just hope no one sees us. I don't need any more trouble, that's for sure."

"We're only borrowing Ben, Lupe, but you're right about breaking into Doc's house. I've never done anything like this, either. If we're careful, we won't get caught. So, be quiet now and try to relax. We only have a couple of miles to ride. You can get nervous when we get close to the Benton ranch."

Tessa had learned from Dorothea that the murdered doctor's wife was staying at her sister's house in town, afraid to be by herself at the ranch. It was hardly a ranch by Western standards, however. The doctor kept only a few chickens and one cow, a small enough homestead to be easily cared for by a neighbor until Mrs. Benton decided whether or not to sell the property. Tessa hoped her information was correct. She didn't want to worry about waking the old woman, who, if she remained at the ranch, would most likely be sleeping with a gun by her side.

As soon as the ranch house came in to view, Lupe once again tightened her grip on Tessa, who bore this discomfort wordlessly. Lupe was frightened, an emotion Tessa now shared. The tiny house appeared as a dark rectangle silhouetted against the semi-darkness of the starlit sky. It was a miniature replica of one of the similarly shaped red rock mesas that rose at random from the desert floor.

Normally, Tessa loved how the desert sky would blaze with stars on a moonless night. Tonight, however, she wished for some clouds to mute their brilliance. She and Lupe had dressed for a cool night and had kept warm for most of the ride. Now, gusts of chilling wind attacked with uncomfortable frequency. Both women shivered from the cold as well as their fear.

"A horse, there," Lupe said, her voice a mere breath in Tessa's right ear.

"It's probably one of the Benton's horses," Tessa replied. The optimism left her voice as she continued, "or, maybe Mrs. Benton asked someone to stay out here. One of the young men from the Silver Spur, or the Lazy Eight. Both of those ranches are close by. We'd best be extra quiet, just in case."

They dismounted before reaching the ranch gate and walked with Ben the last fifty yards. After tying him to the large post by the gate, Tessa reached in her pocket for the feed she had stashed there.

"Good boy, Ben." With a farewell pat on his flank, she led Lupe down the road, listening carefully for any unusual sounds coming from the house.

The women relaxed slightly as they neared the porch. They had neither heard nor seen anything out of the ordinary as they walked up the path from the gate. Tessa motioned to Lupe that they should go around to the rear of the house. Tessa headed left and Lupe right. As soon as Tessa rounded the back corner, she caught her breath. Candlelight flickered from a window at the far side of the house. Lupe would come that way. Tessa sent a silent message to her friend. *Watch out*.

Tessa squinted into the dark night. Lupe's slight form appeared around the corner, then stopped abruptly. She had obviously seen the light, too, and was pondering her course of action. Both women remained frozen at opposite ends of the ranch house, trying to communicate without words.

Tessa hoped Lupe would know to remain still. Rocks and branches littered the ground and the slightest noise would echo in the still night air. She watched in horror as Lupe rose, planted her face against the panes and cupped her hands around her eyes for a better view. *Get down. Get down,* Tessa silently commanded to no avail. Her friend stayed at her vigil, body rigid, each breath evidenced by the tiniest shrug of her shoulders.

Tessa reached the kitchen door in two strides. She decided to risk a try at the knob, but first she quickly and quietly removed her boots. The knob rotated easily and silently beneath her palm. The good doctor must have kept the hinges oiled. Once inside, she let her vision readjust to total darkness.

As soon as she could make out the silhouettes of the

icebox and the large stove, she crept through the kitchen and into the hallway. At the end of the hall, the flickering light from beneath a door painted a pale yellow stripe on the floorboards. As she neared the door she heard the wood-on-wood sound of a drawer opening, followed by the rustle of papers. Tessa leaned in, her ear glued to the door, pondering her next course of action, when the explosion of shattering glass broke through the still night air.

"What the...?" A gruff voice, familiar to Tessa, hollered from behind the door. "I have a gun and I'll shoot. Show yourself, whoever you are!"

Tessa feared that somehow Lupe had fallen, shattering the glass. Without a thought for her own safety, she barreled through the door. Hattie Frye's arm swung quickly away from the window toward the latest crashing noise. She pointed her gun directly at a quaking Tessa.

"You! You're Tessa Crane, one of those *girls* from the Harvey House." The woman's derisive tone told Tessa what she needed to know about this woman's opinion of her and her fellow workers. "What are you doing here? Who else is out there? Someone threw a rock through the window. It couldn't have been you."

"The sheriff is here with me, Mrs. Frye," Tessa lied, proud of herself for such quick thinking, "so you'd better put down that gun. I could ask you the same question. What are you doing here?" Tessa attempted to put a tone of authority in her voice, even as her body shook with fright.

"You think I'm stupid, young lady? Just because you're so pretty and fancy? I know the sheriff isn't out there. It's that Mexican girl, isn't it? She thinks she's so high and mighty 'cause she works at Mr. Harvey's *establishment*." She spat out the last word.

"Her and that no good brother of hers. Taking jobs from God-fearing white folks. They should both be sent back to Mexico. Only he won't live long enough for that."

She turned her head slightly without taking her eyes, or her gun, off Tessa. She obviously wanted her voice to carry out of the window

"You'd better show yourself, little brown girl, or your friend is going to get a bullet right between her tiny breasts."

She raised the gun and fired a shot at the ceiling. Tessa jerked at the ominous sound. Nevertheless, she fervently hoped Lupe wouldn't come out of hiding. If she did, they would both be dead. Before she could decide what to do, Lupe's voice broke through the darkness.

"Quidado. Otra piedra. Watch out! Another rock!"

Tessa ducked as Hattie fired another shot. The next sound was a dull thud, followed by a resounding *thunk,* as the rock found its mark. Hattie crumpled to the ground. Heart pounding, Tessa crawled to where the woman lay sprawled across the floorboards. Blood seeped from a gash above her left ear, but her breathing was strong. She wouldn't be unconscious for long.

"Lupe. Lupe, where are you?" Tessa's voice reached a fevered pitch.

Her friend's beaming face appeared in the window, framed by jagged glass.

"Tessa, are you okay. Did you get shot?" She pointed to the prostrate form on the floor. "That's Hattie Frye. What is she doing out here?"

She continued her nervous chatter without waiting for an answer.

"Joaquin taught me how to throw rocks like that. I'm pretty good, huh?"

Lupe's eyes darted between the prone woman and Tessa, focusing on neither. Tessa recognized the shock in her friend's voice.

"Lupe, stop!" The excited girl had reached through the shattered window, ready to climb into the room. "You'll cut yourself. I'm okay, but I need you to help me. Go around to the kitchen door and find something there so we can tie her up. Then, just follow the light down that hall." Tessa pointed through the doorway, the way she had come in.

"I'll stay here in case she comes around. I have her gun," she held up the small revolver, "but I don't want to shoot her. We need some answers from her and I want to talk to her before the sheriff does."

Tessa's commanding voice and the specific directions she gave seemed to lift Lupe out of her stupor. In a matter of only a few minutes, she came back with a coil of rope in her hand. Hattie started to moan, but didn't open her eyes.

"Hurry, Lupe. We've got to tie her up before she wakes."

The two women set about tying Hattie's hands together.

"Shouldn't we tie them behind her back?" Lupe asked.

"I want her hands where I can see them," Tessa said. "She's a sly one, she is. We shouldn't tie her ankles either. We may need to take her with us and I don't want to carry her, do you?"

Lupe laughed at her friend's question. "If she tries to escape we can certainly catch her."

Of course, Tessa, with her bad leg, might not be fast, but Lupe had every reason to have confidence in her ability to outrun the older, heavier woman.

While they waited for Hattie to regain consciousness, Tessa and Lupe began the task they had originally come to the ranch to do. As they searched through Doc Benton's papers, they discussed what possible reason Hattie Frye had to be there. It was more than coincidence. Tessa was curious about what Doc's papers contained that could be of interest to this strange woman.

"What are we going to tell the sheriff about why we were out here, when we take Hattie to him?"

Lupe's question was a valid one. Tessa wondered the same thing.

"Well, if we find what we're looking for, that will be answer enough. We want to prove your brother's innocence. If we do, I'm hoping the sheriff will overlook tonight's little adventure."

Across the room, Hattie stirred. Her moaning reminded the women that they needed to hurry their search through Doc Benton's papers. Tessa was certain that the doctor had been murdered because of what he knew. She hoped that, when she and Lupe found what they were looking for and could recognize its importance, they could prove the paternity of Deirdre's child. She prayed that the evidence would not point to Joaquin Castillo, and she knew Lupe was doing the very same thing.

"Maybe Doc kept this information somewhere else, not in the medical files. Perhaps it wasn't a piece of paper after all, but maybe an article of clothing, or a piece of jewelry instead," Lupe said.

Tessa nodded thoughtfully. "Hmm, you could be right, Lupe, but I can't think of anything the doctor would have of Deirdre's. It doesn't make sense. Even if she sought his medical advice and paid him with a piece of jewelry, how could that prove Joaquin's innocence? What I can't figure out is what Hattie Frye has to do with this whole thing. Of course, I've heard the gossip about her. Who hasn't? People say that she often does crazy things. Maybe this is just one of those times."

Despite her confident words to the contrary, she felt certain that Hattie's mission to the Benton ranch had something to do with the doctor's murder.

"You no good young tarts! Untie me. You'll be sorry you did this."

Hattie Frey was conscious.

Tessa and Lupe unceremoniously lifted her from the floor and plunked her down in the doctor's office chair, without regard to her comfort. They did, however, tie a bandana around her head to staunch the flow of blood from her wound. The doctor's study was in total disarray, papers scattered everywhere, glass shards crackled under foot.

The two crusaders were even more downcast than the bound woman. They had searched through all of Doc Benton's files, every nook and cranny in his study, and still, they could find no reference to Deirdre Sweeney. They looked at each other. Tessa saw concern in Lupe's gritted teeth and furrowed brow. She guessed her own face mirrored that apprehension. What could they possibly tell the sheriff that would keep them from becoming prisoners too?

Hattie sensed their discomfort and a malevolent grin pricked at the corners of her mouth.

"You two are in an awful lot of trouble. Let me go and we'll forget all about this. Mrs. Benton will think that some thieves broke in when no one was at home. Maybe the sheriff will decide that it was the doctor's murderer come back for something. Then, he'll have to look around for someone other than your brother to arrest." She nodded toward Lupe.

Tessa listened to Hattie and considered their next course of action while she wiped up the tiny puddles of blood from the floor.

There was some truth to what Hattie was saying. The situation appeared hopeless. What could they possibly tell Sheriff Bowman about finding Hattie Frye in Doc Benton's house without incriminating themselves in the process? Hattie's suggestion provided a way out for all three of them, although Tessa hated to free this strange and frightening woman. She also felt responsible for the mess they would leave the grieving widow. She would have to find a way to replace the broken panes without Mrs. Benton, or the sheriff, knowing.

Father would not be proud of me tonight, she thought, and that saddened her greatly.

"Okay, Mrs. Frye, we'll do as you ask, after you tell me what you were looking for out here that couldn't wait until morning?"

Hattie ignored Tessa's question. Instead, she pressed her bound hands to the side of her head in an awkward gesture. "That's quite a lump I've got, Miss Mexican. You should be glad I'm not taking *you* into the sheriff."

Tessa tried again, raising her voice. "What are you doing out here tonight, Mrs. Frye?"

"I don't have to say anything, but since I've got nothing to hide, I'll tell you."

Hattie brought her hands back into her lap with an angry thud, then twisted them back and forth in a nervous gesture. Soon, Tessa could see the raw skin appearing on her wrists. The woman's distress surprised her.

In a condescending *you're lucky I'm telling you this*

tone, Hattie began speaking. "Hiram, he's my husband, you know. Well, he fancies himself something of a card shark. Likes to gamble at the saloon. A couple of years ago he lost a lot of money to Doc Benton. He couldn't pay it back. We never had any extra money and the doctor was too kind to hound him about it."

She looked down at her hands and paled at the sight of the bloodstained rope.

"Untie me or I might take back my generous offer to forget this whole escapade." Her tone was more panicked than threatening.

"Finish your story, Mrs. Frye."

Tessa wondered if this was an elaborate fabrication. She had no way to prove it and maybe the woman was telling the truth. What she said certainly fit with Tessa's image of Hiram Frye.

"All I wanted to do was find the I.O.U. that Hiram gave to the doctor before his wife discovered it and came after us for the money. She isn't nearly as nice as he was. She puts on airs like she's better than the rest of us. She won't even lower herself to speak to me when we see each other in town. Good heavens, a body would think she was the one who was the doctor. Ha!"

Lupe remained quiet during Hattie's tirade. When she did speak, her accusatory tone and gruff voice startled Tessa. "Did you find the I.O.U.?"

Hattie's head jerked toward Lupe. She, too, had forgotten about her assailant. The sound of Lupe's voice seemed to awaken Hattie's memory of the attack. Her lips curled in fury.

"No, I didn't." She spat out the words. "But, I figure if I didn't find it, Mrs. Benton won't either. Maybe her husband tore it up. Come on now. Untie me and let's get out of here. Hiram's at his night watchman's job and little Agnes is home alone. She was asleep when I left, but I don't want her to wake up and not have me there." She appealed to the women's innate maternal instinct. "Let's go." Tessa glanced at Lupe. Her friend shrugged her shoulders. Her eyes were moist, lips pressed tightly together in a thin white line. She was obviously fighting for control, whether over fury or tears, Tessa didn't know. When the two friends planned this night mission, they didn't expect this disastrous outcome. Not only had they not found any evidence to help clear Joaquin, now they were criminals, too. Seeing no alternative, Tessa untied the rope. The freed woman rubbed her wrists, turning the raw skin even redder.

Lupe and Tessa watched silently as Hattie mounted her horse and rode off towards Winslow. As if on a signal, they reached across and squeezed each other's hand.

"Lupe, let's ride over to the Silver Spur and sleep there for a few hours. We can't be seen riding into town with that woman. Plus, I'm so tired I could drop right here. The McAllister ranch is close by, and I know where Anna hides a key. We don't even need to wake her. We'll sleep on the sofa and ride back to town early tomorrow morning. Or is it already tomorrow?"

Lupe, who had no desire to be anywhere near Hattie Frye, was quick to agree.

They rode the short distance in silence over ground as familiar to Tessa as the streets of Winslow. Tessa knew the ranch house would be dark, but she wasn't concerned. She didn't need lights to find her way.

"Shhh. Take off your boots before we walk across the porch. Anna keeps a key on a nail behind the swing."

Anna wasn't as fastidious as Doc Benton about oiling hinges, however. The front door squeaked with dinner-gong loudness when Tessa pushed it open. She only hoped Anna and Johnny were deep sleepers and wouldn't hear this blatant announcement of uninvited guests.

What little luck they had when the night started was long gone. Lace curtains filtered the starlight, casting eerie shadows across the room. Guided by the pale light, the uninvited guests made their way through the maze of chairs and bookcases.

They shrieked when a tousled head popped up from the sofa. Their screams were followed by a coyote-like howl. The size of the head told Tessa that it had to be Johnny. She wondered how such a small person could make such a big noise.

"Johnny, hush. It's me, Tessa. I didn't mean to scare you." She didn't admit to her own fright. "Why are you sleeping down here?"

The boy's eyes and mouth gaped with alarm. Before he could gather his wits to answer, Anna bounded down the steps, oil lamp in one hand, pistol in the other.

"Stop right there or I'll shoot!" she bellowed.

Chapter Twenty-One

"You two just about got shot." Anna's trembling voice still held a vestige of fear. "What in blazes are you doing out here in the middle of the night?"

"I'm sorry, Anna, and you, too, Johnny," Tessa said. "I didn't expect to find you asleep in the parlor, and we sure didn't mean to frighten you."

Lupe gave a nervous laugh. "I thought you were a ghost," she said to Johnny.

Tessa opened her palms toward Anna, in a *please try to understand* gesture.

"It's too complicated to explain the reason for this strange visit right now, Anna. Can Lupe and I sleep here for a few hours? We'll leave before daylight. I put Ben in the corral and we have to get him back to the livery before anyone notices he is gone." She managed a rueful smile.

"Lupe and I are in enough trouble without being branded as horse thieves."

The look Anna gave them was undoubtedly one she used on Johnny when he told a tall tale.

"I promise to ride back here tomorrow and explain everything. But, please don't tell anyone we were here. I really am sorry to do this to you, Anna, but it's very important. Please?"

Tessa saw indecision wash over Anna's face. She couldn't blame her for wanting to know why her home had been invaded in the middle of the night. With a sigh, Anna resigned herself to waiting.

"Okay, Tessa. I'm tired and I can see that both of you are worn out, as well. Come on, Johnny." She motioned to her sleepy-eyed son. "Let's go on up to bed now."

Johnny followed her reluctantly. He sensed that it would be far more interesting to stay downstairs with the intruders.

Anna stopped when she reached the foot of the stairs. She spoke quietly to her friends, indicating Johnny with a nod.

"He fell asleep down here earlier and I didn't want to carry him upstairs. He's quite an armful now."

She fussed at his mop of tangled hair.

"So, I left him in the parlor. I'm glad I did. Otherwise, I might never have known about my unusual midnight guests. I'll see you tomorrow, Tessa. Or actually, later today. Get some sleep. Whatever you're up to, it's obviously worrying you."

She reached for Johnny's hand and two rocks tumbled out, striking the wooden stair with a dull thud.

"Be careful, Mama. Those are my fossils. See, Tessa, I

198 // Susan Tornga

have two of them now and I know I'll find more. I'm going to be famous."

He knelt on the floor to retrieve his treasure, then followed his mother up the stairs. Tessa hoped he would fall asleep again quickly. She didn't want to give Anna any more reason to be angry with her.

The young women curled up at opposite ends of the sofa, neither one expecting to get much rest. Surprisingly, they both dozed, albeit fitfully.

Tessa woke first, disoriented by the strange surroundings. When she remembered where she was and why she was there, she moaned with regret at the previous evening's escapade. Darkness permeated the house, and she was grateful that they had beaten the sun awake.

She nudged Lupe gently.

"Shhh. We don't want to wake Anna."

Her co-conspirator stirred slightly, then sat up, immediately wide-awake.

"Let's go, *amiga*. We need to get Ben back to the livery and us back to the Harvey House before anyone wakes. We don't want to have to explain our disappearance. Or Ben's."

The words squeaked out of Tessa's mouth. She breathed deeply in an attempt to quell her anxiety.

Lupe kept her voice low. "I'm ready as soon as I get my boots on. Now, where did I put my coat?"

The pre-dawn gray was sweeping across the tops of the sycamore trees that lined Main Street when Tessa and Lupe crept back into Winslow. After a night of misadventure, they were grateful to be able to corral Ben in his stall and return to their room without further incident.

Lupe managed another hour of much-needed sleep.

Tessa was more fortunate since she didn't have to work that day. However, it was a slumber punctuated by dreams of rocks, guns and broken glass, and she awoke feeling no more refreshed than she had when she tumbled off Anna's sofa several hours earlier. Her thoughts kept returning to the problem of Joaquin, a problem now complicated by their unwanted partnership with that strange woman, Hattie Frye.

When Tessa told Anna she would visit the Silver Spur that day, she had forgotten that it was Sunday. It would be much easier to see Anna and Johnny in church, saving her another ride to the ranch. She had seen enough of Ben's back for a while.

As she donned a blue summer frock, she thought about her activities over the past few days. Tessa wondered, had she been Catholic, how much time she would have needed in the confessional this morning. She was grateful to do her penitence at the Protestant services this Sabbath. A few prayers for divine intervention couldn't hurt.

"Pastor Wolcott must think the people of his congregation have no Christian kindness," Anna said later, as they left the church.

She and Tessa followed Johnny, who skipped across the churchyard, releasing the pent-up energy from the hour-long sermon.

"He preached charity last week as well, about giving to those less fortunate. Today, it sounded like he wanted us to show charity in our hearts more than our purses. I wonder what he'll have to say next week."

"Charity must be his favorite subject these days," Tessa said, while silently, she wondered if Sheriff Bowman had urged the preacher toward that specific topic.

During the sermon, even before Anna told her that it was similar to the previous week's, she thought the pastor might be directing his words at those who would convict and punish Joaquin Castillo without benefit of a fair trial.

"Maybe he's getting forgetful." Anna continued her discourse on the preacher's choice of sermons. "I liked it last week when he told us to be 'guided by goodness', and, today, he used the same phrase again." She shrugged. "I suppose it *is* difficult to come up with ideas week after week."

"There you have it, Anna." Tessa smiled. "You're being 'guided by goodness' in your charity toward Pastor Wolcott and his repetitive sermons."

"And I'll practice more charity now as I buy my son an ice cream."

Johnny, ever polite, thanked his mother as she handed him the treat. He sat on the steps in front of the General Store, working his way through the enormous ice cream cone. The store was a popular gathering place after Sunday services because that was the day when Mr. Mulliner's two sons were available to crank the freezer.

"Um, peppermint, one of my favorites," Tessa told Johnny as she reached down to wipe flecks of red from his cheek. "I like chocolate, too, and strawberry when it's available in the spring." She smacked her lips, barely masking the rumble of her stomach.

She and Anna sat on a nearby bench, grinning at the boy's obvious delight. One of his pants pockets bulged where the carefully wrapped fossils awaited further inspection, which was bound to happen once the ice cream disappeared.

Anna noticed, as well. "Maybe he'll become a famous archeologist," she said pointing at her son.

"My cousin Sarah often writes of the interesting exhibits on display at the Natural History Museum in New York City," Tessa said. "Maybe some day you and I can take Johnny back East and show him the city. You'd love it, too, Anna."

"I like my wide open spaces," Anna said, dismissing the subject with words that were neither pleasant nor rude, simply matter-of-fact.

Lowering her voice to a whisper, she said, "Now, Tessa, tell me why you and Lupe were sneaking into my house last night, looking like you'd seen a ghost."

"Let's take a walk, Anna." Tessa nodded toward the street. "Too many people are going in and out here."

After cautioning Johnny to stay close to the store, Anna followed Tessa across the boardwalk. They strolled down the street, nodding at several acquaintances. Many of the townspeople were taking advantage of the cool, clear autumn day. Tessa kept her voice low as she explained to Anna about the fiasco at Doctor Benton's ranch house the previous evening. Anna's response was something between a laugh and a cry of alarm. Laughter won out.

"Tessa, I can't believe you stole a horse, broke into a house, tied a woman up, and then proceeded to ride to the Silver Spur in the middle of the night, with no moon. How did you find your way?"

"Ben knows the way," Tessa said. "By the way, thank you again for allowing us to stay. You're a good friend."

Anna paid no attention to Tessa. She continued her recitation, although now all laughter was gone from her voice.

"All that and you still have no proof that Joaquin Castillo isn't a murderer. Tessa, I like the man, too. He's always been a hard worker and, as far as I could tell, trustworthy. But, you have to admit that the sheriff has some strong evidence against him."

"That's not true," Tessa said, ready to defend Joaquin against Anna, the sheriff, and all of Winslow. "He is accusing Joaquin based only on what other people said about him and Deirdre. And, that doesn't explain why Joaquin would kill Doc Benton."

"Maybe because the doctor knew something that would prove Joaquin killed Deirdre, that's why."

"None of this makes sense, Anna. A murderer is still running loose. I know it. We need to find him, not only to free Joaquin, but to stop him before he kills again."

Anna put her gloved hand on Tessa's arm. The women stopped walking and faced each other. Dust swirled across their feet, coating their Sunday shoes with a fine layer of grit. Neither seemed to notice, or, if they did, they didn't care.

"Tessa, you and I are good friends, so I can say this to you. And, please don't get angry. I know you care deeply for Lupe. Maybe you care for Joaquin in a special way, too."

Tessa started to protest, but Anna held up her hand.

"Please let me tell you what I think. You have to let the sheriff handle this. Jed Bowman is a good man. Maybe he's never had to deal with a murderer until now, but he'll be fair.

If Joaquin didn't murder those two people, Sheriff Bowman will find out who did."

"You're wrong, Anna. The sheriff has already decided that Joaquin is the murderer. He won't look any further. I need to show him proof that Joaquin didn't kill Deirdre or the doctor. I know that there is something, somewhere, that will tell me that. You're right that Lupe is my friend and I love Joaquin *like a brother*."

She made sure to emphasize the words that would nullify any ideas Anna had about her relationship with Joaquin.

"More importantly, though, I've lived in the West a long time and I know how Easterners treat Mexicans and Indians. These newcomers think that they are better than the people who have lived here for centuries. If they can blame a murder or two on a Mexican, all the better."

Tessa realized her voice had risen. She lowered it again and made one last point.

"What Lupe and I did last night was wrong and I feel terrible about the mess at Mrs. Benton's house. I'm going to find a way to make that right. However, I won't stop looking for something to help my friends. No one else appears to want to."

"All right, Tessa."

Anna gave her friend's arm one last gentle squeeze and released her hand.

"I understand. One of the many things I love about you is your passion for helping others. The preacher should use you as an example of Christian charity. Please be careful, though. If Joaquin isn't the murderer, and you seem to think that he is not, it means that the real killer could still be walking the streets of Winslow."

As Anna said the words, both women looked up and down the street. When Tessa turned back to face Anna, she saw the fear flickering in her eyes. It matched her own unease.

They returned to the General Store to find Johnny playing a dusty game of marbles with one of his school chums. Spots of peppermint candy dotted his shirt. Anna rubbed at the stains to no avail.

"I wonder if girls get this dirty," she said to Tessa, with an indulgent nod toward her son.

"I know I did," Tessa said. "My nanas would complain to my father that I was a tomboy. I know they wanted him to remarry, so I would have a mother."

"It must've been difficult to grow up without a mother," Anna said.

"Of course, I missed having her to talk to and to help me, but my father talked about her so much that I felt like I knew her. So, I never thought that I didn't have a mother because she was always with me in spirit," Tessa said, and, at that moment, she really did feel her mother's presence.

She said goodbye to Anna and Johnny. The young boy showed her the fossils once more. The knowledge that the desert had once been an ocean captivated his mind.

"Since you are so interested in these things," Tessa said, touching them with the reverence Johnny expected, "I'm going to ask my cousin in New York City to send you a book or two on archaeology. There is so much more to learn by uncovering the past. We can discover things about plants and rocks and people, about events in the past that make things the way they are today."

That is true about so many things, Tessa thought, not for

the first time, as she waved farewell. She recognized how her life had been shaped by past events.

The love shown to her by her Mexican nannies had erased the prejudice evidenced in her peers before it could make any imprint on her life. For that, she was grateful. Thoughts of her life without their love, and without Lupe's friendship, were unconscionable.

And what about George? His death, his murder, had a definite impact on the person she was today. He had been killed before their budding love had a chance to reach full flower. How different would she be today if she were now Mrs. George Bird instead of Tessa Crane, Harvey Girl?

Tessa didn't dally on the street. She was glad that she hadn't needed to ride out to the Silver Spur that afternoon. She had one more place to visit. Several months previously, she had met Lupe's Tia Elena, and she hoped the woman would remember her as a friend. If her suspicions were true, it was possible that this "aunt" would be able to tell her some things that Doc Benton's papers could not.

Chapter Twenty-Two

Elena Mendoza's modest house graced a corner lot close to the Madre de Dios Chapel. Anna knew that *Señora* Mendoza was a devout Catholic, as were most Mexicans. The women went to church daily to pray for forgiveness from, what seemed to Tessa, mostly non-existent sins.

Like most of the Mexican woman in Winslow, *Señora* Mendoza kept her house and yard pristine. It was a matter of pride to them that this was accomplished with little or no outside help. In the front garden, a few remaining yellow and orange daisies glowed in the bright autumn sun, reminding Tessa more of a campfire than a bouquet. In spring and summer, the gardens of the *Norteños* were a riot of color, fragrance and taste. During those months, the cemetery that adjoined the church was vibrant proof of the love and respect the Mexicans bestowed upon their ancestors.

Tessa hesitated as she approached Elena's door. It wasn't that she was afraid of Lupe's aunt, but rather that she feared that what she might learn here would harm, rather than help, Joaquin.

Earlier that morning, prior to church services, Tessa overheard several conversations among the townspeople who were eager to punish Doc's murderer. They weren't inclined to look any further than the young Mexican man sitting in the Winslow jail. She shook off her dread and mounted the porch steps. Soft singing came from inside. She couldn't make out the Spanish lyrics, but the melody and timbre suggested a lullaby.

"Mrs. Mendoza? *Señora* Mendoza? It's Tessa Crane from the Harvey House." Tessa spoke quietly in case a baby slept somewhere in the house.

"*Buenos Dias, Señorita* Crane." Tia Elena appeared at the door so quickly that Tessa guessed the woman had been sitting in the parlor.

"You are Guadalupe's friend, no? We have met once or twice, I think. You'll have to forgive an old woman's memory. Please come in."

Tessa entered a room as orderly as Lupe's half of their shared bedroom. A vase of fiery blossoms glowed on the mantle and a tabby cat, as colorful as the flowers, dozed in the rocking chair.

"I heard you singing," Tessa whispered. "I don't want to wake the baby."

"Baby? No *bambino* here." Elena chuckled softly. "Ah, you'll think I'm silly, but I was singing to El Tigre, that lazy cat over there. He doesn't complain about my voice and I don't complain about him sleeping all day. Please sit down. Can I get you a glass of water or perhaps some coffee?"

208 // Susan Tornga

Elena's thick accent made her English difficult to
understand. Tessa offered up a silent thank you to her nanas
and Lupe for their Spanish instruction and replied in Elena's
native tongue.

"No, thank you, *Señora* Mendoza." Tessa perched on
the edge of a chair, so large and soft that she feared it might
swallow her whole if she leaned back. "How are you feeling?
Lupe said you have been ill."

Elena picked up the sleeping cat, sat down where he had
been lying, and nestled him on her very substantial lap.

"I am much better now, thank you. Just a problem with
my stomach. Perhaps the peppers we put in the tamales were
a little too spicy for an old woman. Now, what can I do for
you, Miss Tessa Crane?"

"I apologize for coming here uninvited," Tessa said,
"but I'm very worried about Lupe and also Joaquin. I was
hoping that you could tell me about Enrique."

Elena's deeply lined brow wrinkled further. She opened
her palms toward Tessa and shook her head in a gesture of
confusion.

"Enrique? Why would you want to know about him?
He is my son and he's only five years old. What in the world
would he have to do with Joaquin's difficulties?"

Tessa hesitated before speaking. She was discussing a
very delicate subject with a woman she hardly knew. And,
although she spoke Spanish well, she worried that this soft-
spoken woman might not understand her questions and she
didn't want to offend her. Tessa had learned that simply
knowing the vocabulary and conjugation of words didn't
guarantee comprehension. Cultural differences in language
usage, if ignored, sometimes led to misunderstandings

as serious as improper vocabulary. She searched for the appropriate words.

"Do you know about Joaquin and the murdered woman? Her name was Deirdre Sweeney. Lupe told me that she often visited you in the company of Joaquin when she lived here. Did they speak of marriage?"

Tessa had more questions to ask, but she decided to let the woman fill the silence. She didn't have long to wait.

"*Señorita* Crane," Elena began.

"Call me Tessa, *por favor.*"

"Tessa," Elena seemed to stumble over the familiarity. "I've borne children and raised a family. I've buried my husband and, *Madre de Dios,* one child." She folded her hands as if in prayer. "I know about life and, yes, I know that Joaquin and the murdered woman were acquainted. That was many years ago."

The woman began to stroke the cat, one gentle movement from ears to tail. Tessa heard the answering purr as El Tigre accepted his due as ruler of the Mendoza casa. Elena continued her tale.

"Joaquin told me about it when she threatened him, demanded money from him because she was going to have his baby. Or, so she said. I was happy, as happy as Joaquin was, when she disappeared. That was the end of it. He doesn't think she ever had a baby. She only wanted him to give her money. He didn't know she had come back to Winslow until after she was murdered."

Tessa cringed inwardly at Elena's words. She knew that Lupe had told Joaquin about Deirdre's appearance before she was murdered. If Joaquin hadn't told Elena the truth about that, what else was he lying about?

"But you said you wanted to talk about Enrique. What does my son have to do with these awful murders?"

Tessa knew she walked on delicate ground now.

"Lupe often talks about you and your family. I'm sure you know that. She enjoys the time she spends with you, especially since her mother and sisters live so far away. Joaquin, too. They both regard you as their aunt. So, of course, Lupe told me that you adopted Enrique from the sisters at the mission when he was only a few days old."

Tessa held her hands in front of her, slightly apart, to indicate how small the child must have been.

"Yes, that is all true, *Señorita* Tessa, but I sense that you are trying to tell me something more, something that has to do with Joaquin and Enrique."

Elena's face gave no hint of either shock or surprise. She continued to speak, in a matter-of-fact tone.

"You think Enrique is Joaquin's son, the son of Joaquin and Deirdre Sweeney, don't you?"

Tessa need not have worried about understanding *Señora* Mendoza. The woman who sang lullabies to a cat spoke slowly and distinctly. Tessa sensed that Joaquin's aunt wanted her to grasp the full meaning of the words, while avoiding any misinterpretation that might harm Joaquin.

"Yes, Señora Mendoza. With Enrique's age and his looks, he could very well be Joaquin's son."

Elena's hands stopped their rhythmic petting of Tigre. She stared at Tessa, dark eyes narrowing.

"Because of his black hair and brown skin? That makes him resemble Joaquin? Look at me. I have the same hair and skin. So does every other *Norteño* in town, and in Arizona. All that means here is trouble for us."

In a matter of seconds, kindness had been replaced by fury.

"Please go now, *Señorita* Crane. My daughter will be returning with Enrique soon, and I don't want them to see you here. She would start asking me questions. I've had enough of that for today. *Adios.*"

Tessa left quietly, sorry that she had upset the gentle woman. She realized, as she walked slowly back toward the Harvey House, that she hadn't learned even one small thing that would help the Castillos. Right now, it seemed like everything she did merely left trouble in its wake.

When Tessa entered the Harvey House kitchen, she was surprised that Lupe was neither washing dishes nor helping Dorothea with meal preparation. She resisted asking Dorothea if she had seen her roommate, a question that might elicit a tirade about the unreliability of help, especially Mexicans. She mounted the stairs slowly, postponing the inevitable. She dreaded facing Lupe with more bad news

She opened the door to an empty room. The relief she felt at avoiding another discouraging conversation was quickly replaced by the guilt of knowing that she really hadn't wanted to see Lupe. At first, Tessa thought that perhaps Lupe had gone to Tia Elena's. She quickly discarded that notion. If that were the case, she would have seen her somewhere along the street.

To fill the time waiting for Lupe to return, Tessa decided to write a letter to her cousin. Putting pen to paper would also help clear her thoughts. Often she wrote lengthy letters to Sarah, only to tear them up. Today, however, she would tell Sarah all that had happened and send the letter, cautioning her not to share the news with her mother. Aunt Rebecca would double her efforts to get Tessa back to New York if she knew that her niece was involved, even remotely, in murder.

Tessa grinned when she thought of how Sarah's mother would react if she had any idea that the two cousins were corresponding about illegitimate babies. To a proper New York matron, that would be far worse than murder.

After locating her writing paraphernalia, Tessa cleared a corner of the table, and began to transcribe the events of the past week. She told Sarah about Anna McAllister's fear and of Lupe's certainty that Enrique Mendoza was her nephew. She also mentioned Sheriff Bowman's concern for Joaquin's safety.

He's a kind man, she wrote, *with a tough job to do.*

She started to tell Sarah how handsome the lawman was, then paused, surprised at herself. Did she really think he was good-looking? She shrugged off the crazy notion and continued her recitation of the murders.

Writing helped Tessa visualize the people involved, giving them personalities, motives, feelings. She had only seen Deirdre Sweeney on two occasions, both of them brief. She knew Sarah would want details, so Tessa rummaged through her mind to recall the young woman's appearance and her manner of speech.

It dawned on her that Miss Sweeney's confident manner reminded her of a successful man. It was a quality possessed by women like Anna McAllister and Hattie Frye, true women of the West. Her original impression of Deirdre had been that of a weak woman, focused on fashion and propriety. She quickly changed her mind, however. The few words Tessa had heard the young woman say were spoken with authority and conviction. Tessa realized, as she scribbled rapidly, fingers trying to keep pace with thoughts, that Deirdre had not been intimidated by either the conductor's threats or her fiancé's indifference. She wouldn't have known that she might be a target for murder.

Would she have been afraid of Joaquin if he had come up to her in a dark alley? *Maybe*, Tessa thought, or was she merely inventing absurd scenes in her mind? The words she wrote to Sarah painted Deirdre as a confident young woman. With such an attitude, she wouldn't have been afraid of anyone, especially a former lover. Nothing that Tessa recalled while reliving these events for her cousin would help free Joaquin or point toward another possible murderer.

Tessa sighed and sealed the letter. She hoped Sarah would recognize the great affection included therein. She freshened up for supper, still wondering where Lupe Castillo had gone now.

"I'm sorry for what I said to you Friday, Tessa. And, to Lupe, too." Dorothea said as she placed a bowl of soup in front of her. "I was shocked by Doc Benton's murder and I lashed out at the first available target."

"I understand, Dorothea. You knew him well, and of course you're saddened by his death."

"I apologized to Lupe, too. I felt so bad, I gave her the afternoon off."

That was all the opening Tessa needed.

"Do you know where she went? She's not in our room."

"I let her go as soon as the second train departed, and she left the kitchen right away. She didn't even take the time to eat. I haven't seen her since. She did the work of two people this morning, so I thought that perhaps she went upstairs for a rest."

"Maybe she went out later and you didn't see her," Tessa suggested.

"Yes, that might be. She's one of my best workers, and I feel bad about the hurtful things I said. You girls are the children I never had. I hope Lupe understands that."

Tessa pushed her empty soup bowl to one side and patted the cook's arm. "I'm sure she does, Dorothea, but if you'd like me to say something to her, I will."

"Thank you, Tessa. Yes, I'd appreciate that."

To demonstrate that appreciation, Dorothea handed Tessa a large slice of chocolate cake. She dug in eagerly.

She was studying the few remaining crumbs on her plate, ready to lick them up, when Lupe walked in, saving her the embarrassment. Without a word or even a nod in Tessa's direction, she ladled out a bowl of bean soup. Then she plopped a thick slice of brown bread on her plate, and poured herself a glass of milk. She shuffled over to the table, collapsing into the chair opposite Tessa. She raised an accusatory eyebrow at the empty cake plate.

"It looks like the cake was good, *si?*" Lupe managed a soft smile, the first indication of any pleasure Tessa had seen from her friend it many days. She was also heartened to see the ample portions that Lupe had dished up for herself. Maybe she had good news to share.

"Where have you been?" Tessa asked. "I was surprised to find you gone when I got back from Tia Elena's."

"You went to see my aunt?" Lupe let her spoon drop into the bowl, where it was swallowed by a quicksand of beans. "Why would you go there?"

"It isn't important," Tessa said, then shook her head. "No, that's not quite true, Lupe. I hoped it would be important but in the end, I didn't find out anything that would help Joaquin. In fact, I think I may have made Elena angry. I thought she would admit that Enrique was Joaquin's son. She didn't, of course." Tessa sighed. "I was wrong to go there. I'm not the person who should discuss such personal things with a woman I hardly know. I'm not sure how it would help if we knew about Enrique anyway. It might even make things worse for your brother."

"Can they get any worse?" Lupe's spoon remained buried in its soupy grave.

Tessa felt bad that she had opened up this topic before Lupe had a chance to eat a decent supper.

"Please eat your soup, *amiga.* You need the nourishment and Dorothea made this pot even move flavorful than usual. Let's not talk about this now."

She changed the subject in an attempt to distract her friend. "I was looking at one of the fashion magazines that Sarah sent me last week. You wouldn't believe what women are wearing in New York. It must take hours every morning to button up those dresses, boots and gloves. You and I would have to get out of bed in the middle of the night." She laughed, aware that the diversionary techniques had worked on her, if not on Lupe.

Tessa chattered away while Lupe retrieved her spoon and emptied the soup bowl.

"You're right, Tessa, the soup was delicious. So, tell me about all these buttons."

Tessa gave Lupe a quizzical tilt of her head. "What buttons?"

Then she realized what Lupe meant. She had already forgotten what she had talked about while Lupe ate. Her mind had already refocused on murder, on Joaquin, and on the muddle she had created for both herself and Lupe.

The women washed their dishes and, by silent agreement, left the kitchen through the back door. Both of them wanted to walk awhile and Lupe was anxious to visit Joaquin. The sun had not yet disappeared over the horizon, and for a few minutes, the air retained some of the day's warmth. In autumn, heat disappeared as rapidly as daylight.

"You asked me earlier where I went," Lupe said as they passed the saloon, cocooned in its Sunday quiet. "To church, of course. I missed this morning's Mass, so I wanted to say my prayers and the rosary. I also wanted to talk to the sisters."

Tessa knew, without asking, what information Lupe expected to obtain from the sisters at Madre de Dios. It was precisely what she had gone looking for at Tia Elena's that afternoon. Were Joaquin and Deirdre the parents of young Enrique?

"Did any of them live at the mission when Enrique was left there?" Tessa asked.

They stopped in front of Dr. Dahlgren's surgery. It was dark and quiet inside, a good sign. Tessa thought back to when she had last seen her father, three days previously, right here at the doctor's place. She longed for his good judgment and his calm manner in the midst of all this turmoil. Lupe's words brought her back to the present. She faced her troubled friend.

"Sister Mary Paul has been at Madre' for more than ten years," Lupe said. "One or two of the other nuns lived there when Enrique appeared, but I didn't talk to them. Sister Mary

Paul remembers that night very clearly. Every year, they find several babies on their doorstep, and she hasn't forgotten any of them. I think she would adopt them all herself if the Church permitted it. She still visits the ones who live close and mourns those who did not survive."

Tessa nudged Lupe back to the subject of Enrique.

"So, did she know who Enrique's mother or father were?"

"She says not and I believe her. I explained how much trouble Joaquin could be in, that he could be hanged. The good sister wouldn't let a man die if she knew something that would help him. However, she's certain that the mother was Mexican. The baby arrived dressed in an intricate christening gown. Actually, it was a three-piece set that we call a *Diego Gown*. It's a popular style with my people because the collar on the robe resembles that of the saints and the pope, a good omen. However, the most important thing was the embroidery on the cap that Enrique wore. It said *Mi Baptismo*. No one but a Mexican mother would use the Spanish words."

"Does the sister still have the christening gown and the cap?"

"She does. It took her awhile to find it. I helped her look through a trunk of items that mothers have left with their babies. Babies outgrow their layette clothes so fast that the adopting families can't use them. Heirlooms or other treasures that are left with the infant are sent along with the new parents, but not the clothes. I suggested to sister that she should give all these extra clothes to Doctor Dahlgren. The doctor could give them to needy families when a new baby is born. I told her not to give away Enrique's christening outfit, however. The *baptismo* cap might be very important."

This new information excited Tessa. "That proves that

218 // Susan Tornga

Deirdre wasn't the baby's mother. So, Joaquin wouldn't have any reason to kill her. Tomorrow, we'll go talk to the sheriff and tell him what Sister Mary Paul told you."

"I was as excited as you are when I first heard the sister's story," Lupe said. "Then I thought about it and realized that it doesn't help my brother. First of all, it's only the sister's word that this baptismal cap belonged to the baby that Elena adopted."

Lupe held up her fingers and ticked off her points one by one. "Even if the sheriff believed Sister Mary Paul's story, it doesn't prove that Deirdre is not the mother. She might have known enough Spanish to embroider *Mi Baptismo* on a baby's cap, if for no other reason than to confuse everyone. The real point here, Tessa, is that Joaquin didn't know any of what Sister told me. If he *thought* that Deirdre had his baby, he would have been afraid of the trouble she might cause him. You know that I don't believe he did any of these terrible things, but I'm trying to look at the situation as the sheriff would. We need hard proof. We need to find the real killer."

Everything Lupe said made sense, but, for the life of her, Tessa couldn't figure out how they might possibly get proof of any of it. She fixed her troubled eyes on her friend.

"Nevertheless, we'll go see Sheriff Bowman in the morning. Perhaps the sister's story will plant a tiny seed of doubt in his mind about who the murderer really is."

Chapter Twenty-Two

The late afternoon sun cast long shadows across Second Street as the two roommates-cum-sleuths left the restive atmosphere of the Harvey House. The morning train from Los Angeles had been delayed, arriving well past the scheduled noon dinner service. The passengers shuffled into the dining room, tired, hungry and peevish. They complained about cold potato soup and warm fruit salad, neither of which was true. Even the always-perfect apple pie drew criticism. Whenever Tessa entered the kitchen, she gave Lupe a resigned shrug, grabbed the artfully arranged food platters and headed back into the tumult.

When the last customer was mollified by the aromatic Harvey House coffee, dishes scrubbed and tables readied for the evening train, Tessa stuck her head in at the kitchen door and motioned for Lupe to meet her by the back garden. She craved a piece of Dorothea's apple pie--she most certainly would not find fault with it--and a chair on which to sit while she ate it.

However, she had promised Lupe that she would accompany her to the jail. Maybe today would be the day when they would actually discover the information they were seeking that would point to Joaquin's innocence. Her deep sigh of resignation drew Dorothea's attention. The cook glanced at Tessa through lowered eyelids, questioning without words as she reached for her cloak.

"Going out again, Miss Crane?"

The amiable cook who had plied Tessa with chocolate cake the night before, had been replaced by an ill-tempered crone, one who undoubtedly had listened to far too many unfair criticisms of her food. It had been that kind of a day.

"Only for a short while, Dorothea." Tessa said as cheerily as she could manage.

"Don't forget that another train will arrive in a couple of hours. I expect you and Lupe to be back here in plenty of time to do your share of the preparation. I'm just wondering when you two women ever rest."

With a smug look of secret knowledge, the cook returned to her pie dough.

Tessa's stomach wrenched. Had Dorothea seen her creep back into the Harvey House early Sunday morning? Just one more thing to worry about, she thought.

"I know the sheriff won't believe me," Lupe said, as they approached the jail.

Her mood was as dark as Dorothea's. Tessa longed for the pleasant days before a murderer had come to town.

Sheriff Bowman listened in polite silence to the story of the baptismal suit and cap worn by the infant Enrique.

He nodded at the significance of the Spanish embroidery. As Lupe feared, however, he refused to draw any conclusions about Joaquin's innocence from this information.

"Ladies, I find what you tell me interesting, but it doesn't prove that my prisoner didn't kill Miss Sweeney or Doc Benton. Five years ago, she tried to get money from him but didn't succeed. She came back here last week to try again, using the same threat, claiming that he took advantage of her, resulting in the birth of a child."

It was obvious to Tessa that the sheriff was uncomfortable with the turn the conversation had taken. He seemed especially interested in something on the bottom of his boots. He moved to a subject more easily discussed with the young women.

"The doctor knew something about Deirdre Sweeney, something that was a threat to her murderer. Joaquin could easily have found out about that from you, Miss Castillo. You were here at the jail that night when Doc told me that he would get information from his files and bring it to me. No one else with ties to Miss Sweeney had any knowledge of Doc's intention. I need a lot more than an embroidered cap that a nun found, *says* she found, on a baby five years ago, to convince me that I arrested the wrong man."

Tessa wasn't going to allow Bowman to brush them off so easily, however.

"Sheriff, I was here when Doc Benton mentioned that he knew Deirdre. I don't remember his exact words, because I didn't think he said anything important."

"I don't understand what you are trying to say, Miss Crane."

A frustrated Tessa tried again to find the right words to convey her intuition about Doc's conversation with Bowman.

"Doc Benton didn't sound excited about whatever file it was that he had at his ranch, so it couldn't have been so important as to convict a murderer, or to set one free, and certainly it couldn't have been anything that would make Deirdre's murderer kill again. Obviously, Doc didn't fear for himself because of what his records said. So, why are you so sure that Joaquin was afraid of what Doc knew?"

His boots forgotten, Sheriff Bowman looked straight into Tessa's eyes. The gaze she returned was defiant and unyielding. He admitted defeat with a blink and a crooked half-smile.

"Miss Crane," he said, then inclined his head toward Lupe. "Ladies. Doc recognized the picture of Deirdre Sweeney as soon as he saw it on my desk. She was his patient when she lived here. She left Winslow a little more than five years ago, so whatever happened had to have occurred before then. That would have been when she was working at the Silver Spur."

Now he ignored Tessa and spoke directly to Lupe.

"The same time your brother worked there, Miss Castillo. Isn't that right?"

The question required no answer. Bowman knew he was right. Lupe did have something else to say, however. Tessa saw her clench and unclench her fists repeatedly in an effort to control her temper. Tessa hoped the gesture worked. She had seen Lupe's temper flare on a few occasions. The sheriff's assumptions were angering her, but no good could come from a torrent of accusations.

"Sheriff, maybe my brother was the father of Deirdre's child," Lupe said, "but he doesn't think so and neither do I. She was an evil woman who wanted money from a poor

Mexican boy. She preyed upon his fear, fear that he would end up in jail, sent back to Mexico, or worse, hunted by a *Norteño*-hating vigilante posse. He worked hard for the life he has today. He wouldn't risk losing it. And, he is most assuredly not a murderer."

Lupe stamped her boot down hard on the floorboard and Bowman's head jerked back. Tessa, too, was surprised by her roommate's emotional display. Pressing her advantage, Lupe shook a finger across the desk at Bowman as she continued to defend her brother.

"Someone else had a reason to murder those two people, sheriff. Maybe you have two murderers running loose in your town. Perhaps you had better find them, instead of sitting here admiring your fancy footwear."

Tessa could see by the sheriff's widening eyes that Lupe's tone had startled him. Even Lupe herself seemed surprised. Not many people ever saw the fiery side of *Señorita* Castillo. Not many wanted to.

Drat! Tessa was afraid this would happen. They didn't need to make an enemy of the sheriff. She knew she needed to do something quickly, even if it meant that she might be the next target of Lupe's wrath.

"*Amiga,* you know that isn't true. Sheriff Bowman is only doing his job."

She gave Lupe's hand a squeeze to soften the effect of her words. She flashed Bowman her most seductive smile, disgusted with herself for sinking to such depths, but willing to do what was necessary not to alienate him.

"Sheriff, I'm sure you can understand why Joaquin's sister is so upset. We came here to tell you why Enrique can't be Deirdre's child. We've done that so we'll leave. I'm sorry we bothered you."

Her tone didn't convey an apology, nor did it hint at irritation. Tessa was careful to remain neutral. They needed the sheriff on their side, but she refused to sweet talk him any further.

He was wrong in thinking that Joaquin was a murderer and also wrong about Enrique being his and Deirdre's child, but Lupe's display of temper was not going to change his mind. She moved toward the door, still clasping Lupe's hand. She looked over her shoulder at the sheriff, a quizzical expression furrowing her brow.

"Sheriff Bowman, what else did Doc Benton say to you before he left for his ranch? Would you please tell us that much?"

Bowman softened at the plea in Tessa's voice. He had already forgiven Lupe her outburst. Two attractive women graced his office right now. He didn't often have an afternoon this eventful. He seemed to ponder the advisability of saying anything, then shrugged his shoulders as if to indicate that it didn't matter what he told them because it wasn't important.

"Well, Miss Crane, I told you he recognized Deirdre Sweeney as a former patient of his. He saw the picture of her taken on her wedding day, the day she married that man, Mr. Smith.

"He knew she left town long before he gave up his medical practice, so he didn't pass along her files to Dr. Dahlgren. What he said, if I remember correctly, were words to the effect, 'I have her medical file at the ranch. The new doctor would have the other records.'"

Tessa and Lupe stared at the man. Tessa spoke first. "What other records? Who was he talking about?"

"Did he mean my brother's file?" Lupe asked before Tessa could say anything else.

"Actually, with everything that has happened, I forgot about the other files he mentioned until now. He might have been referring to Joaquin. It would be someone, or perhaps several people, who still live here in Winslow, or at least was living in Winslow at the time Doc retired."

"He could have been talking about a lot of people, sheriff," Tessa said. "Most of the folks who lived in Winslow five years ago are still here now. You can't use that statement to prove anything against Joaquin."

"Okay, Miss Crane. I agree with you, but I don't need to know who Doc was talking about in order to accuse Joaquin of the murders. I have enough other evidence for that."

He began to shuffle through the papers on his desk. The dismissal needed no words.

"I would like to see my brother before I leave." Lupe's tone was polite, but carried the implication that the sheriff would be looking at her for a very long time if he didn't honor her request.

Bowman grudgingly acquiesced. He escorted Lupe to the cell in the back of the jail. When he returned to the office, he left the connecting door open so he could monitor the conversation between brother and sister.

Tessa felt awkward, alone in the room with the sheriff. His large build and booming voice overpowered the small office. He remained standing, but didn't speak. She wanted to say something to fill the silence, so she spit out the first words that came to her.

"May I see that picture of Deirdre Sweeney? I hardly remember her face."

"I don't see any harm in that, Miss Crane."

He bent over his desk and pulled the photograph from

beneath several newly arrived wanted posters. As he did, two other pieces of paper floated to the floor. Tessa squatted down to pick them up. One of them, a telegram, caught her eye when she saw the name printed on it. She rose slowly, allowing time to scan the telegram. It was interesting, but provided no information that would help Joaquin Castillo. She put it out of her mind and concentrated on Deirdre Sweeney's wedding photograph.

Tessa studied the woman's face. She remembered the stubborn set of her chin and the capricious look in her eyes. Her demure smile seemed forced, as if she was trying, without success, to project the image of a shy bride on her wedding day. Using her imagination to enhance the sepia tones of the photograph, Tessa pictured auburn curls cascading from under the lacy veil.

A slender left hand rested above her right breast, showcasing a diamond ring. It wasn't an extravagant jewel, but eye-catching, the round diamond ringed with tiny pearls. In contrast, the necklace she wore around her neck was quite modest, a tiny heart, simple in design, dangling from a thin chain. Its simplicity and delicate size complemented the bride's long, slender neck.

Two ivory combs held her veil in place. The combs were plain, but with a smoothness that conveyed elegance. The girl had a flair for fashion even at that young age. Tessa wondered what events in this beautiful woman's life had led to her brutal murder in an alley in Winslow, Arizona.

"Even back then, she was a woman who enjoyed pretty things," Tessa said to Bowman, indicating Deirdre's left hand.

"Yes, she did," Bowman said, as he took the photograph

from Tessa. "Mr. Smith very kindly donated her clothes to the ladies of the church. They'll either give them to someone in need or put them out at the rummage sale."

"The rummage sale makes more sense, I think, sheriff," Tessa said. "From what I saw of her clothes, they weren't quite what a poor farm woman would wear."

Lupe returned from the jail cell, dabbing her eyes with a lace-trimmed handkerchief. The dainty square of linen seemed out of place in this building where the ghosts of thieves and killers roamed. Tessa quietly took Lupe's hand. She nodded a good-bye to the sheriff, but didn't speak. Lupe did neither.

Tessa set a fast pace as the two friends headed down the street from the jail, her limp magnified by speed.

"We don't need to walk so fast, Tessa. What about your leg?" Lupe hurried to keep up. "Slow down. I have something to tell you. It wasn't Joaquin."

"Of course, it wasn't Joaquin. That's what we keep trying to tell Sheriff Bowman."

"No, that's not what I mean. When I was talking to Joaquin, I asked him about why he consulted Doc Benton. He never mentioned that he was sick or injured. He told me that he never saw Doc, not as a patient anyway."

Tessa nodded, understanding at last.

Lupe continued. "So, the other file that Doc mentioned to the sheriff, the one that stayed with Doctor Dahlgren, it can't be Joaquin's."

"That's interesting, Lupe, but I'm not sure how that helps us. Doc might have been talking about anyone. He was the only doctor in town. And even if we knew what records he meant, we don't know that it has anything to do with his murder."

Lupe's face sagged, a balloon losing its air. She stopped long enough to stamp her foot, sadness replaced by anger.

"Every time we learn something that might free Joaquin, it turns into another piece of useless information. Nothing helps." Her voice broke.

"We'll help him, Lupe, but right now we need to help Dorothea. I hope the people on the next train don't complain about the food. They may see a frying pan come sailing through the dining room. Now, hurry, so that skillet won't be aimed at us."

The entire Harvey House staff breathed a collective sigh of relief when the stationmaster rang the arrival gong to announce the on-time arrival of the evening train. One train full of disgruntled passengers was enough for the day. Dinner service ran as smoothly as a well-oiled clock, a welcome occurrence on this day of chaos. There was a quiet celebration when the last customer left the dining room to board the departing train.

Only Tessa and Beryl Turner remained in the dining room. Tessa enjoyed this part of the workday. The passengers were gone and clean up was complete. The two women walked around each table, laying out the silver and china for the next day's crowd. As they worked they chatted idly.

"Tessa, do you remember that handsome ranch hand, Lucas Carr, the one who kept smiling at me during last week's roundup?"

"Of course, Beryl. You spent quite a bit of time with him Friday night."

Beryl giggled. "After the cowboys loaded the Silver Spur's cattle on to the train Saturday, he came by here to see me. He said he would visit me again when he had some free time."

She plunked the last of the cups and saucers down on the table with more force than was necessary. It seemed a happy topic, so the anger displayed in Beryl's action surprised Tessa. The love-struck girl's next words explained her fury.

"Not that it will be anytime soon. Thanks to your roommate's brother, the Silver Spur is short-handed. Lucas said that Lupe's brother chased after any pretty girl around. He is surprised that Joaquin hasn't been arrested long before this."

Tessa bristled. The girl was so obviously smitten with her cowboy that she would believe whatever he told her. She just hoped Lupe wouldn't hear any of this malicious gossip.

"How long has Lucas been a ranch hand out at the Silver Spur, Beryl?" Tessa asked, wondering what made him an authority on Joaquin Castillo.

"I don't know, Tessa." Beryl answered in a calmer voice. "It's been a long time, though. His family has lived in Winslow since he was a small boy and I think this is the only ranching job he's had. He knows a lot about what goes on out there. He never liked Joaquin. He knew that man was trouble from the first time he met him."

Beryl echoed Lucas' words as if they were her own. Tessa was annoyed. She didn't care how handsome Beryl's cowboy was, he was conceited and prejudiced. She had known plenty like him all around the West, and, for that matter, back East too. People who think a person's skin has to be lily white or they are no good. Worse yet, if a crime was committed, their fingers always pointed to the one who was different.

She wondered if perhaps Lucas had a fancy for Deirdre Sweeney and was angry with Joaquin for courting her. She would ask Lupe to talk to Joaquin about that. Maybe Lucas had been a patient of Doc Benton's and his file was now sitting in Doctor Dahlgren's surgery. The thought of another suspect energized her.

Chapter Twenty-Three

"Lupe, Lupe, wake up." Tessa, impatient, wanted to tell her friend what Beryl had said about Lucas Carr and her own interpretation of their conversation. "I know you're tired but this is important."

The poor girl hadn't had a decent night's sleep in over a week, what with the extra hours in the kitchen to pacify Mr. Clifton and all of the clandestine activities meant to save her brother from the hangman's noose, but Tessa was too excited to wait until morning.

"It's only half past seven, Lupe. I have something to tell you. Then you can go back to sleep."

"What?" The pillow under Lupe's face muffled her words. She kept her head buried. The hand peeking out from the bed cover motioned her roommate away. Tessa held her ground.

"*Amiga,* listen. You know Lucas, the handsome ranch

hand at the Silver Spur? I think he was in love with Deirdre when she worked out there. Beryl Turner as much as told me so."

Tessa hoped Lupe wouldn't question that statement. Beryl hadn't said any such thing, not in so many words, but Tessa felt certain that was the reason Lucas was intent on convincing everyone of Joaquin's guilt. Lupe stirred as Tessa continued her story.

"Lucas wanted Deirdre for himself. Maybe she loved him, too. The two of them devised the scheme of blaming Joaquin for her pregnancy, which may or may not be true."

Lupe was immediately defensive. "Joaquin did not get that girl pregnant."

Tessa knew that Lupe had no way of knowing that for certain, but she tried to pacify her, anyway.

"What I meant was, we don't know if she was with child, and, if she was, we don't know whose child it is. Maybe Joaquin's, or maybe Lucas was the father."

"And don't forget Hiram Frye. He was seen talking to her." Lupe was fully awake now and warming to Tessa's theories.

"You're right, Lupe." Tessa wrinkled her face at the thought of that disgusting man with the elegant Deirdre Sweeney.

Lupe noticed Tessa's grimace. "You weren't here five years ago, Tessa. Back then, when he was sheriff, he kept himself neat and clean, and was hardly ever seen in a saloon."

"Okay, we still have to consider Hiram, but Lucas has a reason, jealousy, to want Joaquin behind bars, or worse," Tessa said.

Lupe choked at the words. Tessa put her arm around

her roommate. The hope that had crept into her face as they talked, was once again replaced by despair.

"But if Lucas was jealous because Deirdre fancied Joaquin, why would he kill Deirdre?" Lupe asked.

"Maybe she only pretended to love Joaquin so that she and Lucas could threaten him. They would share the money. Then Deirdre disappeared without giving Lucas his portion. So now, he hates Deirdre and Joaquin."

"What about the baby? Enrique can't be Deirdre's and Lucas' child. They would never have a black-haired, dark-skinned offspring."

"Lupe, I doubt there was even going to be a baby, Joaquin's or anyone else's."

"If this is true, Tessa, how do we prove it? I'm quite certain the sheriff won't listen to any more of our speculations."

"You're right, *amiga.* I thought about all of this while I finished setting tables for tomorrow. Here's what we need to do."

She proceeded to lay out yet another of her elaborate schemes.

Lupe listened to Tessa's plan, her eyes growing wider with each word. When Tessa finished, she shrugged with resigned acquiescence, and dressed once again in her darkest skirt and shirt.

The two women tiptoed down the stairs, hunched like a pair of old crones. Hearty laughter from the kitchen told them that Ardella Gibson and Dorothea Parks were trading stories of the day's happenings, and, from the distinctive clink of glassware, Tessa knew that they were enjoying something stronger than coffee to accompany them.

Tessa smiled to herself. Her father introduced her to sherry when she was quite young.

"You might as well know what all the fuss is about," he had told her. "It's what people cannot have that they crave so much. Let good sense and moderation be your guide in all things, my dear Thérése, and you will never go wrong."

Where is my good sense now? Tessa thought, and wondered what Papa would think of her recent nocturnal activities.

When they reached the street, Tessa heard Lupe's sigh of relief. She felt the same way. It was early enough that many of the townspeople were out for a stroll in the mild evening air, which was sweetened by the aroma of burning piñon wood. Tessa breathed deeply.

"I love that smell," she said. "Fort Apache is surrounded by piñon forests, so we would burn the wood all winter. I've never smelled anything more fragrant. The Indian women would harvest the pinecones and roast the piñon nuts, then they would sell them to us. Delicious."

"It sounds like you miss living there, *amiga,*" Lupe said.

"Sometimes, yes," Tessa said, coughing lightly to mask the catch in her throat, "I long for the mountains and the security I felt living at Fort Apache with my father. Then, George was killed and I knew I had to go some place where I wasn't constantly reminded of him."

They rounded a corner.

"This is the street," Tessa said, once again in charge of their plan and her emotions.

"That's the Chamberlain house there," she whispered in Lupe's ear. "The one with the rose arbor. I've bought eggs from her for the Harvey House once or twice."

She grabbed Lupe's arm.

"Wait there by the trellis." Tessa pointed to the white

picket arch that dominated the front garden. "I'm sure Mrs. Benton doesn't want to talk to the sister of the man she thinks murdered her husband."

Lupe nodded and disappeared into the shadows. Tessa stepped onto the porch, smoothing her apron as she walked. She had decided to wear her uniform, thinking she would look more official, as if that would justify the strange questions she intended to ask.

"Mrs. Chamberlain?" Tessa asked when a thickset woman answered their knock. "I'm Tessa Crane, from the Harvey House. I'm sorry to intrude this late in the evening, but it is important. Could I speak to your sister for a few minutes, please?"

Ava Chamberlain puffed out her already ample chest. The effect was intimidating, which Tessa supposed was what the woman intended.

"I remember you, young lady. You bought eggs for Mr. Harvey's establishment. You were always polite and paid cash."

That seemed to have put her in good stead with the lady of the house.

"Come on in, child. My sister is poorly, as you can imagine, but I think she'll speak with you. Just don't upset her and please, don't stay long."

The soft voice that came from the large woman startled Tessa, as did her easy acquiescence. Gratefully, she followed Mrs. Chamberlain into a well-lit parlor where Edna Benton sat, holding an empty embroidery hoop as if it were an open book. The lost look on the widow's face made Tessa want to cry.

Once again, she promised herself that she would

somehow make right the mess she had created at the Benton ranch house on Saturday night. As yet, the poor woman had no idea what had happened. Guilt flooded over Tessa like a river at spring thaw. She introduced herself in a voice so small that even she could barely hear it.

"Mrs. Benton," she said, forcing confidence into her tone. "I'm sorry to bother you at this time, but I need to ask you some questions about your husband's medical records."

The older woman acknowledged her presence with a slow nod, but said nothing. Tessa continued quickly, fearful she would lose her nerve.

"Did he ever talk to you about his patients? The murdered woman, Deirdre Sweeney? I knew her."

During their walk to the Chamberlain residence, Tessa and Lupe had discussed the best way to approach this subject with the murdered doctor's widow. If Mrs. Benton thought Tessa was trying to help Joaquin Castillo, she most certainly wouldn't say a word. Nothing helpful, at any rate. Tessa didn't want to lie, but she hoped to give the impression that she wanted to avenge Deirdre's murder.

"I know about her." Edna Benton spoke to the embroidery hoop. "She was a patient of my husband's many years ago. He came home that night, excited that he remembered her. He went directly to his study, talking to himself more than to me as he walked down the hallway. When he came out, he told me that he had to ride back to town. I said he should wait until morning, that whatever it was would keep, but he wouldn't listen." Mrs. Benton brought a handkerchief to her eyes. "If he had listened to me, he would be alive today."

The bereaved woman's words stunned Tessa. "You mean you saw him again the night of his murder? After he returned from town? The sheriff said he was shot when he was riding from town back to your ranch."

"Oh, no. He rode into town with that cavalry man. He was gone for only a couple of hours. When he returned, he dashed straight to his office, muttering about babies. He was slamming drawers around in there, and when he came out to the parlor, he had some papers in his hand. He said he needed to go back to town to see Sheriff Bowman again. He hadn't eaten supper so I handed him some jerky. He gave me a kiss."

Her eyes glistened with tears. Tessa looked away.

"Well, you know the rest. I'd like to be alone now, please, Miss Crane."

Tessa remained seated. "Just a few more questions, please, Mrs. Benton."

She plunged ahead before Edna Benton could deny the request.

"You said you knew Deirdre Sweeney when she lived in Winslow five years ago?" Tessa phrased the statement as a question, hoping for a more detailed explanation from Mrs. Benton.

"It would have been difficult not to know of her, Miss Crane. You said she was your friend."

Tessa hadn't said that in so many words, but she wasn't going to correct the misunderstanding, especially since she had instilled the idea in the first place. Edna Benton continued.

"Forgive me for saying this, but you and she are an unlikely pair of friends. Back then, at least, she was quite a flirt. Every time she came to town, we would see her with a different man. She worked for Mrs. McAllister out at the

Silver Spur, you know, but she always seemed to be in town on one errand or another."

Tessa wondered if that were really the case. She couldn't picture Anna allowing frequent trips into Winslow when there would be so much work to do at the ranch. More likely, Deirdre, with her good looks and smart clothes, was noticeable whenever she did come to town, even if were only once a fortnight. Well, no matter. She turned her attention back to what Mrs. Benton was saying.

"Curtis wasn't surprised when she came to him in trouble, if you know what I mean. He wanted to have the sheriff go after the man who got her with child, but she refused to say who he was. I think she didn't know. It could have been any one of a number of local men." The widow's pale face reddened with embarrassment as she said this.

Tessa was anxious to get back to Lupe with this exciting piece of news. Thinking it over, though, she realized that what she learned from Mrs. Benton was just more useless information. If there were that many possibilities for the father of Deirdre's child, then it would be impossible to prove which man it was. The sheriff had a Mexican locked up. A jury need look no further.

"Do you know what happened to the baby, Mrs. Benton?"

"All I know is that Miss Sweeney left Winslow long before the baby was due." She wrinkled her brow in concentration. "Wait. I do remember something. Curtis told me that she went to San Francisco and would have the baby there. She felt she could find a better home for the child in San Francisco than in Arizona. It's a big city, you know, and perhaps she hoped to avoid the stigma of an illegitimate birth. Curtis felt sorry for her. Miss Sweeney was alone and scared, not quite the belle of the ball that she wanted to be."

Mrs. Benton's tone indicated that she didn't share her husband's sympathy for Deirdre. She rose slowly, holding out a bony hand.

"I'm tired now, Miss Crane. I'll say goodnight."

Tessa knew that the widow wouldn't want to mention the rumors about her husband and the dead babies. It didn't matter since it had nothing to do with Deirdre's murder and Tessa felt that she had caused enough trouble for Mrs. Benton. She decided the least she could do was to leave now and not upset the poor woman any further.

She took the Edna Benton's hand in hers. It was like holding a butterfly. She let her mouth utter the words that were in her mind.

"Mrs. Benton, when your husband became a doctor, he took an oath to save lives. If you think of anything that could save an innocent man from hanging, please let me know. A tribute to Doc's memory, if nothing else."

Tessa was glad to leave the depressing atmosphere of a home in mourning, but the refreshing evening air did nothing to lighten her mood. She kept compiling information, interesting information to be sure, but nothing that could help Joaquin. She called to Lupe in a whisper. Her friend emerged from the rose arbor, rubbing her hands where thorns had pricked them.

Tessa told Lupe what she had learned from Mrs. Benton. Lupe shared Tessa's despair. Once again, they had learned nothing that would convince Sheriff Bowman that he had locked up the wrong man.

"We need to find someone who lived in Winslow five

or six years ago who could tell us what was happening then. Who is the biggest gossip in this town, Lupe?"

"Miss Parks has lived in Winslow for a long time. She likes to gossip, too. Mrs. Crook, who runs the boarding house, probably knows everybody here, and their business." Lupe warmed to the topic. "Mr. Mulliner talks to a lot of folks when they shop at his store, and I think everyone in Winslow visits the General Store at least once a week. He is as much of a gossip as any woman. I'll talk to him, Tessa. I think he likes me. When I was working for the mayor, I went into his store frequently and he was always giving me something extra, a piece of candy or a length of pretty ribbon."

"Then you should pay him a visit tomorrow," Tessa said. "I'll talk to Mrs. Crook and Mrs. Parks."

"Be careful when you talk to Cook," Lupe cautioned. "You don't want Mr. Clifton to see you gossiping in the kitchen."

Tessa remembered the clink of glasses she heard when she and Lupe crept out of the Harvey House earlier that evening.

"Maybe we can both talk to Dorothea tonight. Mr. Clifton should have left by now. Let's hope we're lucky and Cook is still there."

Tessa led the way toward the Harvey House at a pace that the amazed Lupe had difficulty matching.

Luck was with them. Dorothea Parks sat at her desk in the kitchen. Puffs of steam rose from the cup of tea by her side. She hummed a lively Scott Joplin tune, something Tessa had recently heard coming from the saloon. For the time being at least, the maven of the kitchen was happy with the world.

If she was surprised to see two of *the girls* come into the kitchen from the garden-side door, she didn't show it. She lumbered to her feet and began opening cabinets, in search of makings for a meal. Visitors at this time of night usually meant empty stomachs wanting filled. Tessa put out a hand to stop her.

"We aren't hungry, Dorothea. We've been out for a stroll, talking about the way Winslow was many years ago. I've lived in the West all of my life and I'm interested in how towns change when the railroad comes through. You told me you came west, when was it? Eighteen eighty?"

Deprived of making a meal, Dorothea motioned Tessa and Lupe into two chairs at the kitchen table. She sat down at the head, ready to lecture.

"Earlier. Eighteen seventy-eight, actually, more than fifteen years ago now, and, yes, I've seen this town grow. You're right in thinking that the railroad made a difference. We get so many interesting people coming through here now. Of course, that can be good and bad, but I enjoy meeting most of them. Best of all are the foodstuffs that the trains bring in. Oh, my! Fresh fruit and vegetables, wonderful meat, and herbs. What about the ice cream? We never know when some will come in on a train. When it does, it's like a Christmas gift, a cook's dream. Those wonderful flavors and no cranking required. Mr. Harvey is a hero to all the towns along the Santa Fe line. You can be sure of that."

Her face lit up with delight as her mind danced with pictures of crates of pears, apples and cherries, and boxes of imported chocolates.

Tessa grinned at the cook's obvious pleasure. However, she needed to steer the conversation back to less cheerful topics.

"Miss Parks, last week you said that you thought you remembered Deirdre Sweeney, the murdered girl. You knew her or at least heard of her when she lived in Winslow over five years ago. Am I right?"

"So, you are interested in her, too. I'm not surprised." She looked pointedly at Lupe. "Of course, the sheriff wanted to know if I remembered anything about the time she lived here. I wasn't much help, I'm afraid. Then yesterday or the day before, I forget which, I was in the General Store when several other women were crowded around the counter talking about Miss Sweeney's murder and Doc Benton's too."

The cook wiped her hands on her apron, as if they'd been in soapy dishwater instead of in her lap.

Tessa looked at Lupe. Her friend's eyes glassed over. She obviously didn't expect anything helpful from the cook and had quit listening. Tessa, ever hopeful, kept the conversation going.

"What were they saying? Did any of them know Miss Sweeney?"

"Someone, I can't remember who, it was a woman, for sure, wanted to know if Deirdre left Winslow to have her child. This woman said that Deirdre probably went away because she was afraid to have Doc Benton deliver her baby, after what had happened to Lillian Clark and her baby boy."

The cook's voice caught as she explained, "Not only Lillian, who was a good friend of mine, but within a month another ranch wife lost her baby with Doc attending the birth. The women around here got scared, but most of them didn't have the money to travel to St. Louis or San Francisco. Some did, though. I think all the bad talk about him was one of the reasons Doc Benton decided to quit being a doctor. Poor man. Childbirth is a difficult time and I'm sure he did his best, but people will talk, won't they?"

"Yes, people will talk," Tessa said, thinking of the townspeople who were convicting Joaquin Castillo with their tongues.

The cook continued, "Mrs. Benton didn't have it easy, either. Can you imagine listening to so much malicious gossip about your husband? I'm not saying people didn't have good reason. I really don't know the truth behind it all, but I never found fault with him." She paused and a faraway look came into her eyes. "But then, I was never lucky enough to get married and have a child."

Dorothea's jovial mood had vanished, replaced by melancholy. She shrugged away her sadness, however, and gave Tessa a pat on the hand. She looked from Tessa to Lupe.

"When you two get married and start families, you'll have young Dr. Dahlgren to look after you. She has done a lot of good for the women of Winslow, and I, for one, am very happy to have her here."

Lupe acknowledged the comments with a nod but said nothing. She seemed content to learn what Dorothea knew, without injecting her own memories of earlier days in Winslow. She had been so quiet that, when she did speak, Tessa and Dorothea looked at her in surprise, as if she had just dropped from the sky.

"Do you remember when Elena Mendoza adopted Enrique from the sisters at Madre de Dios? You do know her, don't you?" Lupe asked.

"Yes, I know Elena. I think you call her Tia," Dorothea replied. "She often brings me cilantro and chilies from her garden and I'll buy them from her when my garden is bare. We talk about gardening. When I first came to Winslow, I didn't know how to make things grow in this dry climate. She taught me a lot and not only about plants."

The cook realized that she was rambling and gave Lupe an apologetic smile. "I'm sorry, child. You asked me a question about Elena and I don't remember what it was."

"Enrique," Lupe explained. "Tia Elena's adopted son. Do you remember when she got him from the sisters at the mission? Do you know anything about him?"

"All I know about the baby is what I've heard from the gossip around town. He is obviously Mexican. Some people thought he had an Anglo mother and Mexican father. I never asked Elena. She probably doesn't know either. She is a saint to take in such a young child at her age. *Wherever* he came from," the cook stared at Lupe, "he is one lucky boy to have Elena as his mother. She accepted responsibility when his real parents didn't."

Dorothea's last words dissipated from the air, taking the warmth from the kitchen with them. The timber of the late evening's conversation had gone from intimate to hostile. Her tone made it clear the conversation was over. For emphasis, she rose from her chair and marched toward the door, reminding Tessa of the soldiers on parade at Ft. Apache. She opened the door a few inches, then closed it with more force than was necessary. She turned back toward the young women, and stood, arms akimbo, a school marm addressing her errant charges.

"If you're asking me if I think Joaquin Castillo is Enrique's father," she said through taut lips, "I'll tell you this. I would bet on it. I've heard the talk around town. Bad things are happening here and your brother, Miss Castillo, is up to his neck in them. Good night, ladies."

Like ice in summer, she was gone.

Chapter Twenty-Four

Across town, a dark shadow slithered down an otherwise pleasant street that, in daylight, was filled with the laughter of children at play. It had always provided a sheltered haven for those who lived there, a calm oasis at the end of the day. Always, that is, until now.

The shadow's head, practically swallowed by its hunched shoulders, jerked nervously right and left, fearful of being followed, yet afraid of being alone. Events had gotten out of hand. Good intentions gone bad. *The road to hell...* thought the shadow. *I only wanted what was best for my family. I must protect them at all costs, even if it means taking the life of an innocent boy.* The shadow and its trailing figure, straightening with resolve, moved quickly down the now-quiet street, powered by the evening breeze.

* * *

Tessa and Lupe stared at the door through which Dorothea Gibson had vanished, leaving an echo of angry words in her wake. Without a word, they rose in unison and climbed the stairs to their room. Evening quiet shrouded the Harvey House, giving no indication of the turmoil that accompanied two of its own through the darkened hallways. Lupe closed the door behind her, shutting out the cruel world. When she raised her face to look at Tessa, it was streaked with tears.

"Maybe I have been wrong about Joaquin all this time, *amiga.* If someone as kind as Miss Parks believes he is a murderer, then what else can I think? When people are frightened, they do strange things. I'm going to the jail tomorrow to talk with my brother again. I have to know the truth, no matter how bad it is. He's always been a good Catholic. I'll offer to bring the padre to hear his confession and give him communion. Joaquin needs that peace. Now, *querida,* I would like to say my own rosary and go to bed."

Lupe's acceptance of her brother's fate astonished Tessa. She was envious of the calm that settled over her friend. They were an odd pair, she and Lupe. As Lupe stepped closer and closer to accepting Joaquin's guilt, Tessa jumped away from it. Tessa countered Lupe's tranquility with an uncontrollable urge to act, fast and furious.

Something she had seen or heard tugged at her memory. She couldn't put a name to it at this moment, but she knew that whatever it was, it was important. Before she slept, she was determined to go over everything in her mind. Somewhere in the events of the past ten days, she would find the missing piece. Someone was harboring a secret, and she felt sure that it was not Joaquin Castillo.

"*Bueños noches, amiga,*" she called, softly, into the night. She heard the whispered refrains of Lupe's *Ave Maria* and did not expect an answer.

Lupe's demeanor wasn't the only change wrought in the night. A cold wind blew in from the east the next morning, chasing away the last of the Indian summer warmth.

Tessa had lain in the dark for hours, walking her mind through every detail from the conductor's arrest to Miss Parks' abrupt departure from the kitchen, yet she was unable to uncover even one thing that might provide the proof she needed to save Joaquin.

Lupe, on the other hand, appeared refreshed, although Tessa noticed that her hand frequently visited her apron pocket where Tessa was sure she kept a rosary.

"I have turned my brother's fate over to God," Lupe said, when Tessa commented on her equanimity.

"Perhaps I should covert to Catholicism then," Tessa said, only partly in jest.

"Yes, perhaps you should," Lupe answered, with total sincerity.

Tessa performed her morning tasks mechanically, paying little attention to the sparkling crystal and shining silver. Normally, these symbols of luxury would elicit feelings of pride. Not today. If the crystal was streaked and the silver tarnished, she didn't notice. Her mind still searched for that one niggling detail.

Between train arrivals, Tessa carried a cup of coffee onto the back step, preferring the chill wind of Mother Nature to the icy human atmosphere of the dining room. Apparently, her non-stop questions of the past few days had put everyone on edge. Even always-friendly Beryl Turner returned Tessa's "good morning" greeting with merely a curt nod.

As Tessa sipped the rich brew, she thought over the events of the previous week. She had asked numerous questions, but she wasn't able to put her finger on what one in particular had upset the people around her. She couldn't remember receiving any answers that were the least bit incriminating to anyone except Joaquin, but there had to be something else, something she knew was important. A dull ache started in the back of her head, a response, she was sure, to the effort she had placed on her brain.

Lupe slipped quietly out the kitchen door, sank to the step and hooked her arm through her friend's.

"Amiga, don't look so sad. You have done so much for Joaquin and for me. It's in God's hands now. I'm going to visit Joaquin before the next train arrives. Would you walk with me to the jail? When I go down the street, people shy away from me, like a stream parting for a boulder. I would welcome your company."

It was as close as Lupe ever got to expressing insecurity and Tessa was quick to agree.

"Si, hermana. As you are my sister, Joaquin is my brother. Of course, I'll go with you to visit him."

She drained the last drop of now-cold coffee and returned the cup to the kitchen. She lifted her shawl from its hook by the door and pulled it tight around her shoulders. She'd had enough of the cold wind.

The sheriff wasn't at the jail when Tessa and Lupe arrived. One of the deputies sat in Bowman's chair, feet propped nonchalantly on the desk. Tessa was certain they had wakened him when they entered. He sputtered a greeting, then quickly escorted Lupe to the cell where Joaquin languished. Apparently, he didn't trust the young woman alone with the prisoner because he didn't return to the outer office.

Tessa occupied herself by thumbing through the *Wanted* posters that littered the sheriff's desk. Many of the men pictured didn't look like the murderers, thieves or vandals that they were purported to be. When she reached the bottom of the stack, there it was again, Deirdre Sweeney's wedding picture.

The woman, no, really just a girl, who stared back at her had the look of vulnerability that Tessa had seen on most of the young brides arriving at the Army posts where she had lived with her father. The world was a frightening place to those young women. They were without family in a strange and dangerous part of the country. Some of them did not survive the hardships, and those who did live often returned to the civilized East, perhaps taking a baby or young child with them.

Deirdre Sweeney hadn't survived because someone else had decided that she shouldn't live. Tessa was certain that a baby, or at least the threat of a baby, held the key to this murder. The more she stared at the young face looking back at her from behind the lacy veil, the more she knew the answer lay in a child, a child here in Winslow. Was Joaquin the father? Or Lucas?

A quiet voice broke through her musings. "We can go now, Tessa. I've done all I can for my brother so I'll ask the Padre to visit him. Go back to the Harvey House. I'm going to the church to say a prayer and talk to padre, then I'll join you. Thank you for coming with me. *Adios.*"

Lupe spoke as though she were reading from a book, an impression enhanced by the fact that her eyes never met Tessa's. Puzzled, Tessa watched her friend walk from the jail, and make her way toward the mission church with purposeful strides.

Tessa took a final look at the photograph of the young bride, then laid it gently on top of a picture of a most unsavory character. It didn't seem fitting to leave it there, so she picked it up again and was burying it under a stack of papers when something caught her eye.

The deputy had not returned. *He's probably asleep back there,* Tessa thought. She peered down the hallway to be sure, then folded the wedding photo and tucked it in her pocket. For the first time in days, she grinned, not just smiled, but grinned.

As Tessa reached the garden of the Harvey House, she heard her name called from across the street. She squinted into the bright sunlight. In the glare, she could barely make out the form of Edna Benton walking slowly towards her. The grieving woman had lost so much weight that the hem of her skirt hung low, creating a cloud of dust at her feet.

Tessa hoped that the unexpected appearance of Doc Benton's widow indicated that she had remembered something more about the doctor's last day that would lead to the murderer.

She waited, trying unsuccessfully to curb her impatience, as the older woman lumbered across the street, stopping inches from Tessa's face.

"I've thought about what you told me last night, Miss Crane," Mrs. Benton said, without preamble. "I believe Curtis would want me to do whatever I could to see to it that the right man gets punished for his murder."

She stared at Tessa, eyes narrowed in hatred, hatred toward the person who had robbed her of her husband. As if she recognized that Tessa might misinterpret the malice in her voice, her tone became conciliatory.

"And, that the wrong man doesn't hang," she added, softly.

The widow, of course, didn't know that Tessa and Lupe had rifled through her husband's papers, looking for something that would tie anyone but Joaquin to the murders. Nor did she know that a pile of broken glass and overturned furniture awaited her when she returned to her home. If she had known, she most certainly wouldn't be standing in the Harvey House garden offering assistance. As grateful as Tessa was for any help at all, she wondered what Mrs. Benton could possibly know about Joaquin's innocence that had escaped their search.

"The sheriff gave me back the clothes Curtis wore that night. I suppose he didn't see any need to keep them. He has all the evidence he needs to convict Mr. Castillo. From what you tell me, Sheriff Bowman thought that Curtis was on his way *to* our ranch. I guess that's why he had no interest in his clothing. I was folding his suit when I found these papers tucked in one of the coat pockets."

She held a small parcel in her outstretched hand. The pages were torn around the edges and yellowed with age. Tessa's heart skipped a beat. Maybe Mrs. Benton did know something that could help them after all, information the poor widow didn't even realize she possessed.

"This is what I found. Here, take these and read them." She pulled Tessa's hand toward her and slapped the package into her palm.

"Whatever it means, whatever is in this package is what my husband thought Sheriff Bowman needed to see. I wasn't going to tell anyone about it, because it didn't seem important."

Tessa started to thank the woman, but she held up a hand to forestall the interruption.

"The sheriff arrested the man he thought killed both Deirdre and Curtis. That was good enough for me. What you said last night about saving lives made me think about doing the right thing. Look at these papers and then give them to the sheriff, please." Her pleading voice contained more than a hint of sadness.

"He should see them too. I am entrusting them to you, Miss Crane, because you seem like a caring person and I believe you'll do the decent thing. If I give them to Sheriff Bowman now, I know he won't show them to you. Now, I must go. Good day, Miss Crane." Before Tessa could recover her voice and thank the woman, she had vanished.

Tessa entered the kitchen at the exact instant the familiar train whistle blew. The arrival gong would soon follow.

"Damn," she hissed, then chastised herself for the slip of her tongue.

She remembered the first time she had said the word aloud. It was one of the few memories she had of her mother. Tessa had been very young, no more than four years old. A tower of blocks she built came crashing down. "Damn," she had said, having learned the word and its appropriate use from the men at the Army post. Her mother had been quick to scold her, telling her that a lady should not use such language. Her father attempted to support his wife's discipline, but laughed instead, and soon her mother had joined in the merriment. How could a word be bad when it brought back such pleasant memories?

Her frustration today was with more than falling blocks. She was itching to delve into Doc Benton's parcel, but the ill-timed whistle demanded her attention. She tucked the papers in her pocket, next to Deirdre Sweeney's wedding photograph, where they would stay throughout the afternoon and evening.

For the next several hours, Tessa tended to two trains' worth of hungry passengers. At every interval, when her hands weren't full of plates, bowls or pitchers, she thrust her hand inside her apron, fondling the crinkling paper as a baby would its favorite blanket. It put her in mind of Johnny's fossils, the treasure that he kept tucked into his pocket for safekeeping.

Tessa placed the last gleaming fork on the table and sighed with satisfaction. The room was ready for tomorrow and the remainder of the evening was hers. She hurried upstairs, forgoing dinner in favor of the promise of questions answered and doubts put to rest.

She quickly read the pages that Edna Benton had given her, hoping to have good news for Lupe, who was still scrubbing away at the day's mountain of dishes and cookware. She skewered her face in concentration as she tried to decipher the words that the old doctor had scribbled on the now-yellowed pages. On a second, slower, reading, she was able to make out the words, but their meaning puzzled her. She was deep in concentration when Lupe stumbled through the door and on to her bed.

"I am so tired, Tessa. Tonight we sleep."

There she lay, fully clothed, and would have been asleep in a minute had not Tessa bounced down beside her, exuding excitement from every pore in her body.

"Lupe, I know who killed Deirdre Sweeney and Doc Benton. Edna Benton brought me the doctor's files tonight.

You know, the ones we were searching for in his office? We couldn't find them because he had already taken them from his desk and was riding back *into* town when someone, and I know who, murdered him."

To Tessa's surprise, Lupe didn't share her excitement. She kept her forearm over her eyes and moaned in protest.

"Every night you have a different idea of what we should do to find the killer, Tessa," she said, "and every night we go out, risking our positions, breaking curfew and almost getting shot, for no reason, to say nothing of getting no sleep. And we never learn anything that will help Joaquin. I'm sorry, *amiga,* but tonight I cannot participate in another one of your adventures. I'll listen to your latest plan tomorrow, okay?" Her voice dripped with both fatigue and sarcasm. "Please, Tessa! Please leave me alone."

Chapter Twenty-Five

"When will we ever sleep?" Lupe groaned, but Tessa detected a note of excitement in her voice, and allowed herself a smile of satisfaction. She had ignored her roommate's objections and stayed on the bed next to her. Fidgeting with excitement, she began to read sections of the disintegrating pages aloud. She accented the parts that were most important, like a mother reading a hair-raising tale to her child. Lupe was soon wide-awake and ready, if not anxious, for another nocturnal adventure.

The two women had navigated the stairs in the dark so often recently that they didn't slow down as they descended to the kitchen and slipped out the back door. Both of them still wore their uniforms, although Tessa had removed her white apron, knowing how it would stand out as they moved through the darkened streets.

"The timing must be right, *amiga,*" Tessa whispered into Lupe's ear. "She should be alone, except for the child, who must be asleep by now. We'll listen for a few minutes. If it's quiet, we know it will be safe to go in."

"What do we do if she has a gun with her?"

"We have to surprise her. Everyone thinks Joaquin is the murderer, and he's locked in jail, so she believes that she's safe. Why would she keep a gun by her side now?" Tessa spoke with far more assurance that she felt.

"Why are you walking so fast?" Lupe asked. "What about your leg?"

"It will hurt tomorrow, Lupe, but I don't care. Tonight, there's no time to waste."

Tessa continued her feverish pace, and Lupe hurried to keep up. Their rapid breathing blended with the east wind, one merely an echo of the other.

As they approached their goal, a white clapboard house surrounded by an unkempt yard, Tessa grabbed Lupe's arm, stopping her in her tracks. She reached into her pocket and produced the two butcher knives that she had taken from the kitchen earlier. Tessa heard Lupe's startled gasp when she pressed cold steel into her hand.

"We have to have a weapon of some kind," Tessa whispered.

"Ay, Dios," Lupe said. "Knives are for chopping carrots. I can throw rocks, but I'm not sure I could stab someone."

"This is all we have. Let's pray that we don't need them."

"Ay, Dios," Lupe said again.

The glow of the kerosene lamp provided a beacon for the women as they advanced toward the house. Tessa stopped in the shadow of a large tree to survey the street. Satisfied that they were alone, she signaled Lupe to follow her through the front gate. Once inside the yard, she again looked for shelter, finding only a smaller tree with a skinnier trunk. It would have to suffice. Pointing her knife skyward, she waved Lupe forward, feeling more like Joan of Arc than Tessa Crane.

She put her lips close to Lupe's ear.

"I'm going to look in the window. We need to know where she is."

The wind carried her soft whisper away, but Lupe understood the meaning. She was a foot soldier, awaiting direction from her general.

Tessa tried to tiptoe across the porch, to no avail. Her weak leg couldn't support the toes-only position, so she walked one foot tiptoe, one flat, in what surely, under other circumstances, would appear quite comical. She felt like a child again, back at Fort Apache, pretending to be a horse galloping across the prairie.

The odd gait produced a low scraping sound, but fortunately, the wind was their friend this evening, effectively covering Tessa's footfalls. By the time she arrived at the window, her hands were wet with nervous perspiration. She had never done anything like this and her nerves were taut. She took a few seconds to wipe her hands and the knife handle with the folds of her skirt. She looked back toward the front yard and was reassured by the glint of Lupe's knife as it reflected the starlight.

Tessa peered through the lace curtains. She stared at the woman within, letting the final pieces of the puzzle fall into place. She knew she had been at the window for far too long, but she felt her eyes were the handcuffs that kept the woman in place and unarmed. If she looked away the woman she might disappear, and all of the explanations and proof necessary to free Joaquin would vanish with her.

Finally, Tessa tore herself away from the still life she had been watching and motioned for Lupe to join her. Unnecessarily, she put her finger to her lips. Lupe navigated the steps and the porch quietly and soon stood at Tessa's side. They could see the woman clearly. She sat on the far side of the parlor, slumped in a rocking chair, obviously asleep.

While Tessa watched, pondering the next move, the woman jerked her head up, apparently startled by something she heard. Quickly, the intruders jumped back from the window, covering their mouths to stifle their grunts of surprise. They waited, but nothing happened.

In the light from the window, Tessa could see Lupe's hands shaking. She knew that fear was more contagious than small pox. She hissed quietly at Lupe and, when her friend looked across the expanse of glass at her, Tessa smiled and held her hand to her heart in an expression of friendship. Lupe's answering smile was more like a grimace of terror.

Tessa steeled her nerves for another look through the glass. Their quarry had disappeared. Perhaps the child had called out, or maybe the woman had gone to bed. Tessa hoped it wasn't the latter.

She chewed on her lower lip, worrying about what they should do next. Then her eyes caught movement inside the house. The woman had returned, although her motions made it obvious that she was preparing to close up the house for the night. Tessa knew she had to act quickly. Without a word to Lupe, she went to the front door and tried the handle. It turned easily under her grasp. Lupe took refuge behind her, encouraging her with a slight squeeze. *It's now or never,* Tessa thought, and marched boldly into the parlor.

260 // Susan Tornga

"What's going on?" The words tumbled from Hattie Frye's mouth as she made a movement to reach behind the sofa.

Lupe, quicker than Tessa could ever hope to be, was by the older woman's side in an instant, holding her hands behind her in a firm grip. Tessa came forward and shoved her down into the rocking chair, pulling the butcher knife from her pocket and flashing it in front of Hattie's startled face.

"We know what you did." Tessa hoped they knew. "Why don't you make it easy on everyone concerned and tell us about it?"

Hattie's fangs spewed venom. "And, I know what *you're* doing, Miss Crane. You're trespassing. This is my house and you aren't welcome here. I have nothing more to say to you. And you," she turned to glare at Lupe, "will find yourself locked up with your brother, a couple of no-good Mexicans. Get out!"

Lupe glared back, dark eyes flashing daggers as deadly as Tessa's knife. The pot that held her anger boiled over. Her knuckles whitened as she gripped her tormentor's arms more tightly, pulling them high behind the chair's wooden back.

"You're hurting me, you witch," Hattie spat. "You know you won't get away with this."

A barely audible curse interrupted the heated exchange. "Lupe, are you all right alone with this murderer while I go look for some twine or cloths to tie her hands? There must be something in the kitchen."

"Si, amiga," Lupe said. "You should worry more about this woman's safety than mine. If she gives me any trouble, I'll strangle her by this chain." Lupe jerked at a silver necklace that had been hanging loose around Hattie's neck."

Her prisoner gagged, but said nothing.

"I'll only be a minute. Yell if there is any trouble." Tessa hurried from the room, still mumbling to herself. In their haste to confront this woman, they neglected to plan for what they would do when they actually had her in their grasp. Neither had thought to bring rope for securing their prisoner's hands and feet. *Pinkerton's will never hire us,* she mused.

"Mama, who's there?"

The child's voice broke through the tension-filled air of the living room. Startled by the unexpected words, Lupe loosened her grip on Hattie. The older woman acted quickly, as if she had rehearsed the movement. She wrested herself free then pushed Lupe down on to the floor. A snub-nosed derringer materialized from the pocket of her dress. Hattie pointed it directly at the Lupe's heart. In that instant, Lupe knew that her life would end. She squeezed her eyes shut and prayed that Tessa would find the proof needed to free Joaquin. Her mother couldn't survive the death of two of her children.

"Mama!" The child shrieked in terror. Before Lupe could open her eyes, she heard the sharp retort of the gun firing and felt an intense burning in her left shoulder. She cried out in pain. Everything went black.

A child was screaming. Lupe heard Tessa's soft voice, coming from far away, offering words of comfort. Her eyes refused to open, their lids weighed down by some heavy object. With immense effort, assisted by her arching eyebrows, she was able to peer across the room through narrow slits. Hattie Frye lay on the floor, wrists bound behind her. Tessa bent over her, looping the rope around her ankles, all the while speaking in soothing tones to young Agnes.

Lupe followed the sound of sobbing, rolling over on to her injured shoulder. She groaned loudly as bolts of lightning carved a path from shoulder to toe. The child's crying grew louder. Lupe turned again, this time more gently. She managed a reasonable imitation of a reassuring smile and bestowed it on the frightened girl.

The sobbing stopped as Agnes jammed her thumb into her mouth and, with the other hand, hugged a tattered pink blanket to her chest. The thumb came out as the child once again called for her mother. She didn't move, however, just stood in the doorway, watching Tessa with fear-widened eyes.

Lupe forgot her pain. She ignored the queasy feeling that overcame her as she sat and then stood up. This child needed her help. She walked unsteadily to the girl's side, reaching around the tiny shoulders with her good arm to draw the frightened child to her breast. She prayed that Agnes wouldn't notice her bloodstained dress. She whispered words of consolation as she led her out of the parlor and into the kitchen.

Tessa knew they needed more help. Luckily, Hattie had been distracted by her daughter's cries long enough to allow Tessa to recapture her. She was grateful to see Lupe moving around, but the widening red stain on her shoulder concerned her.

Agnes was obviously, and rightfully, terrified. She shouldn't be left alone. Tessa was worried that Lupe might faint again at any minute. Then what would she do? She berated herself for thinking that two women could take the law into their inexperienced hands, especially against a murderer who had struck at least twice. *Think,* she told herself.

First, she checked the ropes that bound Hattie's arms and legs, tightening them further for both security and as an act of retaliation for Lupe's wound. Then she took another piece of the rope and tied the woman's limbs to the rungs of a ladder-back chair that sat in front of a desk. Tessa was grateful to hear whispers and soft singing coming from the kitchen. She fumbled in her dress pocket and came up with a kerchief that she used to gag her prisoner. It wouldn't do to have Hattie call out to her daughter and upset the young girl all over again.

She backed out of the parlor, keeping her eyes on Hattie. When she reached the kitchen doorway, she stopped. From there, she could check on Lupe and Agnes, while keeping watch over the woman who sat bound and gagged in the parlor.

"Lupe, are you going to be all right?"

Lupe sat by the stove, cradling the distraught child, her own face white with pain and blood loss. She nodded slightly, trying to look reassuring, without success. With a glance toward Hattie to assure herself that the prisoner was secure, she hurried to Lupe's side. The wood stove had been banked for the night, its smoldering embers giving off only a small measure of heat. Tessa draped her shawl over Lupe's slumping shoulders.

"I'm going to Tia Elena's house for help. Don't let Agnes leave the kitchen. Hattie won't go anywhere, so don't worry about her. I'll send Elena over here to tend to you while I fetch Sheriff Bowman. Will you be okay, amiga?"

Again, the barely perceptible nod, and the soft singing. Tessa could see that Lupe was weakening fast. She knew she needed to hurry.

Tia Elena rushed into the kitchen, her face frozen into a mask of concern. She carried a small basket, which she dropped on the table, nearly tripping over a chair leg in her haste to get to Lupe's side.

"Pobrecita," she crooned as she wiped away the tears that streaked down Lupe's face.

"Poor Agnes, too," Lupe said, squeezing the child tight to her chest. "We'll be all right, won't we Agnes?" Lupe asked. She planted a gentle kiss on the girl's pale cheek.

"Aren't you the brave one?" Elena spoke softly. "Would you like a cookie?"

She pulled a small muslin doll and a round cookie from the basket she'd brought. She handed Agnes a snickerdoodle and laughed as cinnamon and sugar snaked a shiny trail from her fingers to the girl's mouth. Agnes licked the sweet goo from her lips and mouth and gave Elena what passed for a tiny smile of thanks.

Gently, Elena pulled Agnes from Lupe's grasp. When she had settled the child in a chair of her own with another cookie, she turned her attention to her surrogate niece. She pulled Lupe's dress off her shoulder, with all the skill of a professional nurse.

"Madre de Dios!" she cried at the sight of all the blood,

much of which had dried. "The bleeding has stopped, Lupe. That's a good sign. Now, let me look at your back."

"Ouch," Lupe screamed at Elena's touch.

A whimper from Agnes reminded the women of the child's presence.

"I'm sorry," Lupe said. "I was surprised by the pain, but I'm ready now." She squared her shoulders.

"Lupe," Elena whispered, "the bullet is still in your back. I can feel it. This is a problem for the doctor. We need to get you there right away, but I'll do the best I can until help arrives."

Elena cleaned the wound with cloths she had brought, grimacing herself as Lupe winced in pain. She located a pitcher of water, poured a glass, then added a light brown powder that she had excavated from the basket.

"Drink this, *sobrina*. It will help ease the pain."

She found milk, which she poured for Agnes. The girl was calmer now, hugging the doll tightly and humming the tune that Lupe had been singing to her just minutes before.

This quiet scene greeted Sheriff Bowman as he thundered into the house, gun unholstered but pointed at the floor, Tessa on his heels. They had come in through the parlor, checking to make sure Hattie was still securely tied, then made their way into the kitchen.

"The doctor will be here soon, Lupe," Tessa said. She knelt by her friend, clasping Lupe's hands tightly in her own. "Your hands are so cold. Let me find you a blanket."

"No," Lupe replied emphatically. "I'll be okay, amiga. Just take care of this poor child, please."

The sheriff's deep voice echoed off the kitchen walls. "All right, Miss Crane. Tell me what this is all about."

Tessa gave Lupe's hand another squeeze. The answering

gasp from her friend told her that she had pulled a little too hard on the wounded arm. "Oh, I'm sorry, Lupe. You're so brave, it is easy for me to forget you're hurt."

Lupe opened her mouth to say something, but the sheriff spoke first.

"Miss Crane," he demanded again, "why is Hattie Frye trussed up like a chicken in her own parlor? And, here's your roommate in the Frye's kitchen with a bullet in her shoulder."

Before Tessa began speaking, she nodded at Elena. The woman needed no further explanation. She took Agnes' hand in hers and led the girl out of the room and up the stairs, carefully positioning herself so that the child wouldn't see her mother, gagged and tied to a chair in the parlor.

"Sheriff, Lupe and I came here tonight to talk to Mrs. Frye." Tessa decided not to mention their uninvited entry. Or the butcher knives. "She became angry when we asked her a few questions. Then she attacked us. When I went into the kitchen to find some rope to restrain her, she shot Lupe. The rest you know."

"No, Miss Crane, I don't think I know anything. You still haven't told me *why* you came here at this time of night to visit a woman you barely know."

Before Tessa could answer, the thud of the front door opening and closing reached her ears. She was doubly grateful for the interruption. She could avoid the sheriff's questions, at least for the time being, and help had arrived for Lupe.

"In the kitchen, doctor," she called. Doctor Dahlgren hurried in, black bag in hand. Without waiting for instructions, she rushed to Lupe's side and began her ministrations.

"Is there someplace where this poor woman can lie down?" she asked.

"In the parlor."

"What happened here?" he asked, pointing to the thin red line around Hattie's neck.

Specks of blood had dried, giving the appearance of ruby-colored stones.

"Um, Lupe was trying to control Hattie," Tessa said. "She grabbed her by the throat. I think she pulled on the necklace, maybe a little too hard."

Tessa offered a silent *thank you* for the kerchief that kept Hattie from contradicting her explanation.

"I'll take your necklace, Mrs. Frye," Bowman said.

He unlatched it and put it into his pocket. Hattie turned her hateful glare from Tessa to the sheriff.

Bowman led her into the kitchen, though not as roughly as Tessa would have liked. Tessa and Doctor Dahlgren carried Lupe into the parlor and laid her gently on the sofa.

As the quintet passed each other in the hallway, Tessa saw Bowman and the doctor trade looks of utter confusion. She couldn't blame them.

After Tessa assured herself that Lupe was now safely in the care of the good doctor, she returned to the kitchen. She would rather have stayed with her friend, not only to comfort her, but also because she dreaded the conversation with Sheriff Bowman. However, there was nothing to do but get on with it. She held her head high as she entered the kitchen, ready to face the angry lawman. She knew she was right, but would he believe her? Bowman wasted no time on niceties.

"Now, Miss Crane, you were saying."

Instead of speaking, Tessa extracted the yellowed papers, the medical files that Edna Benton gave her earlier that afternoon, from her pocket.

268 // Susan Tornga

"You need to read all of these papers, sheriff, but let me summarize them for you."

She handed the papers to the sheriff and spoke from memory.

"Mrs. Benton gave me these. Doc did make it home the night he was killed. He was on his way *back* to town to give this file to you when Hattie Frye shot him."

Sheriff Bowman opened his mouth and furrowed his brow in disbelief. Tessa hurried on with her story before he could say anything.

"These papers are Hattie Frye's medical records, at least the older ones that Doc Benton didn't pass along to the new doctor. He knew what they said and he didn't want to cause any problems for the Frye's. After all, at the time, Hiram was the sheriff."

A half-groan, half-scream came from the parlor. Three heads turned at Lupe's cry of pain. Dr. Dahlgren's soft voice gave words of encouragement, and the room grew quiet again.

Tessa continued. "When you read this, you'll find out that Hattie Frye wasn't able to bear children. She desperately wanted a child, probably thinking that, if they were a real family, she could keep her husband from wandering. Doc Benton must've mentioned to her that there was a young, unmarried woman in town who would soon give birth."

Bowman didn't go as far as to roll his eyes, but the look he gave Tessa told her that he wanted to.

Tessa kept on speaking, hoping that her words would convince him that Hattie Frye, not Joaquin Castillo, was the murderer.

"No one thought it was strange when Hattie Frye

traveled to San Francisco for her confinement, because, at that time, there was gossip that women here were afraid to have Doc deliver their babies. There had been a few deaths, you see, but nothing was ever proved to be Doc Benton's fault."

"I remember hearing something about that, but I've learned never to pay attention to rumors," Bowman said. "Usually, they're started for the sole purpose of hurting someone, and most times, they do. So, you think Deirdre had a child and gave it, um, her, to Hattie Frye?"

"Yes, sheriff," Tessa said. "Hattie came back to Winslow with a beautiful baby girl, a baby with red hair like her own."

The sheriff chewed his lip, giving the appearance of a man deep in thought. Tessa took that as a sign that he gave her story credence. Her hopes dissolved a second later as he shook his head and sighed, now seemingly unconvinced that her tale had anything to do with the two murders. When he opened his mouth to voice what Tessa assumed was disbelief, she rushed ahead.

"Deirdre Sweeney came through Winslow with the idea to get her daughter back, to take her with her to St. Louis. She planned to wed Stanton Perry, conveniently forgetting that she was already married, albeit to a man she never expected to see again. Her new husband-to-be was wealthy and could take care of her and the child in grand style. She confronted Hattie. I think she might have suggested that Hattie let her take Agnes quietly. If Hattie didn't agree, she threatened to tell Hiram the whole story. Hattie would then lose both her daughter and her husband. So she killed Deirdre."

Bowman nodded, in agreement or understanding, Tessa wasn't sure which. She hoped it was agreement. When he spoke, picking up the story from where she left off, Tessa relaxed. Perhaps he would believe her after all.

"Mrs. Frye was at the jail the night Doc Benton recognized Deirdre's wedding picture."

He looked over Tessa's head at nothing, as if reconstructing in his mind the scene in the jailhouse that night.

"She panicked when he said he had some of Deirdre's medical files that could possibly help me," Bowman said, continuing the story. "I'm betting he knew that Agnes was Deirdre's daughter the minute Hattie brought her back from San Francisco."

Tessa took over the telling. "Doc knew about Hattie's faked pregnancy all along. His files," she pointed to the yellowed pages on the table, "indicate that she couldn't bear children. Remember, however, that Hiram Frye was Sheriff Frye at the time and Doc wouldn't have wanted to bring such accusations toward his wife. What was the harm in the deception, after all?"

"If Miss Sweeney would've stayed away," Bowman said, "no one would ever have known."

"Yes," Tessa said, "and Doc knew she was with child. When she disappeared, it was in everyone's best interest if he didn't say anything about the entire situation. He didn't remember all this when he was in your office that night, but his wife says he was excited when he got home. He probably remembered the whole story while he was riding out to his ranch. Hattie couldn't risk exposure from him, especially after what she had already done to protect her secret."

The doctor appeared in the doorway. "Sheriff, will you help me get Miss Castillo to my surgery? She's resting quietly now, but I need to remove the bullet as soon as possible."

It was a demand, masquerading as a polite request. She returned to the parlor without waiting for him to speak.

Bowman looked at Tessa, his eyes softening. "I'll look at these papers as soon as I can, Miss Crane. This is all very interesting, but you still have some explaining to do about what happened here tonight. For now, however, we need to take care of your injured friend."

Tessa followed the sheriff out of the kitchen then rushed past him to Lupe's side. Color had returned to the girl's cheeks. Her breathing, although shallow, had an even rhythm that encouraged Tessa. Whatever was in the powder that Tia Elena brought with her had worked its magic.

Sheriff Bowman waited impatiently by the door, ready to leave the house. Tessa noticed that the big man, who normally stood tall and proud, slumped. She knew that she was the cause of much of his fatigue and frustration. The past two weeks had been very difficult for the man who thought enforcing the law in Winslow would consist of little more than hauling drunks in for a night in jail. His voice, however, was strong and commanding.

"Miss Crane, please keep an eye on Mrs. Frye. I'll get a wagon from the livery. It won't take long. That will be the easiest and safest way to get this poor girl to your surgery, doctor."

He vanished before his words found their audience.

Tessa didn't like being alone in the kitchen with Hattie Frye, whose squinty eyes shot silent curses at the woman who had uncovered her secret. Instead of taking a seat at the table, she elected to stand in the doorway where she could watch for any movement from the prisoner, while at the same time offering words of encouragement to her wounded friend.

True to his word, Bowman returned within minutes. He lifted Lupe as easily and carefully as he would pick up a kitten and carried her to the wagon. The doctor followed, ubiquitous black bag in hand. When Tessa heard the wagon pull away, she said a prayer for Lupe's safekeeping and sent it off on the night air to join the travelers.

Now she was alone with a murderer. Before full-fledged panic could set in, however, the sheriff walked in with a surprisingly jaunty spring in his step. Perhaps he was relieved to have Lupe gone, Tessa thought. One less worry for him. Tessa was grateful to have him back in the house with the venomous Hattie Frye.

By way of explanation for his quick return, the sheriff said, "Doctor Dahlgren drove the wagon. Miss Kingsley will help get the patient into the surgery." The concern in his voice touched Tessa.

When he spoke next, though, his authoritative sheriff's voice had returned.

"I'll take Mrs. Frye with me to the jail, Miss Crane, but I'm not releasing Joaquin Castillo until I can sort this out." He rustled the doctor's papers. "You've given me a lot to think about. Come to my office as early as you can tomorrow and we'll go over your story again."

The emphasis he put on story made Tessa cringe. Didn't he believe anything she'd told him?

The sound of footsteps on the stairs made them turn, bumping shoulders. Startled, they jerked away from each other. The words Elena Mendoza spoke surprised them even more.

"What about the child?"

Chapter Twenty-Six

Bowman and Tessa, deep in conversation, had forgotten about Agnes, upstairs in her bed. A mumbled groan from Hattie's gagged mouth bespoke her awareness of the child's plight. Tears trickled from the corners of her eyes. Tessa felt a fleeting pity for this woman who had taken what she thought were the necessary actions to protect her family, albeit a family formed from a stream of lies and deceptions. Thoughts of Deirdre Sweeney and Doc Benton vanquished that sympathy.

Bowman scratched his chin, seeking a solution to this new problem.

"Hiram Frye needs to be told about what has happened," he said, "but I don't want to take him away from his watchman's duty tonight. I'll send one of my deputies to the Roundhouse tomorrow morning to bring him straight away to the jail. There's another problem with him that's going to complicate this already confused situation."

Tessa decided this wasn't the time to tell the sheriff that she, too, was aware of the complication. She had seen the telegram from the Santa Fe Railroad advising Sheriff Bowman that Hiram Frye had partnered with the conductor in the ticket swindle. It had been among the papers on the sheriff's desk that she had shuffled through after looking at Deirdre's wedding picture.

Frye had been the Winslow contact for Winston McCauley for over a year, letting him know which boarding passengers would be the least likely to notice any wrongdoing when asked to pay their fare directly to the conductor. That was undoubtedly one of the reasons Frye spent so much time at the Harvey House lunch counter. That, as well as the booze. Right now, Bowman had enough to worry about. There was no reason to confess that she had been snooping around his desk.

The sheriff's words broke through Tessa's musings. "So, you see, it's possible that I might have both Hiram and Hattie locked in my jail. What will happen to the child?"

"Perhaps I can help." Elena said, slowly and distinctly, testing her limited English.

Gratitude lit Bowman's face. *"Señora* Mendoza, can you care for Agnes tonight? Maybe longer?"

"Of course, sheriff. She's a sweet girl. Right now, she's asleep and I hate to wake her. My daughter is at my house, watching over Enrique."

She turned toward Tessa and said in Spanish, "Miss Crane, would you please go to my home and tell my sister that I won't be back tonight?"

Tessa nodded. She was weary, but she knew that Tia Elena must be tired as well. She thought of the frightened child upstairs, who had finally succumbed to the healing power of sleep, and of Lupe, wounded and alone, suffering physical and emotional pain. Yes, she would gladly do what she could to right some of the many wrongs that had occurred during the past fortnight.

Despite the exhaustion that seemed to have taken up permanent residence in her body, Tessa awoke early the next morning. She dressed quickly and arrived at her work station long before of the other girls. She told Miss Parks that Lupe would not be able to work for several days. She didn't try to explain all that had occurred the previous evening. Town talk would soon supply those details. She merely said that Doctor Dahlgren was treating Lupe in her surgery.

"You look so very tired, my dear," Dorothea said. "The next train won't arrive for at least another hour. You sit here and I'll bring you a cup of fresh coffee."

The beneficent cook brought not only coffee, but one of Oswald's cinnamon buns as well. Tessa's fatigue was no match for the yeasty roll and the rich, strong coffee.

"Thank you, Dorothea," she said as she licked her icing covered fingers. "You are an angel." She nibbled on a roll, redolent with vanilla and spices, and sipped the rich, strong coffee. It was a good start to a day that she hoped would only get better.

Finally, the busy morning at an end, Tessa was free to leave the Harvey House. She was impatient to visit Lupe, yet fearful of what she might find. As she walked down Second Street, she pulled her shawl tightly across her shoulders, a cocoon against the day's chill as well as the gossip that had already snaked through the streets of Winslow.

Her limp, evidence of weary leg muscles, didn't concern her. It was Lupe's injury that was foremost on her mind. Each step closer to the doctor's surgery brought a new cramp to her stomach. She wiped her sweaty palms on her apron before she reached for the doorknob. Tessa took comfort in the simple *Elsa Dahlgren, MD* etched into the glass inset of the heavy wooden door, but distress again flooded over her with the realization that the shade had been lowered.

With shaking hands, Tessa turned the knob. She opened the door quietly, fearful of waking the patient, or something far worse. The reassuring lilt of Lupe's accented English met her ears. The sound was a panacea for her fear. She smiled broadly, almost a grin, and walked confidently across the room, with an uneven but rapid stride. Anxiety, weariness and pain vanished into the joyous atmosphere of the surgery.

"Amiga, how are you?" she asked as she rushed to her friend's side. Lupe sat awkwardly against the metal headboard of a most uncomfortable-looking bed, balancing a cup of tea on her legs. With her good arm, she gestured wildly, caught in the middle of relating some story to the doctor.

"Miss Crane, please sit down," the doctor said, motioning to a nearby chair, a spindly wooden affair that looked almost as uncomfortable as the bed. "Miss Castillo is doing well. She should be able to return to the Harvey House in a day or two. I'm trying to get her to eat something, but she's too busy telling me about Hattie Frye to pay attention to breakfast. The two of you had quite an adventure. And not just last night from what I hear."

"Tessa, I'm so glad you're here. Doctor Dahlgren said that the sheriff has arrested Mrs. Frye for the murders, just as you thought. Did he release Joaquin from jail? What about Agnes? What will happen to that poor child?" Lupe gasped. She had run out of breath before she ran out of words.

"Lupe, slow down. You shouldn't get so excited."

Tessa proceeded to tell the two women what happened after the doctor had taken Lupe away from the Frye house.

"I'm ashamed to admit that we had forgotten about Agnes," Tessa said. "Tia Elena stayed at the Frye house with her last night. She planned to take the girl home with her today. That poor child needs to feel loved, and Elena is the perfect person to do that. I'm on my way to the jail to speak with Sheriff Bowman. Lupe, you have to rest and eat. Things will sort themselves out."

"*Si*, Mama." Lupe rolled her eyes as she pantomimed the motion of feeding herself. "Please come back and tell me what you learn at the jail."

The young doctor followed Tessa to the door. She obviously had something on her mind that she wanted to discuss outside of Lupe's hearing. Tessa's heart sank. Was her friend in grave danger despite her rosy cheeks? The doctor's weary voice cracked with emotion.

"I had a professor at the Medical College in Chicago who had been a battlefield physician during the War Between the States. He taught us how to treat bullet wounds. I remember one particular lecture where he broke down and had to leave the hall. At the time, I didn't understand his reaction. This week, though, I have treated your father's soldier and now

Miss Castillo for bullet wounds. It is an ugly thing we do to each other, Miss Crane."

With no further words, Doctor Dahlgren turned on her heel and returned to Lupe's side. Her words were sobering, but couldn't dampen Tessa's soaring spirits. Lupe would be fine. Tessa could already see signs that her happy nature was returning. When she turned onto Main Street toward the sheriff's office, her spirits rose even higher. Tied to the hitching post in front of the jail, pawing impatiently at the dirt, stood her father's horse. The handsome steed was decked out in full cavalry regalia. Smiling broadly, Tessa picked up her pace. It was a morning filled with happiness.

She pushed the jailhouse door open with such force that she almost knocked the colonel off his feet. He sidestepped just in time.

"Papa, I am so glad you're here. You don't know what all has happened. Lupe was shot and…"

Her father took her slender wrist in his large, rough hands and smiled at her with such love in his eyes that she burst into sobs, the emotions of the past few days seeking release. When he saw the tears, her father dropped her wrist and swept her into his arms, whispering words of concern that she sensed rather than heard. After a few minutes, Tessa straightened up, gulped in air and smiled back at her father.

"I'm sorry, Father. There is no reason for tears today. Seeing you is one more happy event in a day filled with good news. So much has happened since you returned to Ft. Apache. When did you get back to Winslow?"

"Poor Tessa," Colonel Crane said, pushing her away, ever so gently, so that he could study her tear-stained face.

"Sit down, my dear. Sheriff Bowman had been telling

me about last night. He's not convinced that he should set Joaquin Castillo free. Hattie Frye won't talk and that husband of hers is as mad as a peeled rattler."

Tessa ignored the proffered chair. Instead she paced across the jailhouse floor, ticking off points on her fingers, as Miss Kingsley might do to a classroom full of ten-year-olds. With each tick, she shifted her eyes from one man to the next and back again.

"First," she said, "Hattie Frye murdered Deirdre Sweeney, who threatened to take Agnes away from her."

Another finger came up. "Second, Agnes is Deirdre's daughter, of course." Another finger. "Hattie and Deirdre traveled to San Francisco together. They undoubtedly planned the entire scheme before they left Winslow, over six years ago. They stayed there until Deirdre gave birth. I'm sure Hattie paid Deirdre a goodly sum of money for the child. She probably got the money from Hiram by telling him she needed it for new clothes and doctor's costs."

She reached the end of one hand and began on the other.

"Then Hattie, who told Hiram she was going to have his child, returned to Winslow with Agnes, parading her as their beautiful baby."

Tessa looked at both men to assure herself that they were following her story. She glanced down at her pointed fingers, dropped her hands to her sides, chagrinned, and continued her recitation.

"In the beginning, Hattie's plan worked beautifully. Hiram became a model husband. He stayed away from the saloons, worked hard and bought Hattie and Agnes anything Hattie asked for, especially if it was for Agnes, *his* daughter."

"I remember," Bowman said. "He was a different man than what we see now."

"Yes," Tessa said, "but he couldn't maintain that behavior. He went back to drinking and carousing. At that point, though, Hattie didn't care, because he was still providing well for her and Agnes. Deirdre's appearance threatened that."

"I know that's what you've told the sheriff, Tessa, but you have no proof," Colonel Crane said. He might have wanted to believe his daughter, but years on the western frontier had made him a skeptic.

"You haven't seen the files Doc Benton had with him when he was murdered, Papa. I gave them to the sheriff last night." She fixed her eyes on Bowman. "Did you read them, sheriff? The doctor wrote that Mrs. Frye wasn't able to bear children because of something that happened to her years earlier. He knew why she had gone to San Francisco. In fact, he helped arrange the transfer of Deirdre's baby to Hattie. Doc had only two or three pages from Hattie's medical file with him. If you ask Doctor Dahlgren, I am sure you'll find the remainder of her file intact."

"Of course I'll ask her," Bowman said.

"Doc Benton tried to protect the Frye's from scandal," Tessa said. "Remember, Hiram was sheriff here at the same time Benton was the town's doctor. Doc wrote a few notes in Deirdre's records that indicate that perhaps he was the one responsible for putting Hattie in contact with her, or vice versa."

Tessa saw the confusion on the men's faces.

"I mean that Doc Benton, not Hiram Frye, encouraged Hattie to talk to Deirdre. Hiram thought, and still thinks, at least for the time being, that Agnes is his daughter."

"Maybe she is," Bowman said, under his breath. He reddened.

Colonel Crane looked at Bowman, seemed to notice the man's discomfort and quickly asked, "Why would Mrs. Frye go to so much trouble to get that baby?"

Bowman answered. "Your daughter is correct about Hattie's plan, colonel. Hiram Frye was a terrible womanizer. The entire town heard some of the vicious name-calling battles that he and Hattie waged. She wasn't able to rein him in. Instead, his behavior got worse. But, when he found out that Hattie was with child, he stopped all that and became a devoted husband. I think Hattie expected that to continue forever. The man obviously doted on Agnes. As your daughter said though, it wasn't long before he reverted to his old ways, and that cost him his job as sheriff."

Bowman paused long enough to take a quick breath, but he wasn't willing to give up his position as narrator just yet.

"What Doc Benton wrote in the files that Mrs. Benton gave us," he nodded to Tessa, "made me realize that the doctor thought that he was helping both women. He believed, like so many others, that a child is better off in a home with both a mother and father, regardless of their character. One only has to look at Señora Mendoza and young Enrique to see that Doc wasn't always right about that."

His statement both surprised and pleased Tessa, but still she was troubled.

"The proof is there," Tessa said, pointing to Doc Benton's papers, "so why haven't you let Joaquin Castillo go free?"

"Unfortunately, Miss Crane, nothing that you've told me or that Doc wrote in his files provides any proof that Hattie Frye murdered these two people. Joaquin could be, and probably is, the father of Deirdre's child, whom we now know is Agnes Frye. This Sweeney woman could have returned to Winslow to confront Joaquin and demand the money he wouldn't give her six years ago."

Tessa grinned and raised her eyebrows, a child with a surprise to show two unsuspecting adults.

"Sheriff, do you have the necklace you took from Hattie last night?"

Without answering, Bowman opened his desk drawer and extracted the silver chain, dangling it on his fingers. The locket swung loosely, a shiny pendulum.

"Father, have you seen Deirdre's wedding photograph, the one her supposed husband gave to the sheriff?" Without waiting for an answer, Tessa continued. "I showed that picture to Beryl Turner. She served Deirdre the day she arrived on the train from San Francisco. Beryl swears that Miss Sweeney was wearing that necklace. She noticed it because it caught the sun from the window and glittered 'like a star', she said. No such necklace was found on Deirdre's body or in her belongings. Last night, when Hattie tried to kill Lupe and me, she was wearing that same necklace. She had to have taken it from Deirdre after she murdered her." Tessa sat back, feeling a surge of satisfaction

Tessa pulled Rockwell Smith's wedding photograph out of her pocket, smoothing out the creases. Bowman raised his eyebrows. The last he knew, the photograph had been on his desk. He shrugged, apparently not wanting to chastise the woman who had helped bring a murderer to justice.

He laid Hattie Frye's necklace over the one in the photograph of a smiling Deirdre Sweeney on her wedding day. They were identical. His grimace told Tessa that he didn't want to admit he had arrested the wrong person at first. He might not ever say he had been mistaken, but she knew, as did he, that he would now make it right.

Father and daughter left the jail, arm in arm, Colonel Crane allowing Tessa to lean on him.

"I'd say you've made quite an impression on Sheriff Bowman," he told her.

"Not a good one, I'm afraid," Tessa said. "I've broken into two houses and took Ben from the stable without permission."

She smiled up at him, her eyes twinkling.

"Of course, he doesn't know about most of that yet, and, hopefully, he never will."

"Ben? That's the white mule, right? That's what the sheriff was telling me before you came into the jail."

"He found out that I took him that night?" The smile vanished, replaced by a grimace.

"No, that's not what I mean, Tessa. Bowman told me that every time you return Ben to the livery, you brush him down and give him a treat. He agrees with my observation that those who treat animals well also treat people with the same kindness. He may have talked gruffly to you, but I can see that he respects you. He's a good man, Tessa, and you've done a fine thing in earning that respect."

"Hmmm," was all Tessa said, as she leaned deeper into her father's supporting arm. She said no more as they continued down the street. Her father had given her much to think about.

When they reached the Harvey House, she gave him a big hug. "Thank you, Papa."

"For what?"

"I could say 'for being here', and I do thank you for that.

However, I also know that you practically carried me down the street. I am more tired now than I ever remember being. So, thank you, but there is no need to do it again."

She squared her shoulders and walked determinedly up the steps, turning to give her father a quick wave with her fingers. As certain as night follows day, another train with its minions of ravenous passengers would arrive soon, and she needed to get back to work.

Chapter Twenty-Seven

It was one of those delicious winter days in the high desert, with warm sun, impossibly blue skies, and only a slight chill in the clear air. Christmas was less than one week away and three children expended some of their excited energy by running back and forth, from house to corral. The quartet of women who sat on the porch at the Silver Spur smiled as the active trio climbed the fence railing, then straddled the top as if riding horses. Cries of "giddyap" and peals of laughter filled the air.

"Look at them," Tessa chuckled, gathering her shawl tighter around her shoulders. She wanted to join them in their game. Now, with the leather brace that Doctor Dahlgren had fitted on her weak leg, she felt like a child again herself, willing to try anything. "They look so different, yet they are so much alike in their play."

Indeed, the three children made a strange sight. Tall,

thin and blond, Johnny, as the oldest, played the role of ringleader. First, they were cowboys on the range, then archaeologists, digging in the fallow garden for more fossils. Enrique's straight dark hair and brown skin set him apart physically, but he was as much a part of the play group as the others, running from post to post, determined to keep pace with Johnny. Red-haired Agnes seemed to have forgotten the upheaval in her family. She had lost most of her shyness, bossing the boys around one minute, then assuming the role of protective older sister to Enrique the next.

Elena Mendoza rocked slowly, silently, reticent around the younger women. She was content to listen to their chatter and watch the children at play. Her eyes radiated love. She didn't know if Agnes would be with her forever, but she was trying hard to make that happen. Looking at the fair child, no one would think that she could be Joaquin's daughter, but the possibility lodged in her mind, and heart, and refused to leave.

As if conjured by the Elena's thoughts, Joaquin appeared at the barn door, saddle in hand. As he walked by Enrique, he tousled the boy's hair. *How alike they look,* Tessa thought, and wondered.

~The End~